WITHDRAWN

A Companion Novel
to *Echo North*

WIND
DAUGHTER

JOANNA
RUTH MEYER

PAGE STREET
PUBLISHING CO.

PAGE STREET
PUBLISHING CO.

Distributed by Macmillan, sales in Canada by The Canadian Manda Group.

26   25   24   23   22   1   2   3   4   5

ISBN-13: 978-1-64567-436-8
ISBN-10: 1-64567-436-3

Library of Congress Control Number: 2021937029

Cover and book design by Rosie Stewart for Page Street Publishing Co.

Printed and bound in the United States

For my grandmother Mary Rosamond Briggs Austin:
I miss you.

And for anyone who has ever been told they are too sensitive—
the world needs your great hearts.

PART ONE:
North Story

ONE

M Y NAME MEANS FAIRY TALE, WHICH is fitting for the daughter of a storyteller who was once the North Wind. I was born in the winter in the midst of a howling snowstorm, sheltered from the snow by a reindeer-skin tent and the fierce warmth of my parents' love. My mother laughed and my father cried, and they were, in that moment, wholly happy. They called me Satu. Story.

I loved them from before I knew what love was: my father's rumbling voice and my mother's dark eyes, their presence alone enough to banish my infant fears. I didn't understand my mother's ache of sadness, my father's guilt. They didn't show it to me. Not then.

But my father *was* a storyteller, and he didn't neglect to tell me his own story when I was old enough to understand it: how he was born the North Wind, the youngest son of the Sun and the Moon. How his brothers, East and West and South, hated him. How he was lonely. And how he fell in love with a herder's daughter, a talented weaver who was full to the brim with the old magic.

"Old magic?" I would ask.

My father smiled across the room at my mother, who was always working on something by the light of the fire, embroidering or carding wool or spinning yarn on her lacquered wheel.

"Love," he would reply. "It's the power that created the universe, you know."

After that came the sad part of the story: how my father realized that in order to stay with my mother, he couldn't be the immortal North Wind anymore. So he bargained with a wicked enchantress called the Wolf Queen, who made him human in exchange for all his magic. But with that magic, the Wolf Queen sent my parents four centuries into the future, and my mother never saw her family again.

My mother would turn her head away, at this point, so I couldn't see her tears. But I knew they were there. I hurt for her. I always cried a little, too.

Were it not for my father's stories, I don't think I would have ever come inside. I vastly preferred the wild mountain air to the confines of the reindeer-skin tent. It was so much easier to breathe outside, so much easier to *be*, even when the snows came. The cold didn't bother me. My mother blamed my North blood, but she made me wear a coat anyway. I *was* human, after all.

Even if it didn't bother me, the cold could still kill me. But I always shrugged out of the coat when she wasn't looking.

To hear my father's stories, though, I would stay inside, sitting between my parents while yet another snowstorm shrieked outside our tent, battering the reindeer hide like it wanted to come in, like it wanted me to come *out*. Sometimes, I imagined I heard a voice tangled up with the wind, calling my name.

My parents said I took after both of them, even though I looked more like my mother. I had the same round face as her, the same straight dark hair and light brown skin and wide-set eyes. I saw very little of my father when I peered into my mother's carved bone hand mirror.

"But your heart is full of wind and stories," my father would tell me, kissing my head. "You are the best pieces of us."

And my mother would smile at me over her embroidery and I would wonder what it meant to have stories in my heart.

When I was seven, we moved from the tent into a house on the mountain. It was a lovely house, painted the pale blue of ice in winter, and had latticework framing the windows and doors. There was a weaving room and a book room, a living room with a fireplace, and two bedrooms—one of them for me. It had a writing desk and a brightly painted wardrobe, and the bedposts were carved with images from my father's stories. It was beautiful. But I still didn't like to be indoors unless I had to. Houses suffocated me. The heat and close walls made my heart thump, my skin itch, my mind whir too fast.

One morning, in the dead of winter, my mother set me to work in the weaving room with a huge basket of raw wool and a pair of carding combs. I worked for a while, rocking the combs back and forth until the fibers grew smooth and straight, then setting the carded wool in the spinning basket, ready for my mother's wheel. She was lost in the rhythm of her own work, wheel spinning, foot pumping, wool turning to yarn like magic between her fingers. She didn't notice when I slipped from the room and out of the house. I climbed the winding path to the very top of the mountain, gulping deep breaths of frigid air, tumbling and laughing in the drifts. I thrilled at the icy touch of snow on my cheeks.

When I grew tired, I swept the snow from a wide flat rock shelf that jutted out over empty air and sat to watch the flakes drift down. After a while, lacy white pictures began to form in the snow: sailing ships and great white bears, a princess with a trailing gown of ice, a many-spired castle. My father had told me enough stories by then that I knew this must be magic, though I had never actually seen any before. I was transfixed, and more than a little disappointed when the wind stirred through the snow pictures and blew them away.

It was then I saw the winter demon.

He looked like a man, tall and thin, with long pale hair spilling past his shoulders and ice-shard eyes that pierced mine. Snow danced in his palms, and I knew he was the one who had used magic.

"Will you teach me how to do that?" I asked him, too awed to be afraid.

For a moment more he stared at me, his eyes very hard. And then he dissolved into snow.

I blinked after him, a sadness I didn't understand tugging at my heart.

My mother called me from the path, and I turned shame-facedly to greet her.

"Who was he?" I asked my parents that night after dinner, curled up on the couch as far away from the suffocating heat of the fire as I could get.

My mother frowned, busy carding the basket of wool I had abandoned.

"The Wolf Queen has a winter demon, at her beck and call," mused my father. He steepled his brown fingers and stared thoughtfully into the fire. "I wonder if it was him."

I sat up very straight. He didn't speak about the Wolf Queen very often in front of my mother anymore. It made her too sad.

The crease between my mother's brows deepened.

My father turned up the lamp for her, so she wouldn't ruin her eyes in the dim light. "But she has no cause to bother us," he added, pressing a kiss on my mother's cheek. "I am sure she hasn't thought of me in four hundred years."

The carding combs rocked aggressively back and forth, and my mother's face grew tight in a way I knew meant she was try-ing hard not to cry.

I slipped from my spot on the couch, gritting my teeth at the heat from the fire but bearing it for my mother's sake. I settled by her feet and put a hand on her knee. Her sorrow twisted inside of me, and I wished I had the magic to take it away from her forever.

"Nothing to worry about," my father concluded, in an overly bright tone. "Just be careful on the mountain, Satu. All right?"

"All right," I promised.

But my mother's shoulders stayed tight, and I didn't miss the tear that slid down her cheek before she wiped it hastily away.

EVERY MIDWINTER, OUR REMOTE MOUNTAIN village held a festival to help pass the time and chase away the dark. My father would put on his storyteller robes and spin tales in the inn to a captive audience for hours. I never went—I was painfully shy, and I didn't like the thought of being shut up inside with people I didn't know. But that year, my mother convinced me to go with her. I was old enough now, she reasoned, to enjoy the festival, to feel the pride of my father's storytelling. I *was* proud of him, of the book he'd written at my urging, the one about a girl called Echo and her quest to save the man she loved from the Wolf Queen. It was a true story, as all stories are, really, but only my parents and I knew that.

So I tramped with my mother down the snowy path from our house to the inn, nervousness shivering along my spine. It would be better if my father could tell his stories outside, but no one except me wanted to sit and shiver in the snow. ("North blood," said my mother with a sigh when I told her that, and buttoned me firmly into my coat.)

The moment I set foot in the great room of the inn, I knew it was a mistake. The walls were too close and the lanterns too bright. There were too many people talking at the same time, and too many conflicting smells, from the smoke of the fire to the bundles of dried lavender and other herbs hanging from the eaves. It was too much to process all at once, and it made my breaths come quick and shallow, my heart pound uncomfortably fast. I felt trapped inside my own skin.

Not sensing my heightened mood, my mother gave me a gentle nudge toward the back of the room, where my father sat on a pile of furs, children packed in around him chattering with excitement.

I squeezed through the press of people and found a seat beside the fire. I regretted it instantly—it was far, far too hot. I began desperately shrugging out of my coat, accidentally bumping the arm of the boy closest to me. He glared at me and I sucked in a sharp breath, fighting the sudden urge to cry. I kept my coat on. I tried to ignore the heat and the stifling air. I tried not to feel my skin crawling, my heart pounding, the sharp pulse of a headache. How could everyone else bear it? I didn't understand.

My father began his first story, voice smooth and warm as honey. I had heard it before, the tale of a girl who loved a star and changed herself into a nightingale so she could always see him shining. The familiar words did nothing to calm my compounding agitation, and as they wound into me, I realized how *sad* the story was, how utterly, utterly hopeless. I couldn't hold back my tears any longer. They poured down my cheeks and my father stopped speaking mid-sentence, staring at me in concern and half rising from his seat.

"Satu? Are you all right?"

His words caused every eye in the room to fix on me, which made it all infinitely worse. I leapt from my seat and bolted out of the inn, sobbing and shaking.

I ran up the path to the top of the mountain. I gulped frigid air, thick flakes of fresh snow melting the instant they touched my scalding cheeks. I collapsed on the edge of my rock shelf, crying and crying until it felt as if there was nothing of myself left, as if I'd been ripped to pieces by every thought and tear and intense emotion I couldn't contain and didn't understand.

That's when I saw the winter demon for the second time.

He was there on the far end of the rock shelf, his eyes gleaming, his pale hair and long coat whipping about in the wind. A parade of snow figures unfolded suddenly in the air between us: a peacock, a leopard, a wolf, a shimmering dancer spinning on one pointed foot, an icy rose unfolding its white petals. I got the sense he was trying to cheer me up.

I stood, slowly, my heart a riot in my chest, and took a step toward him. My foot slipped on the icy rock.

I tumbled out into empty air.

All was a sickening rush, a tangle of confusion and terror, the breath ripped so violently from my lungs I couldn't even scream. Snow danced in my vision. It was the last thing I would ever see.

But then something solid and warm slowed my fall. Invisible hands held me tight against a heartbeat that wasn't my own. I was borne swiftly upward, settled back onto the rock, where snow fell gently, on and on.

I scrambled hastily away from the edge, heart raging, breaths coming in quick, frantic gasps. I blinked and saw the winter demon staring at me, stricken.

"Take care, wind daughter," he whispered, words like ice rattling against stone.

Then he was gone, icy fractals curling over the rock in his wake.

I was shaking when my parents found me, moments later, their feet crunching through the snow. My father wore his worry in place of his coat, which he must have left behind in the inn, and my mother clung to his arm, trembling just as much as me. "What happened, Satu?" Her voice was tight and high with panic. "What's wrong?"

A crease pressed deep in my father's forehead, and he scooped me into his arms. "Did I tell the nightingale story so terribly, then?" He carried me down the path to our house, my mother coming just beside him, slipping one of her hands into mine.

The overwhelming sensations of the inn came flooding back. "It is just so *sad*," I whispered, biting back fresh tears.

"It isn't real, my darling," said my mother.

"But it's still sad."

She squeezed my hand. "How big your heart must be, that you would feel so deeply for a mere nightingale."

Exhaustion weighed impossibly heavy; I felt wrung out, like I could sink into the snow and sleep for a thousand years. "I fell from the mountain," I murmured into my father's neck.

My mother sucked in a sharp breath, but my father didn't pause, his arms steady around me as he brought me inside and laid me down on my narrow bed.

"What happened?" he said then, kneeling beside me, stroking my hair. My mother hovered in the doorway and I sensed her horror, her fear, sharp as the vinegar we used to scrub the floors.

"The winter demon caught me."

My father nodded, but there was fear in his eyes. He kissed my forehead, lips warm against my ice-touched skin. "Rest now."

Sleep tugged me under against my will. I dreamed I was flying over a frozen world, snow dancing in my eyes, stars grazing past my cheeks. A nightingale wept as she sang and I fell and fell and fell, but in my dream, there was no one there to catch me.

TWO

I REALIZED, AFTER THAT DAY I FELL from the mountain, that there was something *wrong* with me. I couldn't handle the simplest things, like running errands in the village with my mother, or being around anyone other than my parents, or squeaking out more than a single breathy, terrified word when the apothecary, Madam Zima, asked me a simple question. I went into the butcher's with my mother, once, and the sight of half a pig lying vacant and dead on the table sent me into such a state of overwhelming horror I couldn't speak a word without crying for the rest of the day.

In the autumn, my mother made me go to the brand-new school over the hill, the first one ever to exist in our remote village. The very thought of going tied my stomach in knots and made my heart pound like mad, but my mother wouldn't be dissuaded. She bought me new clothes: a crisp linen blouse and a coat lined with rabbit fur, bright ribbons to tie off the ends of my dark braids, soft-felted boots, a red and gold kerchief. She made my skirt herself, out of beautiful blue woven cloth, and embroidered flowers about the hem. When I was dressed and ready, she gave me a kind but firm kiss on my cheek and shoved me right out the door.

I spent the entire walk to school trying to keep my panic at bay, but my stomach tied itself into tighter and tighter knots, and I darted off the path and was sick in the grass.

Then there was nothing for it but to square my shoulders, send up a desperate prayer for strength, and force myself to step through the red lacquered door.

Inside the school's large single room, a dozen children were already waiting, ranging from age six to perhaps ten. They sat on evenly spaced benches that faced the teacher's desk and the stone hearth—complete with a roaring fire—on the far wall.

There was only one seat left, on a bench nearest the fire, and I slid my timid way onto it, keeping as far away as possible from the girl already sitting there.

I couldn't breathe and I could scarcely think. It was far too hot. Sweat crawled down my neck. I took off my coat and draped it over my knees, shooting furtive, terrified glances at the other children. They were talking and giggling with each other, all of them fast friends. I was the odd one out, hiding on my mountain and rarely coming into the village.

Their voices thrummed inside me like too many heartbeats, and the light from the windows and the fire hurt my eyes. I clenched my jaw against a burgeoning headache. I couldn't *breathe*. How could everyone else stand it in here?

I was distantly aware of the teacher, Mrs. Pasternak, calling the class to order, and I forced myself to sit still, to fold my hands in my lap, to focus on what she was saying. But I couldn't think past the pounding in my head and the absolute, overwhelming awareness of my own body: my flaming ears and mad pulse. The itch of my collar and the hardness of the bench. The oppressive heat from the fire.

Belatedly, I realized Mrs. Pasternak was speaking to me. I stared at her in a wash of blank horror.

She raised her eyebrows. "Tell us about yourself, Satu. What is it like to be the daughter of a storyteller?"

As if from far away, I watched myself open my mouth, listened as words I did not mean to say tumbled out. "He isn't just a storyteller. He used to be the North Wind."

For a moment, every soul in the school blinked at me, confused.

And then they all laughed. Even Mrs. Pasternak.

I wanted to claw a hole through the floor. I wanted to perish in the silence and the dark. But I was frozen there as they laughed, as Mrs. Pasternak reprimanded them for laughing, even as her own lips continued to twitch.

I was so, so hot, tears pouring down my face, my head buzzing like a swarm of wasps. Everything inside of me was screaming.

I don't even remember running out of the school.

The mountain welcomed me, crisp autumn air drying my tears and cooling the awful, awful heat of my body. I sat on my rock shelf and stared down at the tundra below, wishing and wishing I could teach my heart and my mind how to be still.

That was the day the wind sent me the bees.

They came a few at a time, glimmering in the sun, buzzing at my shoulders or snagging in my hair. I didn't brush them away—they didn't frighten me. I felt their kindness.

That's how my father found me, much later, when the sun was nearly down: in a cloud of bees, sitting on the very edge of the jutting rock, my feet dangling out over nothing because somewhere along the way I had lost my fear of falling.

If he was startled, he didn't show it. He simply sat down beside me and said: "I expect we should build them a hive."

I swallowed past the lump in my throat, peering out at the dying sun. "I'm sorry I am so strange, Papa." Voicing my shame made fresh tears bite at my eyes; it was a desperate struggle to keep them in. "There's something wrong with me, isn't there?"

"No, dear one. Your heart and your mind are too big to be contained by the four walls of the school, or the inn, or the village. That isn't strange, and it isn't wrong. Your sensitivity, your empathy—they are gifts, Satu. A special magic all your own."

I scrubbed angrily at my eyes. The bees in my hair buzzed in concern. "It doesn't feel like magic."

His smile was a little distant, a little sad. "That doesn't make it untrue."

I still didn't believe him, but I knew he meant to comfort me, and his steadying presence quieted my heart. We watched the sky until the last of the light faded to black, until the stars came out and the bees flitted away, one by one.

TRUE TO HIS WORD, MY father helped me build the first of my hives the next day, followed by five more over the next few weeks—the winds kept sending me swarms. I knew they were my uncles, the West and East and South Winds, or at least part of their magic. I never saw them in their true forms, but they visited me on the mountain, sometimes. I finally had to ask them to stop sending bees.

"Thank you," I explained, standing as usual on the edge of my rock shelf while warm breezes coiled around my ankles and the yellow insects hummed merry in my ears, "but the whole mountain can't be bees. The villagers would complain."

I got the feeling that the winds were laughing at me, but they listened, and didn't send any more.

I didn't return to school. To my great shame, my parents never even mentioned it again. Instead, I learned mathematics and science and stories—of course, stories—from my father's books. And I told myself that was enough.

For my tenth birthday, my father gave me the most startling present I ever received: a journey with him into the wild north, to try and find the ending to my favorite story. He'd written a whole book about it, the tale of Echo and her enchanted white wolf. I was a baby—far too small to remember—when Echo came to our mountain village, searching for someone to lead her to the Wolf Queen, who held the white wolf captive.

My father volunteered to be Echo's guide, and although he couldn't return to the Queen's court without nullifying his bargain, he led Echo all the long, treacherous way to the foot of the Queen's mountain. Echo went up alone, and that was the last my father ever saw of her. He made up an ending for his book—he didn't know the real one.

Because the Wolf Queen could command time, it was possible Echo was still there on the mountain, fighting her, that she would continue to do so for centuries to come. But it had been nearly ten years, now. It was worth going to the base of the mountain, my father said, to see if there was any sign of her. And I was to go with him!

So he hired ponies and loaded them with heavy packs, outfitted me with a sturdy walking stick and a fur coat—which I stuffed into the packs when he wasn't looking so I wouldn't have to wear it—and we went down the mountain.

My mother stayed behind—it was the first time we had ever been separated. I worried that she would sit too long in her weaving room, that there would be no one there to cry with her or try to make her laugh when she felt too sad, missing us.

Every day, my father and I rode north, from the time the sun rose until it disappeared over the rim of the world and was swallowed by a sea of stars. It was a hard journey; it was long and slow. But it was almost always beautiful.

My only trial during those long cold days were the times my father went hunting or fishing to feed us. I couldn't bear to see the game he caught—rabbits and squirrels with wrung necks or the occasional deer, blood marring its hide.

I cried every time. My father never reprimanded me.

On we went, always, always north. I felt as if I had strayed into one of my father's stories. All was brittle, and lovely, and bright. If I hadn't been missing my mother, I would have wanted the journey to last forever.

"Why didn't she come with us, Papa?" I asked him one night, as we camped on a frozen lake, water restless far below the ice, stars blazing far above.

"She was afraid I would take back my power," said my father quietly, his hands busy with needle and thread, mending a tear in our tent. "Forsake my bargain with the Wolf Queen."

I peered at him in the flickering firelight. "You wouldn't."

He pricked himself with the needle, and I was horrified to see blood beading up on his finger. "I would, Satu. Because as much as she swears she is happy with me, the price was far too high. If I reclaimed the North Wind's magic, I could bring her back to her own time, ease the ache in her heart."

My own heart raced alarmingly. "What would happen to me?"

He shook his head, a sudden smile touching his lips. "*That*, my dear girl, is why your mother stayed behind and sent you with me. So I would never forget what all of this is about."

I swallowed past the lump in my throat. "What is this all about?"

"You, love. It has always been about you. Our very favorite story."

I thought about that long into the night, as I listened to the ice singing and watched the silvery moonlight refracting over the surface of the frozen lake. I found I didn't want to be their story. I wanted to be mine.

When at last we reached the meadow that sprawled at the base of the Wolf Queen's mountain, there was no trace of Echo.

My father read my disappointment plainly on my face. "We'll wait awhile," he said, clapping his warm hands on my shoulders. "It will be good to rest before the trip back."

So we camped there for a week, passing the time with stories and songs, or exploring the meadow and the long wall of the ice cavern that cut this patch of earth off from everywhere else.

Our last night in the meadow, my father slumbered deeply beside our crackling fire, but sleep wouldn't find me. After hours of restless turning, I at last got up and paced to the foot of the Wolf Queen's mountain. I'd sworn to my father I wouldn't so much as touch it, but I stared up the path, squinting at the stars that shone through the trees and looked for all the world like shiny baubles dangling from the pine boughs.

A current of icy wind curled around me, making me shiver. Up on the path it began to snow. I blinked, my heart raging like a wild thing. Pictures formed in the falling white: a ship sailing through an icy sea, a broken crown, a magnificent, galloping horse. I had not seen my winter demon since he caught me when

I fell; he had never come back to my mountain.

"Where are you?" My voice was the barest thread of sound in the snow and the dark.

There was a glitter of eyes, the sweep of pale hair on narrow shoulders. Words as cold as deepest winter: "Come and see."

I took a breath. He'd saved my life, and I trusted him. So I stepped onto the path.

Suddenly the demon was beside me, one cold, cold hand locking about my wrist, tugging me upward. He smelled of smoke and ice. Fear stole my breath away.

And then I was yanked back into warmth and firelight, my father breathing wild and hard, a sword I didn't know he possessed bare in his free hand. He held me tight against him, facing the demon on the mountain with his blade outstretched. "Get back!" snarled my father. "You cannot have her. Return to your mistress—you are not wanted here."

For a moment more the snow continued falling on the path, but the winter demon had already vanished.

Terror clogged my throat.

A warm wind came down from the mountain and blew the snow away.

It was some moments until my father relaxed and lowered his sword. I wept in his arms, frantic and ashamed. I could still feel the cold grip of the demon's hand around my wrist.

THREE

THE MOUNTAIN WAS ALIVE WITH SPRING by the time we wearily trudged up the path to our house, bees happy and humming, busy with their nectar gathering. We'd had honey twice a year since the bees first came—I'd learned how to harvest it by reading books in his office.

My mother came barreling down to greet us, colliding with my father so hard she nearly knocked him over. She wrapped her arms around him and kissed him soundly on the mouth, and I blushed and laughed and squeezed in to hug her, too.

"Tell me everything," she said over our lunch of bread with ham and early strawberries, which we ate together up on my rock shelf, the wind teasing at our hair. "And don't you dare leave anything out!"

My father recounted our journey for her, there and back, but he didn't breathe a word about the winter demon or how I was almost lost forever to the Wolf Queen's mountain because of my own folly. I was more than a little relieved. There was no need to worry my mother, not now that I was safe and we were all together again.

But I saw the lines around her eyes, I felt the pulse of her sorrow, and was sorry we had gone at all.

Spring rushed warm and fragrant into summer, and my bee-hives dripped with honey. I spent every moment possible on the mountain, harvesting the honey and letting the winds sing in my ears. I tried to push away the memories of the winter demon, his cold hand on my wrist, my childish wonder turned to terror. But I couldn't quite forget him, and there was hardly a night where I didn't dream of snow.

On a day in early autumn, a young man and woman appeared at our door, the scent of magic clinging to them. The woman had dark hair and blue eyes and four jagged white scars down the left side of her pale face. The man was tall and thin, with a few odd threads of white in his yellow hair. Both of them seemed tired but content, and their hands were laced together.

I knew at once who they were, peering at them from the top of the path, bees snagged in my hair, my kerchief lost some-where up on the mountain: Echo, and the man who had been her white wolf.

My mother ushered them inside, and it took me several

minutes to gather enough courage to follow. I hadn't been back to the village since my disastrous first day of school. But my hunger for the rest of Echo's story won out over my anxiety.

They were all sitting at the kitchen table, sipping tea, when I came in. I ducked my head shyly, wanting simultaneously to be noticed and to stay invisible. My heart thudded in my throat, and panic pricked at my skin.

Echo spotted me first, a smile pulling up the scars on her face. "Satu! I'm so glad to see you again—this is Hal."

The young man smiled at me, too, color warming his cheeks. I realized he was just as nervous as I was—maybe even more so—and that gave me the courage to slide into the seat next to my mother, who already had a steaming cup waiting for me.

They told us the rest of their story while the tea went cold and the light outside faded: how Echo had broken Hal's enchantment by not letting go of him while the Wolf Queen transformed him into all kinds of terrible monsters. But not before she discovered it was the *second* time she had confronted the Queen. The first time, she'd failed, and so she called on the Winds and begged them to send her back and let her try again.

At this, Hal squirmed and looked unhappy, while I perked up at the mention of my uncles.

"I saw you, Ivan," Echo said then, turning to my father. "You were in a cold room, writing in a book. It was you who sent me on my journey backward in time, though it was the West Wind who carried me."

I felt a pang of jealousy that Echo had seen my uncle West, while I had never met him.

My father's brow creased. "It was my power, perhaps, wearing my face, but I have no memory of that meeting."

Echo nodded. "Then you are still just Ivan. You didn't reclaim your magic."

My father glanced at me. "I did not."

I blinked and saw the winter demon, felt his hand locked cold around my wrist. I flushed in shame and stared at the table as Echo finished her story.

She had lived her life over again, and the second time she defeated the Wolf Queen and broke Hal's enchantment. The Winds had taken the Queen's magic away and borne her daughter Mokosh, who had once been Echo's friend, to safety. The Wolf Queen was nothing more than a beast now.

"But what *did* happen to my father's magic?" I blurted, surprising myself by speaking.

Echo and Hal exchanged glances. "I'm not sure," said Echo.

"It's gone for good, dear one," my father said firmly. "I don't wish it back."

"In any case," Hal put in, speaking up for the first time, "the Queen's power wasn't strong enough to take more than ten years from us."

"From me, anyway," said Echo quietly. "She took far more than that from you."

Pain creased Hal's face, and my heart wrenched. "She took

centuries from you," I realized. "Like she took from my mother."

"Oh Satu," said my mother, her fingers light on my arm. "My story doesn't matter now."

"Of course it does. All stories matter—there isn't one that's not important."

My father laughed. "Wise words from a true storyteller's daughter. But what do you mean to do now, Echo?"

She glanced at Hal, who flushed bright red as he turned to my father. "Actually, sir—"

"Just Ivan, Hal."

Hal gulped and Echo smiled, squeezing his hand. "There's something we were hoping you could do for us," she finished for him.

My father explained over and over that he wasn't a priest, but Hal and Echo didn't mind. "We'll pay our fee to the first priest we find," Echo promised, "but it's you and your family we want to be our witnesses before God."

And that's how, the next morning, Echo and the man who had been a wolf were married on my rock ledge, with my father speaking the words of binding, and me and my mother and the bees looking on. They said their vows and both of them cried, and I felt their joy pulse hot and bright inside of me.

Their wedding feast was a simple dinner in my parents' house: beef and mushrooms and noodles, bread and honey, and tea, of course. We ate and drank and were perfectly happy, and I never wanted the moment to end.

But the following morning, Echo and Hal said their farewells. I stood in the doorway of the house, biting my lip and trying very hard not to cry.

Hal crouched down to my eye level, unexpectedly hugging me. He smelled like winter and wildness. "It was good to meet you, Satu. Don't let your father make any more deals with enchantresses, all right?"

I smiled. "Don't you, either."

He laughed. "I believe I've learned my lesson."

Echo hugged me, too. "Be well, North Wind's daughter. We'll see each other again, I think."

Then Echo and her wolf were gone, winding down the mountain, out of my story and back into theirs.

LIFE SEEMED QUIETER, AFTER THAT. Smaller. Like my existence wasn't worth as much apart from Echo and Hal's larger, grander tale.

Nightmares haunted me, an endless repetition of the winter demon seizing my wrist on the Wolf Queen's path and dragging me to some unspeakable horror. Sometimes I would fall from the mountain, fall and fall and never find the bottom. Sometimes I was trapped in a dark place, encased all in ice. I couldn't hear or see or breathe, but I could feel every beat of my frozen heart until even that grew still, and the only thing left was fear. That was the dream that lingered, even in the daylight.

I spent that autumn and the first part of winter helping my mother in her weaving room. We set the warp threads on her loom, and when that was finished, we began the actual weaving. My hands were clumsy, but she was patient, and the cloth grew, slowly but surely, one thread at a time.

Deep in the winter, a fur trader came up the mountain with a packet of letters. One was from Echo, who assured us that she'd found her father, and that she and Hal were safe and well. The other was from Echo's half sister, Inna, who was almost exactly my age. *Echo thought we might like to be pen pals*, Inna wrote, and then proceeded to ramble on for four pages about her father's bookshop, and how they were all going to move to the city to be close to Hal and Echo while Echo attended the university. I loved Inna instantly and wrote her back at once, although I realized with deep shame that I didn't have very much to tell her. I agonized over two pages that paled in comparison to her four, and after all that I decided not to even send them. But my mother packed them into her letter by mistake, and by the time I realized it, my awkward lines to Inna were halfway across the country.

I didn't expect her to write me back after that. But another letter arrived in early summer, twice as long as the previous one, and even more enthusiastic. *We're friends now*, Inna wrote. *Too late to take it back—you're stuck with me.*

Her words made me happier than I'd been in a long time. But not even friendship with Inna—which grew letter by letter as the months spun into years—could make me brave. I thought perhaps I would learn to be stronger, *better*, until people and noises and small spaces and hot rooms wouldn't bother me anymore. I thought I would find enough courage to visit Inna in her marvelous river city—we wrote lots of letters back and forth, planning out every detail.

But I am only brave, it seems, with the winds, with the bees. Because it is halfway past my seventeenth birthday, now, and I am still on the mountain.

PART TWO:
North Magic

FOUR

THE APOTHECARY REEKS OF HERBS AND honey, and the close
walls feel, as always, like they're squeezing all the breath
from my lungs. I rub the leather strap of my carrying basket, letting the familiar texture ground me, trying not to be impatient
as Madam Zima counts out a stack of paper bills. The apothecary
has been buying honey from me for years now, but I'm no more
comfortable in her presence than I was as a child. I've only been
here five minutes, and I'm already itching to get back outside. I've
work to do, on the mountain—the winds to talk to, more honey to
harvest, a letter to write to Inna. The summer air is calling.

Madam Zima finally hands me the money and I tuck it into
the pocket of my skirt and turn to go, relieved.

"Satu."

I look back, forcing myself not to bolt. My heart thumps uncomfortably.

"I have need of a shop assistant," Madam Zima says with a kind smile. "Someone to help me mix powders and prepare poultices. I can pay you."

I stare at her with a mixture of panic and horror. My pulse rages, my head pounds.

She frowns, confused at my silence. "Well?" she presses.

"I—I can't," I stammer.

"Why ever not? You don't go to school. I can't imagine how you possibly fill your days. You would learn a useful trade. Put your mind to work, interact with people. People *need* people, Satu, no matter how sensitive they are."

I swallow, ashamed, fighting the hot press of tears. I have slowly come to respect Madam Zima, and I appreciate her business. But her words shatter me. Has she only bought honey from me all this time out of *pity*?

I blink at her, my throat working. I scrabble desperately for words that don't come. "I can't," I whisper. "I can't be away from the winds. From my bees."

The apothecary shakes her head. "What a feral girl you are. I'm disappointed."

I bolt from the shop before I start crying in front of her, pushing past a bewildered customer who curses at me for nearly barreling her over.

I don't stop running until I'm on the mountain, until I'm

gathering tools from my supply shed, opening the hives, pulling out the wax-coated frames that bulge with honey. The work steadies me. Calms me. Allows me to breathe again.

But it doesn't keep me from hating myself. I don't care what my parents say. Normal people aren't so sensitive that they can't agree to work a few hours a day in a shop. Normal people don't need the wind and the sky and the mountain to *live*. If it had been me in Echo's place, Hal would never have been freed. The Wolf Queen would have won. And because of me, she very nearly did. I have never deluded myself about what almost happened that night in the meadow. If the winter demon who served the Queen had succeeded in pulling me up the path of her mountain—things would have ended very differently indeed. He must have been destroyed when the Wolf Queen's magic was taken away from her, because I never saw him again. I'm grateful for that. Because some part of me will never forget he saved my life, once, no matter what happened on that mountain path.

I take the frames to my supply shed and begin extracting the honey. It's slow, sticky work, but it teaches my mind to be still, my heart to be steady. It doesn't wholly chase away my shame. I scrape off the wax with a hot knife, bursting the cells and squeezing the honey through a wide sieve to strain out impurities. When today's honey is strained into buckets, I cover it in cloths to allow it to rest. Then, I bottle the honey I extracted a few days ago, encasing the rich amber liquid in glass. I line the jars up all in a row.

I pace out onto my rock ledge to write to Inna, fishing

crumpled paper, a pen, and an ink bottle from my skirt pocket. The ink wasn't capped tightly, and a good amount of it has leaked though my skirt and all down my stocking. Both are ruined. I feel sick—my mother made them for me.

But I try to put that aside as I pen my letter to Inna, bees humming in my hair. I imagine what it would be like to tell her I'm coming to visit at long last, that I might even arrive before the letter. But I don't tell her that. I don't ever tell her that. If I can't work in the apothecary, how can I ever expect to leave the mountain again?

I'm still on my rock shelf, pouring my heart out in ink, when the storm comes. Clouds knot thick and dark over the warm summer sun, and a sudden flurry of snow coils down on the wind. I set my pen down and cap the ink bottle—tightly this time. There shouldn't be snow. Not in June.

I shove the half-written letter into my pocket, smearing the still-wet ink, and tug my kerchief tight over my ears. I race to check the hives, whispering a prayer that my bees had enough foresight to come home before the anomalous storm.

The snow comes thicker, mingled with ice, and worry gnaws deep in my bones. I inspect the hives, alarmed at how empty they are, at how many bees are out in the elements—they might not make it back. My heart clenches. Losing the bees would break me.

I tell myself firmly that this is no time to cry.

"West! East! South!" I shout into the storm. "Please bring my bees home. Please keep them safe."

A breath of warm wind coils instantly around my shoulders, and I know my uncles, at least in part, are here with me.

The coil of warm air slides away, and I strain my eyes through the falling snow, holding my breath until I see the bees, scarce moments later: a glimmering current carried along on the winds to safety. They flit into their hives and I sigh in relief, the fist around my heart easing.

"Thank you," I tell my uncles. The warm wind glances once more past my cheek before vanishing into the storm.

When the last bees are safe inside, I tug rolls of canvas from the back of the supply shed. I wrap the hives, pulling the canvas tight to protect against the snow and keep my bees warm.

I don't have anything to cover my flowers and herbs, which ramble merrily all about the mountain, drooping now under the weight of the snow.

Then I've nothing left to do except collect my honey jars and set them carefully in my covered basket. I grimace, thinking of Madam Zima. I wonder if I will ever have the courage to face her again.

The snow comes faster and thicker as I head down the mountain, clumsy with my laden honey basket. I slip on a patch of ice and go tumbling down the path, slamming into the side of the mountain. The honey spills out and smashes on the rocks. I stare at the precious amber liquid oozing into the snow, wasted.

Tears prick my eyes, and I hate myself. I'm so, so tired of crying.

There comes the crunch of a footstep on the path above me,

and I jerk my head up, startled out of my misery.

The winter demon stands in the snow, no longer confined to the realm of nightmares.

He is just as tall and thin as I remember him, with long white hands and a long blue coat trimmed with white fur. His hair is as long and pale as the rest of him and is tied back at the nape of his neck, not loose like it was before. His jaw is sharp and cleanly shaven, and his eyes are a glittering blue. He cannot be any older than nineteen or twenty—he certainly does not look as old as he did when I was a child, but he *feels* as ancient as the Winds. Magic sits on him as snugly as his fitted coat, and snow eddies around him, seeming almost to caress his cheek.

My heart thuds like a lump of iron in my chest as I stare at him. I remember his voice, cold as time, his frigid hand locked about my wrist.

Terror sears through me.

I pick myself up off the ground and *run.*

Down the path, around the bend, through the howling snow.

I barrel into the house, latching the door behind me with shaking fingers. I gasp for breath, trying to think around my raging heart, the buzzing in my skin, the pounding in my head, the fear that seeks to devour every part of me.

I close my eyes. I tell myself to be calm, calm. I let the familiar details of the house sink into me: the clack of the shuttle from the weaving room, the creak of my father's chair from his office, the scent of tea wafting in from the kitchen.

It was just another nightmare, I tell myself, though I have not dreamed of the winter demon in a long time. *You must have fallen asleep on the rock ledge.*

But there is snow clinging to the window glass, and my knee still throbs with pain from where I skinned it slipping on the ice. I've cut my hand, too, on one of the broken honey jars; blood wells up in a red line.

I'm still shaking when I step into my father's office, when he looks up and lays down his pen. "Satu?"

"Papa, why is it snowing?"

His head swivels to the window and his eyes catch on the frosted panes. He grows very still.

"The winter demon is on the mountain," I whisper.

My father leaps up from his desk and grabs my hand. I have never seen such panic in his eyes and it shakes me to my core.

He tugs me from the office, past our living room—where there is no fire burning because it is *June*—and into the weaving room, where my mother sits behind her loom. Her hand pauses with the shuttle, and she looks up at us with concern.

"Isidor," says my father.

There is a weight of meaning in her name that I don't understand. Her face creases, and she looks to the window. The snow is so thick that the view outside is a blur of white. She stands from the loom, her hand going to her mouth.

"What's wrong?" I say, panic crawling up the edges of my vision. I shake, shake. "Please tell me what's happening." I pull on my father's arm but he's just looking at my mother, completely stricken.

"What's happening?" I plead. I'm only aware that I'm crying again when my vision blurs and I taste salt on my tongue.

"I'm sorry," my father says. His voice breaks. "Isidor, I'm so sorry. This is all my fault."

A tear slides down my mother's face. "I thought it could never reach us here," she whispers.

My father drops my hand and crosses the room, folding my mother in his arms. "So did I."

I stare at them, wholly numb.

I don't understand. I don't under*stand.*

My mother weeps, shakes. My father clings to her and raises his eyes at last to mine. "Satu." He is trying to speak calmly but the tremor in his voice betrays him.

"Papa," I choke out. "What's happening?" I step toward him, and grab his free hand in both of mine.

"The North Wind's magic," he says all in a rush. "It's been unbound for too long. You must—"

A moan rips from my mother's throat, and my father's words choke off as he stares into her face, his own wracked with utter despair. He wipes tears from her cheeks with his thumbs. "Forgive me, Isidor. Forgive me."

Little black lines crawl up and down my mother's arm, my father's whole body. There are hundreds of them, like the ends of snipped-off threads. My parents' forms begin to waver, like those black lines are swallowing them whole.

"Papa! Mama!" I'm sobbing and shaking, utterly frantic.

My mother turns her tearstained face to mine. "Satu," she gasps. "I love you. I love you so much, and I never wanted—" Whatever else she meant to say whistles out of her in a hiss of air.

I hold tight to my father's hand but it grows thinner in my grasp, like he has no weight, no form.

"I'm sorry, Satu," he whispers.

My mother screams, one thin, high note that is suddenly cut off.

And then both of them are gone.

FIVE

I COLLAPSE ON THE FLOOR OF THE weaving room, my head wheeling, my skin buzzing. I hug my knees to my chest as tight as I can, gulping ragged, desperate mouthfuls of air. I shake and shake. I can't stop.

My parents are *gone*. They *vanished before my eyes* and they're *gone*.

Long minutes pass while I feel I am no longer attached to my body but outside of it, looking down impassively at the girl who fractures to pieces on the floor.

Then it feels as if a breath of wind coils around my shoulders, even though that's impossible in this still, close room. It's enough to make me raise my head, to take slow, even breaths. My heart is not calm, but I find I am inside myself once more.

My eyes are drawn to the tapestry on my mother's loom. It is half-finished, the shuttle loose on the floor. Ordinarily, my mother weaves patterned cloth in beautiful, repeating designs. But this weaving depicts an intricate scene of a young woman dressed in furs, one hand on a reindeer's bridle, the sky white with snow. There is a man beside her, and he's silver and strange, curls of wind at his shoulders. I realize that this is my father's original form: how he looked when he was the North Wind. How he looked when my mother fell in love with him, and he traded away his power and immortality to be with her.

The weaving stops abruptly just below the figures' shoulders—the warp threads have snapped. The half-finished tapestry ripples in that impossible wind and I catch the scent of magic: sharp as ice, sharp as briars.

Horror weighs deep inside me, but there is something else there, too: an ember of anger, flaring fierce and hot. That's what makes me drag myself up off the floor, through the house, and back into the swirling snow. That's what makes my feet pound up the mountain path, heedless of the cold even without my coat. I am several strides from the top when great shards of jagged ice burst suddenly from the ground, blocking my path.

I wheel to find the winter demon standing there, his eyes cold and hard, his face impassive.

Panic sears through me, and I can hardly think around the pounding in my chest, the buzzing in my skin, the feeling that I can't breathe can't breathe *can't breathe.*

"That way is not safe," he says, in the same awful, cold voice I remember from my childhood. "Not anymore."

In my mind I scream at myself not to shake, not to cry. I fight to keep control, to stay present, to not let my mind float away from my body. "Where are they?" The words come out softer than I intend, making me sound fragile and small.

The demon raises both his pale eyebrows. "Where are who?"

Breathe, Satu. Breathe. "My parents. Where are my parents?"

The snow comes faster, thicker, filling the narrow space between us.

"I have nothing to do with your parents." There is danger in his eyes, in his frame, in his very being.

The ice blocking my path shimmers eerily in the gray light. I'm shaking again. I can't stop. Tears blur my vision. "WHERE ARE MY PARENTS?" I scream. A wild wind whips up, shattering the jagged ice wall like so much glass.

I take my chance. I fling myself across the broken ice.

For a moment there is darkness, a searing, sucking *emptiness* that winds into my bones. I fracture into a thousand pieces, and every fragment spins out and out, into the void. I am lost. I am unwritten.

And then I'm yanked violently backward, into the gray light of the snowy mountain, and the hand that's locked around my wrist is colder than iron in winter.

"That way," says the demon, "is not *safe*."

I rip my hand from his and shake before him, gulping and

gulping and gulping for air. I cannot find my voice to ask him: *Is that what happened to my parents? Are they, even now, spinning out into nothingness, drowning in pain?* My mother's scream echoes in my ears and I can't *bear* it. "What is that?" I look wildly across the line of fractured ice. The words choke me. "What *is* that?"

The winter demon brushes cool fingers over my eyelids.

The world shifts before me. I *see*, as I have never seen before: shimmering cords of magic, some shining, some pale, some dark. They wind through the demon and through me, through the mountain and the sky and even the falling snow.

But across the shattered ice there is a gaping emptiness, the magic torn and hanging loose, like my mother's unfinished tapestry. And I know that this is the old magic gone horribly, horribly wrong.

I jerk to face the winter demon, the vision of magic threads winking out of my sight. I try to hold on to my anger, try to make it fiercer than my fear. But the horror of it overwhelms me; I can't shut out the echo of my mother's scream, the feeling of being fractured into a thousand spinning shards. "Who are you?" I demand. "What have you done to the mountain? What have you done to my *parents?*"

"I thought you would thank me."

I blink at him, confused.

He nods across the shattered ice barricade. "For saving your life."

A shudder rips through me. I can't think of that wheeling

void. I won't think of it. "Who *are* you?"

"I am the Jökull. The Winter Lord."

"Where are my parents, Winter Lord?"

His mouth twists in annoyance, like he expected his title to impress me.

"WHERE ARE MY PARENTS?" I furiously blink away a fresh wave of tears.

His glance oozes contempt. "There is always a price for magic. This is the price of your father's."

"*What* is?"

Wind and snow tangle in the tails of his long coat. "The Unraveling world."

"I don't understand."

"Of course you don't. How could you?" His eyes bore into mine. "You are only a child."

My face floods with heat. "I'm not a child!"

"Indeed? It is only a child, I think, who weeps over spilled honey and scorns help when it's offered."

The anger in my belly flares hot, but I cannot voice it. If I try, it will only make the tears come again. Emotion leaks out of me in salt water, no matter what kind it is—if I'm happy or sad, pensive or wistful, I cry. The only way to stop it is to shove my feelings deep down, frost them over with layers of ice. Hope the ice doesn't crack. That is what I try to do with my anger. I grit my teeth, dig my nails into my palms, and stare at the Winter Lord as impassively as I can. "No more riddles," I say tightly. "Tell me what's happening."

His pale brows quirk up. "Can't you feel it?"

"Feel what?"

"The ragged remnants of the North Wind's power, seeking to tear the world apart at the seams."

My mother's voice haunts me: *I thought it couldn't reach us here.*

"Old magic," I say.

"*Loose* old magic, with no one to wield it for far too long. It has gone wild, Satu North, slipped out into the world untethered, unharnessed. There is nothing for it to do but destroy. Like it almost destroyed you when you crossed my barrier."

I shudder involuntarily. "How do you know my name?"

"I am the Jökull. I know many things. And in any case, names are inconsequential."

"Names are the most important things of all."

He laughs. *Laughs.* "In a story, perhaps. But this is not a story, for all your sentimental parents named you after one."

I clench my jaw. "What happened to them? What did you do to them?"

"Do you lack intelligence or simply comprehension? *I* did nothing to your parents."

"My father called you a demon. He said you were *hers*. The Wolf Queen's. You tried to lure me up to her when I was a child, and now some strange magic takes both my parents away the very hour you make it *snow* in *June*, and you expect me to believe it wasn't you?" My voice shakes. I bite my lip hard enough to taste blood, but even that doesn't convince my body to be still. *They're gone they're gone they're gone.*

"I have done nothing to them," he repeats. "And I am not a demon." His eyes bore into mine as he plucks snowflakes from the air, one by one. They crystalize at his touch, falling to the ground like bits of broken glass. "Your parents have been Unraveled, just as the mountain has been, as you saw, as you *felt.* The loose magic—the magic set loose by your *father's* neglect—has destroyed them. Unwritten them from the world."

My heart thuds against my breastbone. I see the black lines crawling over my parents, feel again the awful, hungry darkness, taking every piece of me. They are in pain, then. They always will be. The tears come yet again; I think I will drown in tears.

"There is a way to save them," says the Jökull. His glance is one of pity, of revulsion.

"Tell me," I beg. "I will do anything."

"Anything?" He smirks. "A reckless claim."

"Tell me," I grind out. "I will pay any price."

"Even your magic?"

"I don't have any magic."

He shakes his head. "What a little fool you are."

I bristle. I have the sudden urge to *smack* him.

He grabs my hand again, brushes his fingers over my eyelids. The threads dance back into view.

"Look," he says. "Closely."

I peer at him, at the silver-black threads that twist through him. There are hundreds, thousands, never still. I glance down at myself. I don't have nearly as many threads as the Jökull but they're still there, rippling yellow as sunlight in the center of my chest.

I look up the mountain, where the Unraveled threads hang loose; I look down the mountain, where fragments of threads blow about in the snow; I look back at my house, which glimmers with bits of magenta and cerulean. These are my parents' threads, I realize, the only pieces of them that are left.

The Jökull lets go of my hand, and my vision once more pulses with snow. "The Unraveling claimed your parents, first, because they are tangled tightest in the magic that ran wild. It is taking the mountain, now, and the villagers, too. It won't stop until it swallows every human soul, and when they are gone it will take the animals. On it will go, down and down, until it touches the fault lines of the earth below the mountain. It will splinter out and out. It will fracture the world, until there is nothing, *nothing* left. And there is only one thing in the universe that can stop it."

I try to think around the panic, the feeling that the sky is pressing down on me and the mountain rising up, flattening me between them. "And what is that?"

"*You.*"

"I don't understand.

"To save your parents—and the world—you must collect the loose threads of your father's magic and claim them for your own."

"How—how do I do that?"

"Easy." He snaps his fingers, and the snow between us coils into an elaborate depiction of a mountain, *my* mountain, with the land spread out below. "Your father had no magic when he lived here, and so there are no threads here for you to collect. You must leave your village and go and search for them."

I shake my head and back away from him, slipping and stumbling down the path. "No. No, I can't do that. How could I do that? And even if I could, how does that help my parents?" I collapse into the snow, shaking and crying. I've lost all hold over myself. I am not sure I can ever get it back.

But some moments later, I lift my head to find the Winter Lord still there, looking down at me with an expression I can't read.

"Satu," he says. "You are the only one who can collect your father's magic."

I gulp some desperate, damp mouthfuls of air. "Why?"

"Because you are his blood. His kin. There is Wind magic in your very bones. And it could be that with enough magic, you can undo what your father's power has done—even bring your parents back. But you have forgotten the price of my information."

I at last begin to feel the cold, seeping into every part of me. There are no tears left; I am hollowed out. Empty. "What price?" I whisper.

He smiles with thin lips and frigid eyes. "Your magic, of course. When you have collected it—I want it all."

I stare at the Jökull, shock and fear and anger tangling inside of me.

"But there's no need to worry about that at the moment," he goes on conversationally, as if we're sitting together over a cup of tea. "Right *now*, you ought to worry about getting off the mountain before it's too late."

I glance uneasily across the broken ice barrier. Even without the Winter Lord's sight, the top of the mountain is an empty, ragged *nothing* now. My heart cries out for my bees, frozen, Unraveled, *gone*. As I watch, the nothingness creeps toward me, swallowing the ice entirely. I take an involuntary step backward—I know what it will do, if it touches me, and I don't think the Winter Lord would save me a second time.

He laughs, snow dancing around him. "Run, North's daughter."

And I turn, and I run.

SIX

I SLIP AND SKID DOWN THE MOUNTAIN path, tumbling into the house. I battle the panic that floods through me, pounding in my head and searing my skin like a thousand biting ants. My heart is too heavy, too erratic, too wild.

Run, North's daughter.

I am afraid to look out the window, afraid to do anything but curl up in a ball and go into the darkness whimpering, but I can't do that, I *can't*. Because all I can think about is the pain of fracturing to pieces in the sucking, wheeling void. All I can hear is my mother's scream. My parents were afraid. And if there is anything I can do to help them—I have to try.

I grab my father's weather-stained traveling bag from deep in my parents' wardrobe, and pack in a whirlwind, shoving in anything I can think of. Then I step outside again, horrified to see that the Unraveling has already swallowed the path I just came down.

I bolt into the village, trying not to think about the unstoppable tide of those grasping, broken threads.

I skid to a stop in the middle of the street, fighting through my pounding fear. What do I do? What do I need?

I realize that the village is wholly, eerily silent, and then I see the tiny black lines hovering in the air, settling slowly like ash onto the cobblestones.

The Winter Lord's voice echoes sharp in my mind: *It won't stop until it swallows every human soul, and when they are gone it will take the animals.*

I gasp for air. *Breathe, Satu. Breathe.*

I run to the inn, ducking around the building to the stables, where a single black pony is munching grain from his manger. I shake as I urge him out of his stall, as I bridle him and saddle him and cinch the girth with trembling fingers. I don't look at the empty stalls beside us.

Back outside, half the street is gone. The pony blows out a bewildered breath, and I swing up into the saddle. "I'm sorry," I whisper to him, "but we're going to have to run."

And he does, feeling my need, understanding the urgency. Or perhaps he's just afraid of the roaring, Unraveling dark.

He charges down the street and the mountain path, surefooted on the rocks and the snow. I dare a look over my shoulder and gasp at the nearness of the loose magic. It comes faster and faster, ripping through the world as if it really were made of cloth.

I sob on the pony's neck. We're not fast enough. We can't possibly outrun it.

The path grows steeper, slicker, and the pony skids, throwing me off balance as he fights for his footing. I try desperately to hang on but I fall anyway, landing with a painful thud in the snow. The pony whinnies unhappily. I lift my head, look back up the mountain. The Unraveling billows toward us, the wild magic shredding stone and snow and air. I can't escape this. Perhaps I was never meant to.

The fear is cold, dull. It numbs me.

I scramble to my feet, place one hand on the pony's heaving side. "I'm sorry," I tell him again. "I wanted to save you."

And then I close my eyes and wait for the Unraveling to fracture me.

But it does not.

There is a smell of fire, a whir of wings, and I open my eyes to find the West Wind standing before me, breathing hard. I know my uncle from my father's stories. Wide white wings grow from his shoulders, and his skin has a golden hue. He's wounded: Gold blood drips from cuts on his face and his arms.

"Uncle," I breathe. "You're hurt."

West waves a dismissive hand. "All that matters is you're safe, Satu."

The Unraveling shimmers behind him but does not advance,

like it's being held back by an invisible wall.

"We're fighting to contain North's errant magic," says West, wind stirring through his wings, which he has folded back on his shoulders. "South and East and I. But it's strong and wild and has been unbound for far too long. We couldn't save your parents, or the village. We cannot hold it back forever. But *you*, Satu. You are saved. And now you can save the rest of us."

I shake my head, my vision blurred with snow and tears. "I can't save anyone."

"It has to be you, Satu. You were born to take up the mantle of the North Wind. You are the only one who can bind your father's power and repair the Unraveling world."

"Can't you bind it?" I say desperately. "You and my other uncles?"

West shakes his head. "Attempting to claim more magic than we were given at the beginning would rip us apart, and the world would soon follow. There is only you."

I choke on a sob, and my uncle puts both hands on my shoulders. "The loose magic will be drawn to the places your father walked, the places he once wielded his power. Follow his paths, Satu, and you will find his magic. You can do this. You are far stronger than you think."

I don't have the words to tell him how utterly, utterly wrong he is.

Behind him, the dark mass of the Unraveling world slams against its invisible barricade; bits of writhing, frayed nothingness leak out into the snow. West glances back, jaw hardening as he unfurls his wings.

"Please don't go," I beg. "Please don't leave me alone."

One last flash of his eyes, and his wings bear him upward. "Farewell, Satu."

Then he's gone, one lone, white feather fluttering down in his wake. I catch it, and threads of magic dance all at once across my vision, like they did when the Winter Lord touched my eyelids. I hold tight to the feather, tilting my head upward. I see West flying into the writhing dark, where the South and East Winds are waiting. Something like lightning splinters across the sky. And then the three Winds hurl themselves into the darkness, and it devours them.

NUMBLY, I STUMBLE OVER TO the pony and climb back into the saddle. The Unraveling doesn't reach for us anymore, but my heart still thuds in my chest as we wind our way down the mountain. I am afraid for my uncles. Afraid for myself.

But slowly, the snow stops, and the air grows warmer. By the time we reach the base of the mountain, it smells like summer again. The tundra stretches before me, scattered with wildflowers, and the sun shines clear. My coat is suddenly suffocating. I shrug out of it and look back the way we came.

The mountain rises before me, disappearing into fog. I wrap my hand around West's feather and see the dark cloud of wild magic that has swallowed the top of it, punctuated by distant lightning. My parents are gone, my bees are gone, and the sweet-smelling air can't cheer me.

You were born to take up the mantle of the North Wind, says my uncle's voice in my head. *You are the only one who can bind your father's power and repair the Unraveling world.*

And yet here I am staring uselessly up at the mountain.

"There's a bee in your hair," says a voice out of nowhere.

I yelp and nearly fall off the pony again. "Who's there?" I squawk, pulse raging.

"I would think you'd be more concerned about the bee. Or doing anything besides just sitting there. The Winds can't hold back the Unraveling forever, you know. Aren't you supposed to be doing something?"

"Who's *there?*" I repeat, the words rankling, even as I find the voice is correct: There *is* a bee in my hair. A queen bee, buzzing contentedly. I swallow past a sudden lump in my throat—whenever a queen appears, her hive is sure to follow. Did my bees escape the Winter Lord's storm and the Unraveling after all? Hope thuds through me.

"Are you from the village?" I call, terrified at the idea of having to talk with someone, but hopeful that I might not have to do this all alone.

There's a shimmer in the air where the mountain path spills out onto the tundra. I squint and the shimmer resolves itself into a boy about my age, or at least something *like* a boy. He has brown hair and pale, freckled skin.

I can *see through him.*

I choke back a cry as he approaches me, his feet making no impression on the ground. "Well?" he says. "Are you really going to just sit there gawking?"

"What *are* you?" I whisper, every nerve inside of me screaming.

He frowns. "What do you mean what am I?"

He comes closer and I begin to shake. "Are you a ghost? Did the Winter Lord send you? I don't have any magic. Not—not yet. I can't do anything, I can't stop the Unraveling, I can't—please leave me alone. *Please.*"

The translucent boy stops, tilting his head to one side as a smile tugs up the corner of his lips. "What *are* you going on about? Winter Lord? I've never heard of him. *You*, on the other hand, clearly have some kind of bee magic."

The queen hums at my cheek, her whirring wings whispering past my skin. I dig in the pack for the jar of honey I brought and uncap it, pinching it between my legs and the saddle horn. The bee flits down and starts eating.

"It's not magic," I say. "We're just friends."

The boy laughs a little. "If you say so. But why do you think I'm a ghost?"

I don't reply, just point at him.

He finally lifts his hand into his sightline. He swears, viciously, and scrabbles backward. I am gutted to see tears gleaming on his ghostly cheeks.

"Who are you?" I whisper.

"I don't know who I am. I don't understand what happened to me." He sinks to the ground and bows his head into his hands. He shakes.

Tears run down my own cheeks as I feel his horror, his confusion, his panic. I take a shuddery breath and climb from the pony, setting the honey jar with the queen bee inside gently in the grass.

I kneel beside the boy, reaching out one hand to touch his shoulder. I swallow a scream when my hand passes right through him. He doesn't notice, rocking back and forth on his heels.

"Let me help you," I say. "I want to help you."

He raises his head and looks at me with sorrowful eyes. "How could you possibly help me? I'm a—I don't know *what* I am." His tone is bitter. Hopeless.

I study him, trying to reconcile how I can see him and see *through* him at the same time. It's almost like he was painted in loving detail on a pane of clear glass. His hair, which curls ever so slightly at the ends, flops down over his eyes. He's dressed in a plain white shirt, the kind that ties at the neck. His trousers are frayed at the hems and have holes in the knees. His feet are bare. He has a sharp jaw and green eyes, with freckles scattered liberally over his nose and cheeks. The barest hint of stubble dusts his chin.

"It can't be a coincidence that you appeared the same day the Unraveling came," I say, shoving away the memory of my parents being taken from me, of the wild, awful magic ripping me apart. "I don't know how to help you, but I know I have to try. I *want* to try." I realize I'm talking about more than just the ghostly boy. I also mean the task the West Wind has set me: collecting my father's magic, winding it into myself.

"Thank you," says the boy. He attempts a smile.

"I'm Satu," I tell him. "Satu North. What's your name?"

Something flashes across his face that I don't have a word for, but it feels frantic and wild, like the magic on the mountain. The next moment it's gone.

"I don't know," he says. "Maybe I am a ghost."

I imagine him dead somewhere, cold bones under earth. Bile burns in my throat. My resolve hardens. "I'm going to help you," I say. "I'm going to—"

He vanishes from sight like a candle flame blown out and I scream and leap back. It's only then that I see the cloud of bees coming toward me, glimmering and golden as drops of sunlight.

SEVEN

THE BEES HUM ABOUT MY SHOULDERS and tangle in my hair, as overjoyed to see me as I am to see them. Their arrival tempers my shock at the ghostly boy's disappearance, but I can still feel his lingering presence, pulsing with strangeness, with sorrow. He must be connected to the loose magic, to the Unraveling world—maybe even to the Winter Lord. But whatever he is, wherever he came from, I don't know how to help him. I don't even know if he will appear again, or if meeting him was some errant chance. That makes me sad.

The world is wide and welcoming, down here on the endless tundra. Grass ripples over the ground in waves of dark green and brittle yellow, with pockets of red moss and stubborn purple flowers. I ride south, adrift in a beautiful sea, the threat of the

Unraveling mountain fading with every breath of wild air. But nothing dulls the ache of my parents' loss.

West's words wind through me: *The loose magic will be drawn to the places your father walked, the places he once wielded his power. Follow his paths, Satu, and you will find his magic.*

I know the places my father walked, because all my life I've listened to his stories. They are part of me, wound into my very bones, and I will let them be my map, my compass.

My heart pulls me to the House Under the Mountain, where Echo lived for a year with her white wolf. Part of my father's power was bound into the form of a gatekeeper there, and the House held the library he had made for my mother. It was filled with enchanted book-mirrors, a dazzling feat of magic that speaks to how strong his power was.

But of course it's strong. Because of his magic, the world is Unraveling.

I would guess I have a few solid weeks' worth of riding ahead of me before I reach the House Under the Mountain. Which means that somewhere out here in this tangle of summer tundra, I am going to have to secure more supplies. I'll have to hope I bump into a trader or happen upon a village.

But it's hard to worry about all that with the bees buzzing in my ears and the rich scent of summer grass filling my nostrils.

The day slips away almost without me realizing it, the pony plodding steadily along. Light fades fast across the tundra, and I'm suddenly aware that I have nowhere to camp, no tent and no bedroll, and hardly enough water for my tea in the morning.

But almost like a miracle, as the last of the sunlight drops from the horizon, I come upon a tangle of bushes and a quiet pool of water in a hidden hollow. I slide from the pony, relieve him of saddle and bridle, and leave him to graze or drink, as he wishes. I whisper to the queen bee, and she flies sleepily into one of the bushes, followed by her swarm. I think of the ghostly boy's words, and wonder if I really do have bee magic.

Then it's dark and I don't know what to do with myself. I fumble in the pack for matches and a beeswax candle, which I drive into a soft place in the earth. The small tongue of light does little to combat the dark, but it shines in the water and makes me feel vaguely safer than before.

"I'd light a fire if I were you," says a voice behind me.

I screech and wheel about to find the ghostly boy tangled up in the bushes, which are thick with thorns the size of my fingers and would be causing him incredible pain if he had the usual amount of human substance.

"Bound to get cold in the night, no matter it's summer," he goes on, a smile pulling up his translucent lips. His form is more smoke-like than it was during the day, and the candlelight wavers through him.

My pulse returns to normal and I attempt a smile back to keep him from realizing how much his sudden reappearance frightened me. He's right about the fire. If I don't build one, I could freeze to death by morning—I just hope the bees will be all right.

I pace about the clearing, tugging loose branches from the bushes and dragging them into a pile. I can't avoid the thorns, and by the time I feel I've gathered enough, my arms are scratched raw. "Where did you go?" I ask the boy as I coax the fire to life—I have to use three matches before it finally catches.

"I don't know," he says.

His sorrow tugs at me—I want so badly to help him, but I don't know how. I touch West's feather and peer at the boy in the firelight. There are no magical threads twisting through him. He's a blank, his body hollow.

Out over the darkened tundra, the winds howl. I shudder at the noise, at the vastness of the world, at the immensity of all the things I don't understand.

Hunger gnaws. I fill my waterskin and the cookpot from the stream, then boil lentils and spices over the fire—I'm thankful I thought to pack them in my desperate rush to leave the house.

The boy leans toward the flames, almost glowing in the orange light.

"Can you feel it?" I ask him.

"No," he says. "But I yearn to. I have never wanted anything more. Wherever it is that I am, I think I am cold."

My heart twists. I wish I could command the threads of magic like my father once did—I would tie them to the boy; I would make his body solid again, until whatever other magic pulls on him is forced to relinquish its hold. I don't know how to put all that into words so I just stare at him. His mouth twists and he ducks his head.

The lentils begin to burn and I take the pot off the fire, only to realize I didn't bring a bowl, so I'll have to eat the scalding, half-burnt, half-raw mess straight from the pot. I set it down and it sizzles in the dirt.

"I'm going to find a way to help you," I say at last, crunching on lentils that are so hot they sear my tongue.

"If only you could command the world as easily as you do your bees," he replies a little petulantly.

"I have no wish to command the world."

"Then what are you doing out here?"

I squirm. "Seeking the North Wind's power."

It sounds more than foolish, spoken out loud, but he nods, taking me seriously.

"I don't want to," I go on in a rush. "I didn't ask for this. But my parents are gone and—and there is no one else. So I have to try." Fear is a dull lump in my chest.

I glance up to find him smiling at me. "You're braver than you think."

I don't believe him, but I can't help smiling back.

"What am I supposed to call you?" I ask him, later, as the crackle of the flames and the soft ripples of the pool drag me swift toward sleep. The boy crouches beside the fire like some kind of guardian angel, and I'm not afraid to close my eyes out here with him watching over me. "I can't keep calling you 'ghost boy.'"

"Is that what you call me?" His voice is laced with amusement. "I don't hate it."

I'm so tired I don't even care about the lumps in the ground, or how my pack makes a terrible pillow. "Not really a name, though," I murmur.

"You can call me Fann," he says, right as I'm on the edges of unconsciousness. "It was my name, once. Or part of it. But what about you? I'm sure you have a name other than 'bee girl.'"

I would laugh if I wasn't half asleep. "I'm Satu. Satu North."

"North Story," he muses.

His voice follows me into my dreams, and when I wake, deep in the night, he's gone. Loss pulses through me. What if he really is some kind of phantom, and the last threads of his soul have spun away from the world?

It takes a moment for me to realize that the fire has died. Smoke curls up from the ashes, and the moon floods my little campsite with silvery light. It takes another moment for me to notice the ice fractals creeping over the ground, to realize I am not alone.

I jerk up with a sharp hiss, swallowing a scream.

The Winter Lord is sitting in the middle of the frozen pool, his long legs crossed over each other, watching me with his disconcerting eyes.

"You sleep very soundly in strange places," he says. Danger coils off of him like vapor, despite his jovial tone, and snow eddies about his knees. The air is sharp with his cold.

My pulse rages as I untangle myself from the coat I've been using as a blanket, and I step toward the bushes where my bees went to nest. The thorns are encased in ice and the bees are scattered all over the ground, motionless, frozen.

I wheel on the Winter Lord, who eyes me with one brow raised, unconcerned and unthreatened by my fury. I have never hated anyone in my life. But I hate the Winter Lord.

"You *killed* them!" I cry, angry tears pressing hard behind my eyelids.

"Insects do not concern me. Magic concerns me." He presses his fingertips together. "And right now I am concerned that you have forgotten your promise."

"*What* promise?" My heart is a feral, wild thing. I feel torn to pieces, but my rage just turns to salt and pours down my face. My bees are gone. My first and best and truest friends, returned to me after I had lost all hope—gone.

"To relinquish to me all the North Wind's magic, when you have collected it."

I just stare at him, dumbfounded. "I made no such promise."

His smile is thin and glitters with ice. "You asked me to tell you what happened to your parents. You said you would pay any price for that information, and I am here to ensure that you are upholding your end of the bargain."

"I. Made. No. Bargain."

He yawns, like I'm boring him. "All right then. How about a new bargain? I will help you find your father's magic. I will help you remake the Unraveling world. And when you've done it, I'll have the magic as payment."

"I will *never* bargain with you." My voice is high and tight and thin. "I will *never* give you my father's magic."

He cracks his knuckles, and snow falls from his hands. "And you will never harvest honey again, either, but I couldn't have you distracted from your quest by a bunch of annoying bees."

A scream rips out of me and I lunge at him, slamming into him so hard we fall together onto the frozen pool. The ice splinters out in spiderweb cracks, and the Jökull grabs my wrist, yanking me away from the largest fracture.

"LET GO OF ME!" I snarl, jerking out of his grasp and scrabbling backward. I breathe hard, wrestling with the beast of my fury, scarcely aware of the tears blinding my vision.

"The pool was Unraveling," he says tersely, standing straight and cold. "I iced it over for you. You're welcome."

I glare at him. "What are you? You were hers, once. The Wolf Queen's demon. What are you now?"

The Winter Lord's face darkens, moonlight sharpening his edges. He seems gilded all in ice now, like the dead thornbushes, like my dead bees. He's suddenly beside me, gripping my arm, his fingers burning cold down to my bones. "That witch has no hold on me anymore. She means *nothing* to me. I am my own. I have always been my own."

I twist in his grasp but he doesn't release me and fear pounds sharp against my breastbone. "You're a liar," I whisper. "You belonged to her. Maybe you're still serving her, even though she's gone. But whatever you are, I will *never* let you have my father's magic."

"*Let* me?" he snaps. "*Let* me? Your father's magic will rip you apart if I'm not there to take it from you. You don't have the capacity in your foolish, fragile body to hold it all."

He flings me away from him and I fall into the dead fire, scattering the ashes in a choking gray cloud. I shake with anger as I drag myself up again. Hatred winds into my bones. "*You* told me I was the only one who could collect my father's magic."

His smile is cruel. "But I never said you would survive the collecting. Do you really think you're the hero of this story, North's daughter? Do you really think you actually matter?"

"You're clearly the villain, so I don't know what else I could be." My hand goes to the thread at my throat, where I strung West's feather to keep it safe and close.

I shouldn't have touched it.

"What do you have there?" says the Jökull, brows raised. "A magical token to help you on your journey? Tsk, that won't do at all."

Quicker than a heartbeat he's at my side, snatching the feather from my neck. He looks me dead in the eye as he freezes it, crushes it, flings the fractured pieces to the ground, and grinds them under his heel. "If you want to see the threads of the world," he says viciously, "you'll have to call for me."

I am not sure if my anger is hot or cold, if I want to scream or cry, run or hide. Perhaps it is all those things at once. Perhaps it is more.

"*Leave*," I spit out at the Winter Lord. "Leave *now*, before I do something I might regret."

He throws back his head and howls in laughter, and in that moment I think I could legitimately kill him, no matter how much it might make me shake.

"Do you think you command me, little bee?"

At that I fling myself at him again, no thought in my mind but to hurt him, to drive him under the Unraveling ice.

But he dances out of my way, snatching my arm and jerking me back to keep *me* from the fate I meant for him.

For a moment we are frozen together, suspended in time, and I don't think I breathe, I don't think my heart beats. Fear of him crawls up my throat. He could kill me in an instant if he wanted to. But he doesn't. His eyelashes look pure white in the moonlight. His eyes are softer, younger, sadder.

"I will have the North Wind's magic," he says quietly, "whether you are willing to give it to me or not. Fly away now, little bee. Fly swiftly."

And then he's nothing but snow, swirling into the night.

The ice on the pool cracks, breaks, and even without West's feather, I sense the darkness there, the frayed edges of powerful magic, seeking to draw me in.

I grab my pack and shove all my belongings into it, then rouse the pony. I whisper a eulogy for the dead bees as I saddle him, and my tears freeze on my cheeks.

I ride south under the stars, until I have gone far enough

I can no longer sense the Unraveling magic. But I can't out-pace the feeling of the Jökull's cold touch, the terror that he will encase me too in ice and shatter me to pieces like West's white feather.

EIGHT

HALFWAY THROUGH THE MORNING, I HAPPEN upon a woman on the tundra. She's kneeling in the grass, a ragged pack beside her, and she's weeping like her world has ended.

I slide from the pony and crouch beside her, her sobs catching at my heart. Under other circumstances, a stranger would tie my stomach in knots. But I understand the language of tears better than anything else. I want to help her.

I wait until she raises her head, takes shuddery breaths, wipes her eyes with the back of one hand. She is not old and not young—my mother's age, perhaps; her eyes are dark circles of unfathomable grief.

"What has happened?" I ask her gently.

"I've lost my husband," she whispers.

Her sorrow stitches itself into my bones. Her grief shatters me. "I'm so sorry."

She sniffs, her fingers winding tight about the strap of her pack. "He went outside the wards. There's magic in the earth, you know. Wild, angry magic. It took him."

Panic sears down my spine. "How can the Unraveling have gotten so far from the mountain?"

The woman shakes her head, not understanding. "I didn't want to stay with the others. They told me not to leave, but I can't go on living as if he doesn't matter. I can't—" She chokes on another sob and bites her lip. "I'm hoping that I'm wrong," she goes on in a quieter voice. "I'm hoping he got lost, that he's out here, somewhere. And if he is, I mean to find him." She squares her jaw, but the grief doesn't leave her eyes.

"I hope you do," I tell her.

Fresh tears cloud her eyes. "I won't. But I'm going to try anyway." She hauls herself stiffly to her feet, shrugging into her pack. She leaves without another word to me and walks north.

She fades into the rolling tundra and I weep for a while in the grass, because I can't shake away her sorrow.

A flurry of snow nips at my heels, and I jerk my head up. But my terror subsides when the Winter Lord doesn't appear. All day his presence, his cold, has haunted me, and everywhere I look I see my bees, dead and frozen in his ice.

I pick myself up. I whistle for the pony, who is grazing

contentedly a few paces away. He trots over and I lean against his neck, breathing in the strong, horsey smell of him. It calms me, bit by bit.

"Do you know that woman?"

I jump at the ghost boy's voice, turning my head to see him standing there with his hands in his translucent pockets, the waving grass blowing through him.

I try to calm my jittery nerves. I climb onto the pony and click at him to walk. He does, and the ghost boy—Fann, I remember—keeps pace beside us.

"No," I tell him. "I never met her before now."

"But you were crying for her."

A fragrant wind stirs through my hair as another flurry of snow catches in the pony's mane. I glance at Fann sideways, wondering if he's part of the Winter Lord's magic, if he's part of the Winter Lord himself. Maybe that's why, when I held West's feather, he had no threads in him.

He's still looking at me, waiting for my answer.

"Sometimes I feel other people's emotions," I say. "Like they're my own. It overwhelms me."

"How do you live like that?"

The pony plods along and Fann walks beside us, his bare feet not even bending the grass.

"I don't very well." The truth in this accidental confession startles me.

"I'm sorry for it," he says.

I bite my lip. "Thank you."

We continue on some minutes in silence, until Fann looks up at me, his brow creased. "Why are you looking for the North Wind's magic?"

I blink at him, considering. If he was part of the Winter Lord, he would know the answer already. "Because the North Wind is my father."

Understanding softens his face, and he looks to me with awe. "*That's* why," he muses. "It isn't bee magic at all, is it? It's Wind magic. You're a Wind!"

I'm seized with a sudden, unexpected anger. "No I'm not—I am just myself. I didn't plan this journey, I didn't want it, just like I don't want my father's power. But my parents are gone and the world is falling apart, and if I can help in this small way, I will." The weeping woman's words echo in my mind. "Or at least I will *try*. But that doesn't make me some—some storybook magical being." Tears catch hard in my throat. "I'm sorry," I grind out. "I don't know why I said all that."

"You don't want to be told what you are or are not," Fann says. "You want to simply *be*."

I gulp, reexamining him. I have never had someone put into words something that burns so fiercely inside of me. "That's what you want, too," I realize. "Just to be."

He smiles aside at me. "Yes."

Wind ripples across my shoulders and snow swirls at the pony's feet. Hope blooms inside of me. I don't have all the answers right now—about myself or Fann or my father's magic. But I don't need them yet. "Then let's both of us just *be*," I tell him. "Come on this journey with me, Fann. We can help each other."

"I'd like that," he says.

JUST PAST MIDDAY, THE JINGLE of bells and tramp of many feet echoes over the tundra. A large group of reindeer and herders come into view against the western sky, whole families dressed in bright colors. There are adults and children of all ages, ranging from babes strapped to their mothers' backs to toddlers just learning to walk to nine- and ten-year-olds coming along at a more dignified pace, clearly wanting to appear more grown-up than they actually are.

Most of the herders walk, while a handful ride reindeer in beautifully crafted saddles. A few of the older herders sit in wagons mounded high with furs and supplies. The whole mass of people and animals is vibrant and jangling and loud, making my heart jump in panic and anxiety buzz through my body as I try to absorb it all. I want to jerk the pony around and ride hard in the other direction, but I tell myself, firmly, that their presence is a godsend—I need supplies.

I'm vaguely aware of Fann saying "Satu? Are you all right?" just as our path intersects with the herders' and I climb from my pony's back and start babbling about needing food for my journey. I hardly understand the words pouring out of my own mouth, feeling as if I'm outside myself, watching a foolish girl stammer and shake. The herder at the head of the group, an older woman with silver hair and a proud set to her brown chin, peers at me like I'm not even speaking her language.

"Satu," says Fann. "Slow down. I don't think she's going to eat you."

I take a breath. I blink at the herder woman, who doesn't seem to have heard Fann, her gaze not even flicking to him. My eyes catch on the embroidery around the neckline of the woman's blouse, stitched in a pattern of red and blue reindeer. My mother embroiders in a similar style, and thinking of her gives me the courage to collect myself. "Beg pardon," I say. "I'm Satu North, and I was hoping to buy food and supplies, if you have any to spare. I can pay."

The herder woman smiles, taking my hand between both of her own and pressing it warmly. "I am glad to meet you, Satu North. I am Taisia, the leader of the herders."

"I told you she wouldn't eat you," puts in Fann.

Taisia still doesn't look at him, and I get the sudden idea that she doesn't hear him—that she can't even see him.

There comes a loud, undignified *squawk* from just behind Taisia, and a girl about my age pops up, her eyes round as twin moons. "*What* did you say your name was?" she demands of me.

I blink, utterly confused. "Satu?"

"SATU!" the girl cries. "I CAN'T BELIEVE IT!" And she

throws herself at me, nearly knocking me down in the ferocity of her sudden hug.

I pull away, bewildered, while she just grins, her generous allotment of freckles standing out starkly on her pale skin.

"I don't—" I stammer. "Do I know you?"

I think her grin might split her face in two. "It's Inna, Satu! Inna Alkaev!"

And then it's *my* turn to squawk in amazement, because somehow my only friend in all the world is *here*, exactly when I need her.

Taisia looks between Inna and me with an amused smile. "It is clear, Miss North, that you and Miss Alkaev were destined by the Great Weaver himself to meet today. We were about to stop for our midday meal—join us."

Without waiting to hear my answer—which, at the moment, I am incapable of giving anyway—Taisia turns and calls instructions to the rest of the herders, setting off a flurry of activity that makes my head spin. The tundra explodes into a cacophony of shouting and laughing, grunting and swearing. Reindeer are driven off to graze, wood is unloaded from wagons, fires blaze up and pots are suspended over them.

All the while I'm staring at Inna and she's staring at me, and for a solid five minutes, we're both in too much shock to say anything more.

But then Taisia beckons us through the chaos and I follow her, fighting the panic that's squeezing my chest, my hand tight on the pony's bridle. Fann moves silently on the other side of the pony, with Inna bouncing on my right.

"I can't believe this!" she says, over and over. "I can't believe this!" She squeezes my arm. "To find you here, after everything!"

And then we've reached Taisia's fire, and the herder waves the pair of us onto low cushions in the grass, while calling to a half-grown boy to take my pony.

Fann is not offered a cushion, and my earlier supposition that Taisia can't see him seems to extend to everyone else. I glance at him and he shakes his head, firelight flickering through his translucent form.

"But how did it happen?" Inna asks, leaning close, her long brown braids swinging. "How are you here? Does it have anything to do with the wild magic?"

"Yes, North's daughter," says Taisia, settling on a cushion across from us. "What brings you so far from your mountain?"

Her dark eyes pierce me, and the chaos of the camp and pointed questions make me want to crawl out of my own skin. The mention of wild magic unsettles me almost more than anything else. I fight to concentrate, to tamp down my anxiety and keep control of myself.

"Are you all right, Satu?" says Fann low in my ear.

Heat pours through me, and I feel worse than before. But I force myself to focus on Inna, on Taisia. "How did you know I'm North's daughter?" I ask the herder.

"The magic tangled inside of you is brighter than a lantern in a blizzard. There's no mistaking your heritage."

"Do you have *magic*, Satu?" says Inna, clearly delighted.

My outburst to Fann is fresh in my mind, and I squirm, uncomfortable. "I don't know."

A woman who looks like a younger version of Taisia ladles stew into clay bowls. A boy and girl close to my and Inna's age, who look like younger versions of Taisia still, plop down on the remaining two cushions, elbowing each other in the ribs.

"My daughter, Sanya," says Taisia of the woman. "My grand-children Manya and Miron, the imps." She smiles at the three of them fondly.

Sanya hands round the bowls of stew and I eat mine slowly, savoring the meat and vegetables, the thick, savory broth. It set-tles warm in my stomach.

"So," says Inna, bouncing and impatient, "you still haven't told us how you're here!"

"How are *you* here?" I retort, laughing. "You're much farther from home than I am."

Inna makes a face. "Don't remind me. Papa and Echo are going to *kill* me when I get back. Are you coming for a visit? Did I miss a letter from you telling me you were on your way? Or—" She studies my face, concern pinching her own. "Or is it something else? Something to do with the wild magic?"

I swallow, the stew turning to lumps of beeswax in my belly. "I met a woman this morning who said her husband was taken by the wild magic. She said she was looking for him."

Taisia nods, grim. "That was Nika. She wouldn't listen to reason. She would have been safer, with us. Inside the wards. Beyond them, we can't protect her."

"Wards?" I ask.

"Magical protections around the camp," Inna supplies. "Taisia weaves them every night."

I am not used to the idea of seemingly ordinary people with that kind of power. It sobers me. "And the wild magic?" I say carefully.

Taisia's eyes bore into mine. "I think you are the one to tell us about that."

I twist my hands in my lap. "I don't know how it's out here, beyond the mountain. But—but my uncle did say it would be drawn to the places my father walked. The places he once wielded his power. He was here, wasn't he? The North Wind?"

"The North Wind has not existed as such for a very long time," says Taisia.

"The wild magic is your father's?" asks Inna.

Beyond the fire, Fann paces, and the movement distracts me. How can I see him when no one else does?

"It used to be," I tell Inna. "But when the Wolf Queen was defeated, there was no one there to bind his power. So it's loose. Wild. Hungry. It's tearing the world apart. My parents were Unraveled before my eyes and my uncle West says that my only chance at bringing them back is if I collect the pieces of my father's power. Bind them to myself. *That's* why I'm here."

The fire leaps and pops, Inna and Taisia's family quiet with the horror of it. Taisia, however, doesn't seem surprised.

"What does it mean to be Unraveled?" asks Inna softly.

"It means you are unwritten from the universe," Taisia says. "Purged from existence."

I battle the tears with everything in me, but a few squeeze out anyway.

Inna takes my hand, her face a wreck of anguish. "I'm so sorry, Satu."

Taisia studies me. "You will travel with us," she decides, "for as long as our paths align. But I will require something of you in return."

I order myself not to shake. "What's that?"

"A story," she replies.

NINE

Taisia doesn't tell me what she means right away. She says it will keep until evening, and then gives the order to break camp. The herders douse their fires and are on the move again faster than seems possible. They turn south, like Taisia knows where I'm headed without me telling her. I walk with Inna and my pony, whom I have decided to christen Honey, because he's faithful and sturdy and sweet. Fann ambles along beside me, invisible to everyone else. I can't talk to him now—Inna would think I was off my head. But I desperately want to know what he thinks about all this, if he remembers anything about himself that he didn't before. He seems content enough for now, though, and keeps flashing me encouraging smiles.

I try to push my worries away, focusing on the providential

appearance of my dearest friend. "What *are* you doing here, Inna?" I ask her as we go.

She adjusts her kerchief, which is bright blue and yellow and is tied haphazardly over her braids. "I wrote you a letter before I left, but you know how slow the post is."

I nod. It takes half a year, sometimes, for our letters to reach each other. Our written conversations happen all out of order.

"It all started at school," Inna tells me.

"The fancy one by the university?" I say. "Filled all with rich kids except for you and one other person, who are there on scholarship because you're geniuses?"

Inna blushes. "I'm not a genius. But yes. That school. Illarion—he's the other scholarship student—we've been in competition with each other for years, and when I told him that I was going to be an ethnomusicologist, *he* said I didn't have it in me, that I would never leave the city, that I was too much of a coward, but I know what he was *really* saying was he didn't think it any kind of occupation for a girl. So—"

"Inna."

She looks at me. "An ethnomusicologist is a person who travels to remote parts of the world to transcribe music and folk songs in order to preserve cultural heritage—"

"Oh yes, you've told me. I'm just hoping you're not about to say you ran away from home because of a boy."

I'm aware of Fann, walking beside us and privy to every word.

Inna chews on her lip and avoids my eyes. "Well, not *directly* because of him. I read in the newspaper about remote groups of reindeer herders that migrate relatively close to the city during the spring, and I thought I could find one of them and maybe go and visit you at the same time, and—"

Fann is laughing on the other side of Honey and I have to fight to hide my own smile.

"—well yes, I wanted Illarion to know how serious I am. No one has ever transcribed these herders' folk songs before. When I come back to school with my arms filled with music, no one will be able to dismiss my aspirations anymore. I'll prove to Illarion that I mean what I say. I'll prove to the university that I deserve to attend. And I'll prove to history that"—she spreads her arms out wide, nearly knocking me in the head by accident—"that I belong here, in this world, doing what I love to do."

Inna's fiery zeal swells inside of me, intoxicating. It makes me feel as if I could conquer all the world, and never be afraid of anything ever again.

"That's amazing," I say.

She grins. "Isn't it?"

"But did you really leave without telling anyone?"

"I left notes for Papa and Echo. They'll be angry, but they'll understand—won't they?"

I shake my head, in absolute awe of my passionate and reckless friend. "I'm sure they'll forgive you, eventually. How long have you been gone?"

She grimaces. "Four months, now. It took quite a while to

find the herders in the first place, and it's been an enormous task coaxing them to sing or play their music for me, but I'm nearly finished with my transcribing, now. I'll have to go home soon. Face Papa. I'm thankful that you've come, Satu. That you're here with me."

I smile. "I'm thankful, too."

And I am, more than I can say, but my mind still snags on the loss of my parents and the Unraveling magic and my bees, my bees, dead and frozen in the Winter Lord's ice.

"But can I ask you something?" Inna says.

"Of course."

"When you first found the herders, you seemed . . . terrified. Like you wanted to run away."

"I was. I did."

"Why?"

I never told her about this aspect of myself in our letters. I never knew how. Now I grasp for the words to explain. "New people, new situations—they overwhelm me, especially if there's a lot of noise and activity. It's like my mind tries to absorb every-thing, all at once, and it makes me feel like I'm suffocating." That's not quite it, or at least not quite all of it, but it's as close as I can manage.

Inna nods thoughtfully. "Is that why, whenever I wrote about you coming to visit, you always put me off?"

I don't know where to look, and I fiddle with a loose thread on my sleeve. "Yes."

"That makes sense," she says unexpectedly. "I appreciate you telling me."

My stomach wobbles. "You're not going to say I'm being stupid and too sensitive and need to get over it?"

"Why would I do that? Your mind behaves how your mind behaves—that doesn't make you broken."

Tears smart my eyes.

She smiles at me. "I'm terrified of talking in front of my class, you know."

"*You?*"

"Yes! All those eyes staring at you! It's terrible. But I learned to cope with it, eventually."

"How?"

"Well first of all, and most important," she says, "I learned not to eat any breakfast beforehand if I don't want to lose it."

A laugh bubbles out of me and she laughs, too. My heart warms that my dearest friend now knows the worst about me and accepts me anyway.

BY THE END OF THE day, I have learned two important things about Inna: I love her so much I would die for her, and *by the Good Lord, she never stops talking.*

It's delightful, filling each other in on all the details we were never quite able to fit into our letters, but the constant, intense conversation exhausts me. I feel awful that I want to retreat into a corner by myself for a while, and yet that is the *only* thing I want to do—and it's an impossibility in the middle of a company of reindeer herders.

Just as the sun is slanting over the horizon, Taisia calls a halt, and I remember she has yet to tell me what story she wants to hear. My stomach tightens.

The herders erect reindeer-skin tents to shut out the cold that will come with the night, and she invites me to share her family's, which Inna has already been doing for some weeks. I tell her I would be easier under the sky and ask for a place by her fire instead.

For dinner, we eat brown bread with butter, toasted over the fire, and strips of salted meat and pats of reindeer-milk cheese.

"I'm sorry I talk so much," says Inna, around mouthfuls. "I know I've talked you half to death." She quirks a smile at me. "Echo's always saying I could have defeated the Wolf Queen just by talking at her for half a day. I *know* I talk too much. You can just tell me to be quiet for a bit, and I'll do my best. I won't be offended, promise. I know you need that—space. Silence."

Her thoughtfulness squeezes my heart and I smile back. She hasn't forgotten what I told her today. "Does Illarion talk as much as you?"

She laughs. "Nearly. And always with a scowl, though he hasn't anything to scowl about that *I* know of."

We finish eating, and Inna slips away to transcribe a lullaby one of the herder women just remembered.

Fann crouches on the ground beside me, wavering like flame in the firelight.

I seize my moment. "I'm the only one who can see you, aren't I?" I say in a low voice. "Not even Taisia can, and Inna tells me she has a magical Sight."

He nods, the set of his jaw evincing his unhappiness. "I think we're connected, Satu," he says quietly.

"Connected how?"

"I don't know, really. Some kind of magic."

I study him across the fire, waiting for him to say more.

His eyes catch on mine and they're filled with a frantic desperation. "When I'm not with you, I'm not anywhere, Satu. Like I'm caught in a nightmare I can't wake up from. But I hear you calling me, calling my name, and I fight through the darkness to reach you, to wake up. It's like there's a thread. Tying me to you."

My throat catches, my pulse thudding quick. "Old magic," I whisper.

"Miss North?"

I jerk my head up to see Taisia standing by the fire, her eyes traveling to the place Fann sits and moving on past him before returning to me. "About that story."

One last look at Fann, who gives me a quiet nod, and then I push to my feet and follow Taisia into her tent.

It's not as large as the reindeer-skin tent where I was born, but the dome-shaped space is welcoming and comfortable. A lantern glows from a hook at the peak of the roof, illuminating baskets piled with wool and other weaving supplies, and a heavy wooden chest beside them. My heart hurts at these reminders of my mother; I almost expect her to come in after us.

Taisia kneels beside the chest and hefts the lid up, while I hover hesitantly behind her. Inside are books and cylinders that must contain maps or scrolls. She uncaps one of the cylinders, crouching back on her heels as she slides out a parchment. She unrolls it, and I stumble back in bald shock.

The parchment depicts, with some ancient artist's brush, the exact image on my mother's unfinished tapestry: the young woman dressed in furs with her hand on a reindeer's bridle, the silver man beside her wrapped in winds. But where the tapestry was incomplete, this picture shows the entire scene. The two figures are holding hands, and the man wears a woven belt that matches the embroidery on the woman's skirt.

"What is this?" I blurt. My heart is racing so loudly I can hardly hear anything else.

Taisia studies me, her dark eyes seeing deep. "The story I asked for, Satu. I will tell you the beginning, and you will tell me the ending. This is not the first time my people have met the North Wind. We are descendants of your mother's family, the one the North Wind stole her away from. The one she never saw again."

TEN

"BUT IT WASN'T LIKE THAT," I say, hands wrapped around a tea mug, steam curling up. We are back outside by the fire, watched over by cold stars. Taisia said we needed tea if we were to talk properly. She sits across from me with her own mug, but she doesn't drink from it.

"My father didn't steal her away," I go on. "He traded his power to the Wolf Queen so he could be mortal. So he could live out his life *with* my mother. It was the Wolf Queen who tricked them, who tore them from my mother's time."

Taisia regards me through the flames, and I am aware of Fann, hovering at my shoulder, our unfinished conversation still pulsing between us. Inna hasn't come back yet, busy at her transcribing. A high female voice spools toward us through the camp, repeating the same haunting melody, over and over.

"But that was a wedding portrait," I say quietly. "A wedding portrait of my parents. Which means—"

"Which means you do not know the whole story."

I had always thought my parents were married after my father's bargain with the Wolf Queen. I never realized my mother's family knew the North Wind, that he lived with them for a while. My parents had never told me that. I try to fight the numbness, the tears. I want to flee the herders' camp, seek solitude and peace on the open tundra. But that wouldn't give me true peace. And even if my parents' story is painful, even if everything I always thought is a lie—I still need to hear it. "Please tell me."

Taisia closes her eyes and lifts her face to the sky. I close my eyes, too, so I can listen with all that I am.

"Once," she says, "there was a girl who fell in love with the North Wind. This is how it happened:

"The girl was one of many children in a large family of herders who crossed the great expanse of tundra year after year, seeking grazing for their reindeer and scraping out a life from the harsh ground. Her family were creators, given sparks of magic by the Great Weaver himself. They were painters and potters, musicians and storytellers.

"The girl was a talented weaver. She saw beautiful things where others noticed nothing out of the ordinary, and she wove them onto her loom: sunsets and wildflowers, honeybees and reindeer calves, the mountains, stark against the sky.

"And she noticed the beauty in the wind that brought the winter snows, that changed the world from green to white. It was the North Wind, of course, whom she took notice of, and the North Wind, for his part, had never been noticed by a human before, let alone a beautiful girl with a compassionate heart.

"So he appeared to her in the form you saw in the painting: his Wind body, given to him by his mother, the Moon, and his father, the Sun. The North Wind and the weaver girl walked together over the cold earth for many months, sharing their hearts and their minds, their joys and their sorrows. And they fell in love, or perhaps it is better to say that love was bound fast between them.

"The girl asked him to come and meet her family and he obliged her, though he was afraid at first that he might not be accepted. Perhaps it was the sparks of magic in the girl's family, perhaps it was their great hearts, but they did accept him, welcoming him as one of their own.

"And so the girl married the North Wind, and one of her brothers painted their wedding portrait. That same brother heard them, not many months later, arguing under a crescent moon. The girl wanted to seek out the Great Weaver, and the North Wind your Wolf Queen. Her brother never did understand why. And then the North Wind took the girl away in the dead of night, with no explanation. Her family never saw her again."

My heart wrenches, and I open my eyes again to see Taisia staring into the fire. My mind is reeling with the revelation that *my father took my mother with him* when he made his bargain with the Wolf Queen. She was *there*, in the Wolf Queen's court, there to see my father be made mortal, there to feel the full weight of the Wolf Queen's betrayal. When my parents came down from that mountain and made the long, long journey home, had they realized right away that the Wolf Queen had stolen centuries from my mother? But the thing that shakes me even more is the understanding that the Wolf Queen's magic was not my father's only choice.

"So tell me," says Taisia. "The ending of their story."

I do, in halted phrases, my heart breaking. When I'm finished, I don't speak for some minutes, trying to settle my thoughts. "Who is the Great Weaver?" I ask Taisia at last.

Fann shifts where he sits, staring moodily into the fire. I wonder why he's been able to stay for so long this time, without vanishing.

"The one who, in the beginning, spun the first threads of magic, and wove them together to make the world."

I sip my tea, which has grown cold. "My mother wanted to go to the Weaver, to petition him to make my father mortal. But my father chose to bargain with the Wolf Queen instead. Why would he do that?"

Taisia shakes her head, her eyes once more passing over the place Fann sits, as if she's drawn to his presence even though she can't see him. "Perhaps he was too proud, or too afraid. Or perhaps he could not bear the thought of the Weaver's price."

"What is the Weaver's price?"

"No one knows except the person who stands before him. But it is said to be very heavy."

"My mother knew where to find the Weaver?"

"It seems so."

"Maybe my parents did look for him, and couldn't find him, and so went to the Wolf Queen out of desperation."

Taisia fixes me with a pitying eye. "Perhaps."

I stare at the ground, gripping my tea mug too tight. "My father didn't mean for it all to go so wrong. I know he didn't."

"Perhaps not," says Taisia. "But it did. He caused Isidor great hurt, and her family has not forgotten it—nor have they forgotten her. I am the twelfth great-grandchild of Isidor's brother, the one who painted that portrait. I am glad to know, at last, the ending to Isidor's story. But I am grieved beyond words that it is not a happy one."

I bow my head into my hands, no longer able to hold back my tears. I think I could fill all the sea with them.

"It isn't your doing, North's daughter," comes Taisia's soft voice at my ear. "None of this is your fault."

But that doesn't matter, because this is the story I'm caught up in, the one I can't escape. And the knowledge of my father's betrayal has shattered me.

Taisia doesn't speak again, just lays something gently on my knee and disappears into her tent. I examine her offering in the firelight and find it is a woven belt, the same one my father wore in the portrait. I know at once my mother made it, made it for him, and I bunch it tight in my hands and weep for a while under the stars.

FANN VANISHES SOMETIME DURING THE night, our last conversation haunting me. I reach out for him in my mind, grasping for the thread connecting us, calling his name. But he doesn't appear, and I feel his absence as keenly as a missing tooth.

It's a relief to get moving after breakfast, to ride Honey in the midst of the herders, with Inna beside me on a reindeer. I can't help but soak up some of her good cheer.

She explains that the herders will be traveling south for another week or two, at which point she will have to head home.

"I'm going to miss all this," Inna sighs, her twin braids swaying as she throws her head back and smiles up at the sun. "Papa is going to shut me in my room for the rest of my life."

I have to laugh. "Which you would sort of deserve."

"Which I would sort of deserve," she acknowledges.

The world doesn't seem quite as awful as it did last night, and I allow the tide of reindeer and people to carry me along like a stone in a river. It's comforting, to not have to worry about the path I'm taking, for now. I tell Inna what Taisia told me, the betrayal I feel from my father.

"The Great Weaver is not a myth, then," she muses, stroking her reindeer's neck. "In the city, they speak of God as a distant figure, an uninterested deity who has forgotten the world. But out here on the tundra, the Weaver is alive and well in the herders' songs and stories, in the patterns they weave into their clothes, in the way they speak and dream and discern. It has shaken me, touched me like no stuffy city sermon ever has. But I still never quite imagined . . ."

Something stirs inside me as I study her, a deep, certain *knowing*. "That he was more than a story?"

Inna nods. "And the fact that as recently as four centuries back, your mother believed she could find him and speak to him, that's—well I don't know quite what it is."

"It shifts your understanding of the world," I say.

"Yes."

"Why didn't my father want to find him, though? What could be a terrible enough price that he risked bargaining with the Wolf Queen instead?"

"Perhaps he was simply afraid that the Weaver would say no and tell your father to return to the tasks of the North Wind, for which he was created."

"And he knew the Wolf Queen would never turn him down," I say heavily.

"Love is a powerful force," says Inna. "But so is fear."

I tangle my fingers in Honey's mane, thinking about the panic that so often overwhelms me. "But the Weaver might have said yes."

Inna meets my glance with a quirk of a smile. "And if he

had, you would live in a long-ago time, and we would never have met."

This conversation is starting to make my head hurt.

"But what is done is done," Inna continues. "All we can do is look ahead. Move forward. Forge new paths out of the old ones."

"How are you so wise?"

She laughs. "I'm rehearsing my speech for my father. Do you think he'll buy it?"

And then I'm laughing, too, so hard that for a while I forget everything else.

When we've sobered again, I find myself telling Inna about Fann.

"Completely see-through?" she says, with some mixture of horror and elation. "*Completely?*"

"It's not like I can see through his *skin*," I explain, wondering why Inna is blushing. "It's more like . . . like he's a stained-glass window. Detailed, and yet not wholly *there*."

Inna gives me a wolfish grin. "Are you saying he's *beautiful*, Satu?"

I blink at her. "Sunsets are beautiful. Honey in glass jars are beautiful. Boys aren't beautiful."

Inna cackles. "Oh how very wrong you are, though I don't expect you had a very wide sampling on that mountain of yours."

I flush, realizing what she means. Unbidden, I see the Winter Lord on the mountain, ice tangled in his hair. I shove the image away as fast as I can, unsettled and bewildered.

"Granted, I've only kissed the *one* boy," Inna is saying, "and it *was* Illarion, but——"

"You *kissed Illarion?*" I demand.

Inna turns so red I think her head might explode. She tells me the rest in a squeaky, embarrassed voice, how it was raining in the city just before she left, how she appeared outside the door of Illarion's parents' bakery and informed him that she was off that very morning to prove him wrong. He stared at her, hair dripping, and he *kissed* her, and it was overwhelming and perfect and strange and sent heat pouring all the way down to her toes, even though the cold and the damp made her shiver.

"And you still *left?*" I say, awed.

"I wasn't going to go back on my word *then*. Not for a *boy*."

I laugh. "Isn't he the reason you're here in the first place?"

Inna tries to scowl at me but can't hold it in, a grin breaking through. "It's still been a marvelous adventure, no matter how it started."

No matter how it will end, I think.

ELEVEN

THE DAYS SLIDE INTO A STEADY rhythm of moving and camp-
ing and eating, of songs and stories around the fire. Of
company, warmth, family. I try to make myself useful whenever
I can, helping knead dough or mend reindeer harnesses or weave
cloth—which reminds me painfully of my mother. I trail along
after Inna as she double-checks her transcription work and collects the last few folk songs. Her careful process fascinates me: She
listens to the herder play or sing for her, then scribbles down the
notes and sings them back until she's confident she transcribed
the melody correctly.

The songs are sad or funny or sweet by turn. There are
drinking songs and love songs, milking songs and weaving songs,
dirges and lullabies. There's a song about a woman who becomes

a nightingale and flies among the stars to be with the man she loves—the origin, I realize, of my father's story. There's a song about the North Wind that's sung as a tragic ballad and paints my father as a villain. There are many, many songs about the Great Weaver. And there are even a few about a winter demon, who stops the hearts of naughty children and freezes them in their beds. Those songs make me shudder, because there is only one winter demon I have ever heard of, and his ice does indeed have the power to kill.

The work fills up Inna's whole being, and I can't help but feel a little jealous. She has found her place in the wide world, and I am drifting farther and farther from mine.

Still, there is peace among the descendants of my mother's people. Kinship with my many-times-removed cousins. If the world wasn't in danger and my parents lost, I could almost see myself staying with the herders forever. They don't judge me for my quirks and my need for solitude. They're happy to give me space; they don't mind that I'm awkward and uncertain and talk quietly. But for all that, my heart is restless. It tugs me onward.

Manya and Miron, Taisia's grandchildren, often ride or walk with me and Inna. They're twins, just sixteen, and both extraordinarily brilliant. Manya is a mathematician, and she's always working out complicated equations on scraps of paper. She confesses to us that she's trying to find the courage to tell her mother and grandmother of her wish to leave the herders and attend a university. Inna invites Manya to come with her back to Gradeslav, the river city where Inna lives, and apply to the university there.

This clearly makes Miron unhappy, but he supports his sister's dream anyway. He has a thread of Taisia's magical Sight, and tells Manya with confidence that it will happen, just as she wishes. I'm jealous at the thought of Inna and Manya traveling together, while I must continue on my quest alone.

For Miron's part, he wants to leave the grazing lands where he's roamed all his life and see the rest of the world.

"I can't," he says, when Inna invites him along, too. "Grandmama is counting on me to be the leader of the herders one day."

Manya chews on her lip. "We should both be able to go. It isn't fair for you to have to stay if you don't want to."

Miron shrugs, patting the neck of the reindeer he's riding today. "I don't mind, Manya, honest. It's more important that our way of life isn't forgotten. That Grandmama's legacy is upheld."

My mother's legacy, too, I think. *My legacy.* It's a strange idea.

Manya sighs, scuffing her shoes in the grass. She's usually too antsy to ride so she's walking while the rest of us do. "But isn't that what Inna is doing? Helping to preserve our way of life so it's never forgotten?"

"That doesn't mean we abandon it entirely, Man."

"Then let *me* stay," Manya says.

Inna rolls her eyes at me and I swallow a laugh—we've heard this exact argument every single day since I've been traveling with the herders. It always ends with Manya declaring she'll stay as long as Miron does, and Miron telling her hotly that she oughtn't waste her brain, and anyways he's Seen it, at which point Manya berates him for bringing up his magic when she doesn't have any, and how does he even know his blasted Sight is real, anyway?

"Have you ever seen Miron or Taisia use their Sight?" I ask Inna a few days later, while we're sitting on a rock that juts out over a little stream. We're carding wool because Taisia called a halt for the rest of the day to restock water supplies and do a bunch of other things that need doing, and she won't abide idle hands. I try not to think about my mother as I rock the combs back and forth, pulling the fibers straight and smooth, then laying the carded wool in a basket and grabbing another handful of the unprocessed stuff.

"I don't think so," Inna replies. She's doing more musical notation work than carding, but I don't mind. I'm just glad she's with me. The rest of my journey pulls me on, and I know we can't be together for much longer.

"Although maybe it's not really something other people can see," Inna goes on.

"Can they seek out Sights?" I ask. "Or do they just come on the Weaver's whims?"

Inna fixes me with a critical eye at my word choice. "Just ask Taisia, Satu."

I look away, down into the bubbling stream. I've avoided

Taisia since the night she told me the rest of my parents' story. But it hasn't made her words untrue, and it hasn't eased the ache inside of me.

"What do you want her to See for you?" says Inna carefully.

I don't know how to tell her I want Taisia to See another way, someone, *anyone* else who can collect the North Wind's power and heal the world. I want her to See a different path for me.

"I just wish I could come with you," I say at last, avoiding the question.

"Then come! After you've found what you need at the House Under the Mountain, of course. Bah, I'm so jealous *I* can't come with *you*. Do you know how infuriating it is to have a sister who has been on a literal magical journey when you haven't done anything more interesting than feud with a boy at school?"

I laugh, but my heart isn't in it. "You're having an adventure now," I point out.

"Yes, and I don't want it to end."

"Satu?"

I shriek and drop my carding combs in the water, and Inna grabs my arm to keep me from falling, too.

I gulp air and stare at Fann, who has appeared just beside me, looking shaken and scared. I haven't seen him in weeks and I was beginning to think he was gone for good.

"Fann," I breathe, telling my heart firmly to stop pounding out of my skull.

Inna's brows go up. "He's here?"

I nod but don't look at her, my attention focused wholly on the see-through boy. He shakes and gasps, wavering in the light. But at last he seems to grow calmer, looking to me with gray eyes.

My heart grows calmer, too, my gaze fixed on him.

"I'm Inna," Inna offers, following the line of my sight.

"Satu?" says Fann.

"My friend," I explain. "I told her about you."

"I can't see you," says Inna, sighing. "I'm disappointed."

Fann glances between us.

"You've been gone a long while," I tell him. "I was worried."

He sobers again. "There's been something . . . keeping me back."

"What's he saying?" asks Inna. "How handsome is he?"

Heat floods my whole being—doesn't she know he can *hear* her?

A smile tugs at Fann's lips, but he doesn't remark on her horrifying comment.

"Are you going to translate, or what?" says Inna.

I sigh at her overenthusiastic nosiness but oblige anyway. "He says he hasn't appeared in a while because there was something keeping him back."

"That would be the wards," says Inna, nodding. "Taisia renews them every time we make camp." She fixes me with one of her intense looks. "Something else to ask her about, Satu."

I grimace.

"What are the wards . . . meant to keep out?" asks Fann, avoiding my eyes.

I repeat his question for Inna's benefit.

She holds up her hand and ticks things off her fingers: "Wild magic. Winter magic. Dark magic. Wind magic. No offense, Satu."

"I'm not any of those things," says Fann, tightening his jaw.

I tell Inna.

She cocks her head, and I'm not sure she quite believes him. "What are you, then? Where do you come from, and why can't you remember anything?"

"Inna!" I say desperately. Sweat pricks at my neck and I'm pressing so hard against the rock to try and dispel my anxiety my fingers are starting to hurt.

"I don't mind her questions," says Fann. "She just wants to protect you."

"Do I need protecting?" I blurt, starting to shake.

Inna puts a hand on my knee and I focus for a moment on breathing, so all the pieces of me don't float away.

"Tell her what I told you before," says Fann. "That I don't know where I am when I'm not with you. Tell her it's like I'm caught in a nightmare, and in that nightmare I hear a voice calling a name. Your voice, Satu. And I just assume it's my name—what else could it be?"

I repeat his words for Inna's benefit, my voice wobbling.

Inna swears. "That's horrid."

I gnaw on my lip. "I'm sorry," I tell Fann.

He gives me an odd smile. "Why do you apologize for things that aren't remotely your fault?"

"What did he say?" Inna asks.

I swallow the lump in my throat and tell her.

"Fann, you can stay," Inna declares in his general direction. Then turning to me: "He's right. Why do you apologize so much?"

My face flames. I feel like I've been slapped. I shrink into myself, fighting sudden tears and the sensation I am suffocating, though out here under the sky I have a whole world of air to breathe. I gnaw on my lip and try not to hate myself and I fail. "I don't know how else to say it," I grind out.

Inna's hand moves to my shoulder, and her voice goes gentle. "How else to say what?"

I take a shuddery breath and focus on Fann. "That I hate that this is happening to you, that you're caught in this in-between state, that you have no control over when you disappear and where you go when you do. That I'm the only one who can see you but can't help you at all. That—that it isn't right to only know your name from a nightmare. That I—I *feel* your fear like it's mine, only it's not, it's yours, and I don't mean to take even your feelings from you when you hardly have anything at all."

Both Fann and Inna *stare* at me.

Inna, naturally, is the first to recover. "Satu, I've never heard you say so many words all at once before."

Fann nods, his eyes catching on mine. "Thanks for explaining."

Inna wraps me in a hug and I relax against her. For a moment, all my tangled-up feelings melt out of me, and there is nothing left but release.

I FINALLY SUMMON THE COURAGE to speak with Taisia after dinner, encouraged by Inna, who refuses to let me stay to help her scrub out the stew pot, and Fann, who promises to stay with Inna until I get back.

Taisia is waiting for me as I step past her fire and into the midst of the camp. She turns to me with a quiet nod, and beckons for me to follow. I do.

"I feared you would leave this conversation to our very last night together," she says as she paces through the camp, past other fires and around little knots of giggling children.

Her tone seems to indicate that this *is* our last night together, even though our paths run the same for at least another week. I'm afraid she knows something, something she Saw, and I already regret approaching her. I can't ask her about that. Not yet. "Tell me about the wards," I say instead.

Her eyebrows arch in the gathering night, face illuminated by the mingled light of a dozen leaping fires. "I will do better than tell you. Come."

She leads me past the line of tents to where the tundra grass rustles in a breath of wind so cold it makes me shiver.

Taisia glances at me as she kneels in the grass, as she works to tug something out of the earth. I crouch beside her, watching. She draws her hands up from the ground as if she's cradling something precious, but whatever it is, it's invisible to me. She twists her fingers, like she's tying a knot in the air, and I realize that's *exactly* what she's doing.

"The wards are threads of old magic," I say. "You tie them up around the camp to keep out anything you don't want in."

Taisia nods, intent on her work. When she is done with her knot, she presses the invisible threads back into the ground again. She takes a breath and straightens up, brushing dirt off her hands. "Come. There are nine more wards to bind anew before I can sleep tonight."

I follow her around the camp as she works her magic, peering at the invisible threads and willing myself to see them. By the tenth ward, I almost think I *can*—a shimmer of silver in the light of the rising moon.

When she's finished, Taisia sinks to the ground, and I sit next to her, staring out into the wide and quiet night.

"Inna says the wards keep out wild magic and dark magic. Winter magic and Wind magic, too."

Taisia nods, a little breeze teasing through her hair. "My people would not have endured so long, without them."

"Are the Wind wards because of my father?"

"Yes," says Taisia.

Shame curls through me. I press my fingers into the soft earth, imagining I can feel little whispers of magic against my skin. "And the winter magic?"

"Over the centuries, your Wolf Queen sent her winter demon to attack us, to steal our people away to be her playthings, her jesters, her slaves."

My heart is overloud in my ears. "She is not *my* Wolf Queen. And besides, she's gone."

"Is she?" says Taisia. "My Sight whispers to me that some of her power remains yet in the world, that she's trying to claw back inside her original form, that she might have already found a way."

Ice sears through my bones.

But Taisia isn't finished with her story. "We learned, from earliest childhood, to beware when the first snows came. I saw the demon once, when I was no older than you are now. Winter was early that year, and there was a reindeer calf who came late. It was a hard birth for a new mother and both of them died in the first snows. I had attended the mother because I was the one who found her, strayed apart from the herd for the birth. When she breathed her last and I lifted my head, he was there.

"He looked at me, and then at the dead reindeer and her dead calf. 'Come with me,' he said. 'Come with me, and you will see no more death.'

"I was terrified, but my sorrow over the reindeer made me angry. 'Go back to your mistress,' I told him. 'I won't fall for your tricks.'

"He turned away without another word and vanished into the snow. The next day, three children vanished, one of them my own sister. I know it was him who took them. We never saw them again. I am sure they are long dead now."

Her grief, and my answering horror, makes me shake. "I'm sorry," I say.

"Oh dear one." Taisia's voice is the gentlest I have ever heard it. "None of this was your doing."

"And yet I feel the weight of it as if it were," I answer.

"That means you are strong, you know," says Taisia.

"Then why do I feel so weak?"

But she has no reply to that.

It is only later, when we have returned to her fire and she makes tea to hand round, that something occurs to me. We are no longer alone, Manya and Miron arguing about something or other while Inna squints at a sheaf of music in the flickering light and Fann paces silent and see-through just past the tent.

"Who was my mother?" I ask.

"The herd leader's daughter," Taisia tells me. "She would have become the leader herself, if your father had not taken her away."

If he would have chosen the Weaver instead of the Wolf Queen, who stranded my mother centuries away from the original threads of her life. I wish I could talk to my parents. Wish I could rest my head on my mother's shoulder and feel her warm fingers in my hair while my father told one of his stories, his melodic voice spinning out the magic he traded away. I wish I could ask him why, *why.*

But they are lost to me, now. Even if I succeed in gathering my father's power, there is no guarantee I can save them.

"Would I be here if my father had gone to the Weaver?" I

whisper. "Would I even exist?" Flames leap up into the night while tea slowly cools in clay cups. Tears prick behind my eyes.

"I am not that kind of Seer," says Taisia. "My Sight shows me only what is ahead, not what is behind."

I try to shove down my grief. "And have you Seen what is ahead for me?"

Taisia meets my eyes in the firelight. "Ice, Satu. Ice and snow and a cold, cold wind."

I think of bees, dead and frozen, scattered across the earth. My vision blurs. "Is that all?"

"No," says Taisia. "But beyond that, my Sight grows less clear."

I shake as I cry, as I fight *not* to, because I don't want Manya and Miron staring, I don't want to pull Inna away from her work. "Tell me," I beg. "Please."

"There is also darkness," says Taisia. "Darkness and sorrow and power. Power beyond all imagining. *Your* power, Satu."

I weep under the stars because I don't want it, don't want it, and yet there is no other path for me to take.

TWELVE

I WAKE TO THE SOUND OF SCREAMING, to a cloud of choking ash, to a red rising sun.

I jerk upright—the camp is in chaos. Reindeer are running loose from their pickets, and herders are pounding between the tents, dousing fires and shouting at each other. I can hardly see through the smoke and ash of the dead fire beside me, but the camp is not as full as it ought to be.

The screaming comes again, twined with the high wail of a child. Both sounds are suddenly cut off, and horror sears through me.

Then Taisia is beside me, pulling me to my feet, her long hair gray with ashes. "The wards have failed," she says. "The wild magic has found us. You must go, as quickly as you can."

"But—"

The herder woman grabs me by my shoulders, her grip so tight it's almost painful. "I will try and bind up the magic. I will try to seal it here, so no more leaks out. But you have to go, North's daughter. Go and gather your father's power. Fix this." The Unraveling. It's here.

For an instant, I look past her. I see Manya dissolve into a thousand black threads, torn and frayed. The pieces of her float in the air and blow away with the dust.

"Go!" says Taisia, shoving me away.

But I'm frozen in place, horror rewriting every part of me as I realize who's missing. "Inna!" I scream, tears pouring down my cheeks. "INNA!"

"Here, Satu." She touches my arm, and my vision clears.

She has Honey and one of the reindeer, loaded with packs. Numbly, I climb onto the pony while she mounts the reindeer. There is a flicker beside her, a shadow that resolves itself into Fann. My panic eases a little.

Inna gives me a grim nod, and then both the reindeer and the pony lunge into motion.

Come with us, I think to my ghostly boy. *Don't leave me. Don't fall behind.*

The sun rises higher, red light dancing through the smoke, like the sky is streaked with powdered blood. I look over my shoulder as we ride away from the camp. Threads dance in my vision. Thousands upon thousands of them. All of the herders are gone. In a moment.

I don't know what Taisia did, or how she did it. But the Unraveling doesn't follow us. It doesn't touch Inna or Fann or me. I feel sick. Utterly broken.

They're gone, they're gone, they're gone.

I don't even realize I'm crying until I can't breathe, tears and mucus plugging my nose and throat. I choke and I gasp and then Inna is tugging me down from Honey, wrapping her arms around me as I sputter and shake like a fish in the grass.

"Breathe," says Inna, her hands firm on my shoulders. "Just breathe."

It's some minutes later that I come into myself enough to lift my head, to wipe my eyes, to see that the sky is no longer red and we're adrift in a sea of grass, Inna and Fann and me. Honey and the reindeer Inna's been riding are peacefully grazing. A gentle breeze whispers past my cheek.

"I killed them," I say. "I killed them all."

"No, you didn't!" says Inna fiercely, her voice thick with tears. "This wasn't your fault."

"You didn't kill anyone," Fann agrees. His translucent form wavers in the wind, and I wish, I wish I could hold him here.

"Taisia," I gasp. "Manya and Miron. The whole camp, Inna!"

"I know," she says. "I know. Taisia knew, too." Her forehead creases. "She Saw this, Satu. She Saw it all, and she woke me early this morning, told me to grab our gear and get you out. She saved us both."

I shake, desperately trying to fight off the pins and needles buzzing along my skin, the pull of my panic that wants to unravel me every bit as much as the loose magic. "She saved us over her own kin? Why?"

Inna shakes her head. "Because you're the only one who can fix all this. And I think—I think Taisia knew you couldn't do it alone. And you *are* her kin, Satu."

A wild wind whips across the tundra, so cold it makes my teeth hurt. I catch the scent of ice. "It was him." I push to my feet, fear pulsing in my throat as I peer frantically across the tundra, searching for the Jökull.

"Who?" says Inna.

"The Winter Lord. He must have found a way to break Taisia's wards, to let the Unraveling magic in."

Inna frowns, the wind tugging strands of hair loose from her braids. "Why would he do that?"

I think of my bees, their frozen bodies littering the ground beneath the thorn bushes. "He loves chaos. And he wants to get at me. To drive me on."

Fann shifts where he stands. The wind blows blades of grass through him, like he isn't there at all. The thought makes my heart stutter.

"Why?" says Inna.

"He wants the North Wind's magic. He wants me to collect it, and then give it to him."

"You would never do that."

"No."

Fann looks stricken, terrified. "You can't let him."

"Never," I say fiercely.

"Fann's here," Inna realizes. "What's he saying?"

I tell her, then whistle for Honey, who picks his shaggy head up from the grass and ambles over to me with obvious reluctance.

The wind grows even colder, and a snowflake melts on my cheek.

"Time is running out," I tell Inna. "What happened at the camp is going to keep happening, until I find a way to bind my father's magic or die trying."

She clenches her jaw, like she knows what I'm about to say and is gearing up for a fight.

"You have to go home." Tears stick in my throat but I push past them. "You'll be safer there, away from me and the Winter Lord and the Unraveling."

She shakes her head. "I'm coming with you, Satu."

I stand my ground, as much as it costs me. "No. You're not. I'm sorry, Inna. I'm so very sorry but I can't let you come. I couldn't bear it if the Winter Lord hurt you, if the Unraveling magic tore you apart. This is not something you can help me with. I have to go on alone."

"You won't be alone," says Fann quietly.

Inna bites her lip. "Satu—"

I launch myself at her, wrapping my arms around her and hugging her fiercely. "I don't *want* you to leave me," I choke into her hair. "But I need you to be safe. Please, Inna."

She hugs me back, so tight I can hardly breathe. "All right," she says. "I'll go."

We draw apart from each other and it kills me to see the tears trembling on Inna's lashes. "Just promise me something," she says. "When you've found the House Under the Mountain, when you've done what needs doing there, come to Gradeslav. Echo traveled with your father for months—she might be able to help you find the rest of his magic and bind it, or at least have an idea of how to stop the Unraveling."

"I'll come if I can," I promise. Grief makes my throat close. "I don't want to say goodbye."

A tear drips down her cheek. "Then let's not. It's a gift from the Weaver that we found each other, and we won't be apart for long. I'll see you soon, Satu."

I force a smile. "I'll see you soon, Inna."

And then she climbs onto the reindeer and rides east, while I mount Honey and just sit there for a moment, watching my friend grow smaller and smaller, until I can't bear it anymore.

The wind whips wilder, colder. I wrap my hands around Honey's reins. "Come with me, Fann," I tell the ghostly boy. "Don't leave me alone."

"I want to stay with you forever, Satu," he says quietly. "Don't let me fall asleep."

We go south, the icy wind biting at our heels.

THAT COLD WIND CHASES US all day, and by the time the sun is setting, the grass behind us is brittle with frost. Honey can't go on through the night and neither can I, but it feels wrong to make camp, when Taisia and all the herders are gone. I hope Inna is safe on her westward road. I hope she's not too lonely.

I wish Taisia had taught me how to set wards to protect myself from the Jökull, but she didn't, and in any case I have neither the knowledge nor the magic. Honey and Fann and I are on our own.

Fann has been quiet all day, sensing, perhaps, that no words could drive away my grief, my guilt. But his presence has comforted me all the same.

I free Honey of saddle and bridle and open my pack. There's no wood for a fire, which means a cold night ahead and no tea in the morning, but the pack is stuffed full of food: strips of dried meat, pats of reindeer milk cheese wrapped in cloth, and bread rolls, brown and sweet. I wonder with a pang if it was Taisia or Inna who packed it up for me. The wedding belt my mother made for my father is there, too. I cinch it around my waist, a piece of my parents to carry with me always.

I eat, and though I've been too numb all day to feel hunger, my head is clearer when I've finished. Then there's nothing to do but shake out my bedroll and stare up at the glittering stars.

"Taisia and the herders weren't your fault," says Fann, stretching out on his back beside me. "I hope you know that."

I turn my face away from him, trying not to feel the rapidly dropping temperature, or the ice forming under my cheek.

"Everything is my fault."

"You're wrong. You are responsible for your choices and your choices alone. If this is anyone's fault at all, it's your father's."

I hunch in on myself. The ice crackles over the grass and I catch the scent of winter as I ask myself a question I don't really want the answer to: Is my father the villain of this story? He could have gone to the Weaver to be made mortal, but instead he bargained with a wicked sorceress and gave her the power to control time. Because of him, my mother was ripped away from her family. My father always told me he atoned for his sins, but did he really? What about all the other people the Wolf Queen cursed or killed with the North Wind's power? Were they all just hapless victims of my father's choice? Is the world, Unraveling at the seams, another casualty? And if my father is the villain, what does that make me?

I breathe out, long and slow. "I know it's not my fault," I say. "But I feel the pain of it. The injustice, the tragedy. It's too heavy for me."

"Then let someone else help you carry it."

I turn to study Fann in the dark. "I don't know how to let it go. I don't know how to not feel everything all the time. I don't know *how*." My voice cracks.

"Just know," he says seriously, "if something is too heavy for you, it is okay to set it down."

Tears prick at my eyes. "I'll try," I say. "I just—I wish I was brave, Fann. I wish I was brave and strong and—I wish I was more. I wish I was *better*, and I'm not. I'm not." I'm crying now, frost melting beneath my cheek.

"You are braver than you imagine, Satu North," says Fann softly. "And you are full to the brim, you know."

He's so hard to see out here in the frigid dark. I reach out one hand—I wish I could touch him. My throat catches. "Full of what?"

"Of life," he says, "of magic. Of stories."

I take a shuddery breath. My heart beats a little quieter. "Fann," I say.

He stretches out his fingers, like he wants to touch me, too. "What is it?"

"I'm going to find a way to help you."

He smiles. "I know."

The night runs still and dark between us. Sleep tugs at me, and I let my eyelids drift shut.

"You're very slow, in your journeying," says a cool voice above me. "I thought you would have collected at least a *little* magic, by now."

I jerk awake and am on my feet the next moment, pulse raging. The Winter Lord stands in the dark with his coat flapping about his knees and his hands shoved deep in his pockets. He eyes me with a hint of boredom, but I can sense the magic lurking beneath his skin.

I scream at my heart to be quiet, at my body to be still. I force steel into my voice. "Why are you here?" I demand. "You've done enough for one day."

"Oh?" His pale brows tilt up. "What have I done?"

I'm aware of Fann, standing at my elbow. His wavering presence makes me braver than I would be alone. "You broke the wards. You let the Unraveling magic in. All the herders are gone, because of you."

His eyes narrow and he smiles thinly. Snow swirls around him, but none of it touches me. "Why would I have done that?"

I meet him glance for glance. "To drive me faster on my way?"

He laughs at the wobble in my voice. "There is some cause for haste, yes. But—" His glance slides over to Fann, and fixes there. "Have you picked up a stray, North? That seems unlike you."

I suck in a sharp breath. "You can see him?"

"Of course I can see him." The Jökull paces over to Fann, who shoots me a terrified look. "Fascinating."

"What do you want?" Fann asks, tight and cold.

The Winter Lord passes one hand through my ghostly companion, who leaps backward and curses at him.

"Why are *you* here?" the Jökull returns. "Who are you, exactly?"

"He doesn't know," I offer. "He can't remember."

The Winter Lord scoffs. "Indeed."

Fann folds his arms tight across his chest. "Leave. Now. Satu is under my protection."

The words warm me from the inside but they make the Jökull throw back his head and howl with laughter. "Under your protection? How? You can't even hold a knife, let alone use one."

A darkness comes into Fann's face. "You shouldn't be here."

"And *you* are a new trick entirely," the Jökull returns. "Clever. There isn't enough of you present for me to freeze—my magic can't touch you." Wind rises swift and cold around him. He glances at me with a question in his eyes, but I have no answer for him. I wouldn't give it even if I did.

"What are you playing at?" Fann says. "If it's magic you're after, you're not going to get it."

"I am going to take whatever I please."

Fann takes a step toward the Jökull. "I told you to *leave!*"

"Fann," I say quietly, afraid of what might happen if he antagonizes the Winter Lord further.

"What did you call him?" The Winter Lord looks like he's been slapped, or some nightmare has appeared suddenly to torment him. But what does a demon have to fear?

"My name," says Fann, staring him down. "She called me by my name."

Snow falls thick and fast around us, obscuring the stars. My hands and feet grow numb, but I don't want to give the Winter Lord the satisfaction of watching me pull my coat tight against his storm.

"That is not your name," says the Jökull. "I knew someone who had that name, or one like it, long ago. It wasn't you."

The temperature drops even more, and the snow that falls against my cheek stings with ice.

"Perhaps I *am* that person you knew long ago," says Fann, eyes boring into the Winter Lord's.

"You know nothing about him."

Fann turns his gaze to mine. "I'm beginning to remember, Satu. Do you want to hear?"

"Of course I do."

"I loved the sun," Fann says. "I loved to ride in the meadow or fence with my brothers in the gardens. I—" His brow creases, like the memories pain him. "I was a painter. I would stand out on the terrace for hours and paint."

I am aware of the Winter Lord in my peripheral vision, a towering pillar of cold rage, but I keep my glance trained on Fann. "What did you paint?"

"The woods. The lake. The sky."

His words transfix me. "The sun?"

He smiles. "The sun, too. But that was before."

"Before what?"

"Before Father sent me away to the army."

My heart is a flittering creature in my throat. I'm afraid for who he was then. I'm afraid for what he might be now. "Did you go to war?"

"Did I die in battle, you mean," says Fann.

I grimace. "Did you?"

"No. I ran away."

His sorrow twists through me. It makes me *ache*.

"That's enough," says the Winter Lord.

I turn toward him; snow drifts up to his knees, icicles jangling together in his long hair. His face is dark with fury.

Fann smiles coldly at him, lifting his chin in defiance.

"Go," the Jökull commands.

Fann folds his arms across his chest. "I'm not going anywhere."

"I SAID GO!" the Jökull shouts. He lifts his hands, hurling snow and jagged spears of ice toward Fann, who screams and winks out like a lamp.

"FANN!" I cry, leaping to the place where he stood.

But he's gone, and I'm left to face the Winter Lord alone.

He looks at me over the snow that swirls between us, and there is something strange in his eyes that makes my stomach twist.

"What did you do to him?" I demand. "You said your magic couldn't hurt him. What did you do?"

"He means you harm, Satu," says the Jökull.

Tears freeze on my eyelashes, giving me a frosted view of the world. "What harm could he do me?"

"More than you think. Don't stay with him, don't talk to him, don't trust him."

"I don't trust *you*. The herders sing ballads about you freezing children in their beds, you know. About being the Wolf Queen's servant and carrying out her evil bargains."

He grimaces. "I don't do that anymore."

Taisia's words curl through me: *Some of her power remains yet in the world. She's trying to claw back inside her original form. She might have already found a way.*

"Don't you? Why else would you break protective wards and let loose magic Unravel the whole camp?"

"That wasn't me."

"Leave." I lift my chin.

He takes a step forward. "Satu—"

"WHAT DID YOU DO TO HIM?"

He looks at me, his eyes searching, deep. "I cut the thread," he says.

"What thread?"

He blinks, and his snowstorm lessens, a little. "The thread connecting him to you."

Grief and anger clog my throat. "You sent him into a nightmare."

"No I didn't, North's daughter. There's only one nightmare. It's mine."

He turns with a swirl of his coat and is gone, icicles clattering to the ground after him.

THIRTEEN

O N MY MOUNTAIN, WITH MY BEES, I only ever wanted solitude. I didn't know I was lonely, then. I know it now, and it
threatens to crush me.

I'm a day on my own. Three. Four. The tundra is crisscrossed
with streams, and as I pick my slow way south, the ground gives
way to hills and valleys, pockets of forest and wide, windswept
plains. I meet no one and could easily imagine I am the only
soul left in all the world who hasn't been Unraveled. That is my
deepest fear. The reason I sleep in fits and starts. Because what if
I'm already too late?

I miss the sense of family, of togetherness I had with the
herders: Manya and Miron's constant bickering and Taisia's
astute observations. I miss Inna's constant chatter and fierce

friendship. I miss Fann's steady presence, the words he spoke in the icy dark that comforted my very soul. And I miss my parents, so deeply and so desperately that I can't, can't, can't bear it. So I shove my missing them down into the core of my being—if I didn't, I could never move on.

I'm horribly afraid that Fann won't be able to find his way back to me, that the cord the Winter Lord severed can never be mended. I call to him every day as I'm riding Honey, every night as I'm staring up at the sky while sleep eludes me. I hope and I hope and I call him.

But he doesn't come.

I've been a week traveling by myself when I camp on the edge of a wood, grateful for abundant kindling, even though the nights are not so cold as they were closer to my mountain.

My fire pops and sparks; above the trees the stars shine cold. Honey dozes on three legs and I nibble the last of the bread rolls from the packs, grown stale now, along with a few strips of dried reindeer meat and a bite of cheese. I boil water over the fire to make tea and spoon leaves into a battered copper pot, silently thanking Inna or Taisia for their foresight in making sure I had all the necessities.

"Satu?"

I squawk and jump, scattering tea leaves on the ground.

Fann crouches on the other side of the fire, translucent as ever, his bare toes leaving no mark in the soft earth.

"I didn't mean to scare you," he says.

I gulp mouthfuls of forest air as my heart rate slows down to normal and a grin splits my face in two. "I didn't know if you'd come back. I didn't know if you *could*, after what the Winter Lord did to you."

His jaw tightens. "He tried to make it so I couldn't. He nearly succeeded. How long has it been?"

"A week."

He shudders and shudders, and I want to wrap my arms around him, hold him still and safe, and I *can't* and I *hate* that I can't.

"I only exist when I'm with you," Fann says. "Without you, without the thread of magic connecting us—I would be trapped forever in the dark."

"I'll find a way to make it stronger," I say fiercely. "I won't let him send you away again, I swear to you, Fann. I'll protect you. I'll keep you here."

He nods, without quite meeting my eyes.

"Don't you believe me?" I ask him softly. My heart is pulsing wild and scared and I find I can't quite bear the thought that he doesn't trust me.

"I'm afraid, Satu. Afraid the pull of the nightmare will be stronger than the pull of you."

The trees murmur in the dark; the flames of my fire twist into impossible shapes, imprinting behind my eyelids.

"Stay awake then," I tell him. "Stay with me. Don't fall asleep."

His smile is as gentle as it is sad. "I'll try, Satu."

But I don't do a good enough job holding him there with me, because by the morning he's gone again, back into his nightmare, and I'm left here, alone, in mine.

I NEED MAGIC, I REALIZE, to bind Fann here. And if I'm right, if there's plenty of my father's power waiting for me at the House Under the Mountain, I can use some of it to hold Fann back from his nightmares. I'll find a way to tie enough threads between the two of us that not even the Winter Lord can sever them. If I pour enough magic into him, maybe I can even make him solid. Human. Whole.

That's the hope that keeps me going for the next five days as I tramp through a forest vastly larger than it looked from the outside. The trees are so tall, the branches so thick, that only the barest hints of sunlight slip through. It's quiet enough I can hear the faintest drip of water, and every branch that crunches underfoot is thunderous. I begin to think I will always be walking here, steeped in the scent of leaves and loam.

But on the evening of the fifth day, I at last reach the far border of the wood. Beyond the trees, stars glow soft over a rolling meadow.

A sudden tugging sensation in my heart makes me stagger and gasp. There are remnants of my father's magic here; I can sense them like a lodestone pulled to the earth.

That *tug tug tug* draws me forward and I obey, leaving Honey to graze as he pleases.

In the center of the meadow there is a small mound under the grass—not a hill, certainly not a mountain, but I know in the depth of my bones that this is all that's left of the wolf's house. The pulse of my father's magic is strong here, as if the very air is made of it. It calls to me, calls to me. I am desperate to answer but I don't know *how*. I curse the Winter Lord and the loss of West's white feather—if I still had it, I would be able to see my father's threads, maybe even draw them inside of me where they belong.

But there is only me, out here in the waving grass. Empty and powerless.

Wind murmurs through the meadow, whispering past my shoulders.

"I don't know how to bind you," I say bitterly. "I don't know *how*."

Something shines in the grass, a jagged shard that reflects a glimmer of stars. I peer at it, my heart thrumming against my breastbone, and begin to dig. My fingers pull at cool earth, digging deeper and deeper until the shard is loose enough that I tug it free.

It's a piece of broken glass the size of my hand. It winks and shimmers, and the memory of a story coils through me. Because it's not just a fragment of glass—it's a mirror.

I suck in a deep breath and touch the center of the shard with my fingertips.

The cool rush of magic creeps up my arm and races through my body. The world wavers around me, and everything goes black.

For a moment, I am nowhere, a place beyond darkness, beyond air, beyond life. It is emptier even than the Unraveling because there is nothing there at all. The terror of it crushes me, but I have no breath or body to scream.

And then I'm lying on a cold marble floor in a ruin of dust and broken glass, my heart thundering through my bones. I sit up, gasping, fighting the panic, the lingering emptiness I can't quite shake away.

It's some moments before I come back to myself, enough to realize I've cut my hands on the broken glass surrounding me. The bite of pain clears my head, and I wipe my palms on my skirt.

I'm in a huge, airy room, high paneled ceilings stretching at least twenty feet above me and hung with broken chandeliers. I know this place: the library my father enchanted. Once, every inch of the walls was covered in book-mirrors that swept a reader off on marvelous adventures with a single touch. Now, the mirrors that remain are cracked, huge pieces fallen away from leather frames or shattered on the floor. I stand slowly, aware of every pulse of my heart.

Whatever broken magic brought me here, I feel as if this library is a gift from my father, a sign that wherever he is he's watching over me, helping me. That maybe he's not the villain after all.

Perhaps here I can learn how to gather up the threads of his magic and bind them in my heart, where I am certain now they belong.

I pace around the room, wincing with every crunch of glass underfoot. I tell myself the story of the House Under the Mountain, how the Wolf Queen collected rooms from hundreds of different places and bound them together with magical threads. The library was one of them—my father made it for my mother when he was still the North Wind. He enchanted books to live and breathe and be, from all periods of the world—past and present and future. That was when he could command time, one of the main threads of the North Wind's magic. He told me he could wind it back or forward if he wanted to.

"Did you ever?" I asked him once when I was small, snuggled with him in his office chair.

"I only ever tried it one time," he returned, kissing my head. "Your mother had a dog she loved—a half-tamed wolf, more like—but it got swept away by a river and drowned. I turned back time to get him back."

I breathed in the scent of my father, his steady heart beating against my ear. "Did it work?"

"The threads of time are curious things, Satu. Pull on one, and you fray a hundred others."

Sorrow bit at me. "What happened?"

"A boy drowned in the river," my father said quietly. "The dog tried to save him and died anyway."

I ponder this now as I circle the library, brushing my fingers along the frames of the ruined book-mirrors. The Wolf Queen stole the library when she took my father's power. I thought it was lost forever. Yet here it is: broken, but not wholly gone.

I touch every mirror I pass, but evidently they're too shattered for their magic to work anymore. I try the blue door at the back of the room—the one that should have led to a storeroom full of more book-mirrors—but it doesn't open. Neither does the door that once led to the rest of the house. I fight back the flash of panic at the thought of being trapped here forever, surrounded by my father's magic and yet eternally cut off from it.

I tell myself to be calm, be calm. To keep looking.

I pick through a pile of broken mirrors in one corner of the library and find a book-mirror that looks quite a lot better than the rest: There's a crack down the middle of it, but none of the pieces are missing. It tugs at me, like my father's magic in the meadow. I can scarcely breathe around the pounding of my pulse as I reach out to touch the glass.

Once more, magic rushes through me, shivering and cool, but it is not broken and empty, like the shard of mirror that led me to the library.

I blink and find myself in a huge, echoing chamber. Stone arches and pillars stretch up into darkness, and the entire back wall is open to a calamity of wheeling green and violet stars. This place brims with magic and the ancient weight of time. It tugs at my soul and I know it, though I have never been here before: the Temple of the Winds. All of my uncles have stood here. My father, too. The awareness of them, of their lingering power, buzzes all up and down my skin.

I pace through the temple, trailing my hands along the stone pillars. Threads of magic burst in front of my eyes, neither West's white feather nor the Jökull's touch needed here. The threads whisper and dance in every color imaginable, some I'm not sure I have ever seen before. They're beautiful, and for the first time I feel the certainty of my heritage, an echoing hollow inside of me that longs for magic to fill it up.

I approach the empty wall, the spinning stars that mesmerize me with their age and their beauty. They are pure magic, I think, untouched by anything else. Perhaps they are what I need; perhaps they are the reason my father sent me here.

A flash of movement knocks me backward and I spin across the floor, thudding hard against the base of a stone arch. The stars pulse and sear, and a violent vision unspools before my eyes:

My uncles stand on my Unraveling mountain: the West and South and East Winds. West's white wings are unfurled, luminous against the dark, and he holds a spindle of glimmering thread that is only half full. Gold blood drips down scores in his face and his arms.

The South Wind wields a vast spear that he uses as a needle, sewing up the great rift in the universe with West's thread. Behind him comes the East Wind with his earth-shattering sword. He keeps the broken threads of the Unraveling from lashing out, from wrapping around the Winds and pulling them into eternal darkness. But though the South Wind works quickly, every stitch he sews with his spear comes undone the next moment.

And West's spool grows emptier and emptier. Soon it will run out entirely, and the fabric of the world gapes open wider than before. My heart cries out that there is no North Wind to help them, that without my father's magic, they are doomed to fail.

And then the vision is gone, and I am alone in the temple, the green and violet stars raging beyond the empty wall.

"Story."

A cry tears out of me—I know that voice, though it is strangled and far away.

I turn my head and glimpse my father, or the shadow of my father, peering past me with eyes that do not quite seem to focus on mine.

"Papa!" I choke back a sob. "Where are you?"

"Story?" he says again.

I step away from the stars, toward my father, but some trick of the light pulls him back from me. I run, trying desperately to close the gap between us, but he remains always just out of reach.

"Papa," I whisper. Tears pour down my cheeks, salt thick on my tongue. "I can't touch you."

"I hear your voice," says my father. "I know you are there."

I shake and shake. "I'm coming to find you, Papa. I'm coming to save you and Mama. I'm going to bind up your power and become the North Wind. I just don't know how. You have to tell me how."

He doesn't seem to hear me. "Every story has an ending. If this is my ending, know that I love you. That I would do it all again—for you, for your mother. That I'm sorry."

"You didn't have to bargain with her," I whisper. "You could have gone to the Weaver. Why didn't you go to the Weaver?"

His eyes fix suddenly on mine, his face drawn and sad. "I was afraid, Satu. Afraid of what it might cost."

I can hardly speak for crying. "What could it possibly have cost that was worth giving your magic to *her*?"

"It could have cost you, my darling girl. I was afraid the Weaver would charge me to return to my realm, to my duties. I was afraid he would deny my request and send me back to the sky. And I could not have borne it. To leave Isidor. To leave *you*, growing already in her belly."

I will drown, I think, in tears.

"There is great power in you," says my father. "There always has been. I didn't want this for you, the burden of magic, the weight of the Winds. But it's yours. It was always meant to be yours."

"Where are you, Papa?" I wrestle the words out, strangled and damp. "How can I find you?"

"Beyond even the reach of a story, I fear. I am a place between."

"Between what?"

"Between the warp and weft of the universe itself, caught up in the Great Weaver's tapestry. All paths lead to him, in the end. I am thankful to see your face one last time—don't weep for me, Satu. Take up the mantle of the North Wind's power. Stitch the world back together. See it made whole again."

"Papa."

He smiles, but his face is steeped in sorrow. "You have always been my favorite story. Goodbye, Satu."

And then he's gone and the Temple echoes around me, stars pulsing at my back.

"PAPA!" I scream. A great wind rushes through the Temple and danger pricks along my skin.

For a moment, I don't understand, and then my eyes make sense of what I'm seeing. Of what I'm *not* seeing.

The Temple of the Winds is Unraveling, frayed and ragged at the edges, every thread pulling away. Pillars and archways vanish before my eyes. The view of the stars through the empty wall is obliterated as the very air pulls itself to pieces.

Then I'm running, running, away from the Unraveling threads and the desperate pull of unbound magic. A glimmer of glass winks at me from the wall. I hurl myself toward it.

FOURTEEN

I'M NOT SURE HOW LONG I lie there, sobbing in the ruined library. Glass shards are embedded in my arms and my face, and it's the pricks of pain that bring me back to myself, little by little. I lift my head, shake glass from my hair, and turn to face the door that once led into the rest of the house: There's a sliver of mirror hanging on it that I didn't see before. I force my trembling legs under me, force my feet to bring me to the door, my hand to touch the piece of mirror.

The magic is swifter and colder than before, but it doesn't feel as broken; it doesn't seek to rip me apart at the seams.

Then I'm back in the starlit meadow, fingers drawing away from the mirror shard I dug out of the earth. I pull my kerchief off, wrap it around the piece of glass, and shove this key to my father's library deep into my pocket. I struggle to think beyond his confession, and his farewell, but I know I cannot dwell on it—if I do, it will shatter me as surely as his ruined book-mirrors.

That's why it takes me longer than it should to glance to the border of the woods and see that I'm not alone. The Jökull lounges against a tree trunk as if he owns the whole world.

I swallow a yelp and jerk upright, my knees damp with earth, my arms and face scored with cuts from the glass shards.

The presence of my father's magic pulses around me, insistent, strong, and I realize that's why the Winter Lord is here, watching me with his glittering eyes and pale, arrogant smile.

Not even my hatred for him can quite dull that *tug tug tug* of my father's magic. My jaw goes hard. "I don't want you here."

He doesn't reply, just pushes off from the tree and stalks toward me across the grass. Fresh snow swirls around him, ice tinkling in his long hair. "I hope you're not still upset about your ghostly stray. He was using you."

The Winter Lord closes the distance between us and crouches at the base of the little mound that was once the white wolf's House. His long legs stick out like a grasshopper's, making him look gangly and almost awkward. It softens his edges, and nearly startles me out of my anger.

"I'm not giving you my father's magic," I say tightly. "If that's why you're here—"

"How could you give me something you don't even possess?"

"His magic is here."

"Of course it is." There's a challenge in his eyes that makes me want to strangle him.

"You can see it."

He doesn't deign to answer that, just lifts his eyebrows and stares me down.

He's going to make me ask him. I clench my fists and bite my cheek to keep from screaming. I try to call my father's magic inside of me but nothing happens, nothing changes. I can't do it on my own.

"Do you need my help, little bee?" His tone is mocking but his glance is fixed. Certain. Like he understands something I don't.

I war with myself. I lose. "Show me my father's magic."

He doesn't wait for me to ask again. He shifts closer, folding one hand around mine and grazing my eyelids with the other.

The threads of magic dance into my vision and I gasp in wonder. They are all of them a vivid cerulean blue, twisting and shining but ragged, unsure. My father's magic. The North Wind's magic. The threads pulse like a heartbeat, calling me.

But seeing them doesn't change the fact that I don't know how to gather them, how to stitch them tight into my heart where they belong.

The Jökull knows.

He watches me between my father's twisting threads, his own silver ones shimmering through every inch of him. "Well, wind daughter?"

"I'm not giving you my father's magic."

"And I am not helping you collect these threads unless you give me something in return."

"You killed my bees and Unraveled the herders and sent the one friend I had left into darkness. If there is any payment required, it is *you* who owes *me*."

He smirks. "Have you grown a spine, oh spineless one? I *am* impressed."

I want to jerk my hand from his, but I can't bear to part with the sight his touch gives me, not yet, so I force my fingers to be still. I take a breath of icy air. I glare at him. "Help me," I say through gritted teeth.

I expect him to smile again, to mock me, but he doesn't, a fierce hard look coming into his face. "Ask the magic to come to you," he says. "Remind it that you are the North Wind. That it belongs to you. And it will come."

"That's it?" I'm startled at the simplicity, and my eyes snag on his.

He nods.

I take a breath and close my eyes, reaching out for the cerulean magic that swirls around me, broken and yearning. *You belong to me*, says my heart. *I am the North Wind. You belong to me.*

Let us in, let us in, let us in, sighs the magic. And it comes. I tug the threads in, in, wind them about my heart. I reach and I pull and I wind. The threads come and come. They are not enough, not yet. But they are a beginning, a taste of power. A few precious drops of water in an empty well. I gather them to me until I can sense no more of my father's threads in the star-drenched meadow.

Only then, do I open my eyes. I feel quieter. More at peace with the world, with myself.

The Winter Lord is watching me intently, and there is danger in his face. "I require something in return."

My heart thuds too quick and I hate that I am still afraid, that this taste of power has not swallowed my fear, has not even made a dent in it.

"I need your magic, wind daughter," he says quietly. "You can no longer claim you don't have any."

I reach for that place inside of me, the threads all whispering silk, fusing together, learning how to be strong, how to be *mine*, clamoring for more, more. "You can't have it."

He is all pale, cold lines in the dappled dark. "Not even if I told you I could bring your parents back from Between? That I could fix the Unraveling world?"

I tremble under his gaze. "What do you care about the world? I thought you were only trying to save your own skin."

"It is hard to go on living if there is no world in which to live."

My father's voice echoes in my ears, and for a moment I'm tempted to say yes, to agree to any bargain the Jökull offers, if only he will save my parents and take the burden of the world away from me.

But the threads inside of me tug and *pull*, and already I know

I could never bear to be parted from them, even if I believed the Winter Lord could do all the things he claims—which I don't.

"You can't have my magic," I repeat, infusing my words with steel.

"Very well." He stretches out one long hand and tucks a loose strand of hair behind my ear. "Just this once, I will accept a different price."

I repress a shudder at the terrible cold of him. "What price?" I whisper.

"A kiss," answers the Winter Lord.

I recoil, jerking away from him.

He just raises his eyebrows. "A kiss," he repeats. "Or I will take your magic whether you offer it to me freely or not."

Heat boils inside of me to match his wretched ice. I have never kissed a man before. I have never thought about it, apart from Inna's tale of Illarion. Something jumbles around in my stomach and I realize that this frightens me far more than any other price the Jökull could have asked for.

He doesn't smile. He doesn't do anything. He just looks at me, waiting.

Magic stirs and whispers inside of me. I can't bear to give it up. I won't.

So I scoot back toward him, the grassy earth soft beneath my knees, and I peer into his cold face and colder eyes.

Still he waits, watching me.

"Kiss me, then," I whisper, heart frantic in my throat.

At once, his long fingers cup my cheeks; his ice seeps under my skin. He draws my face to his, and his lips are shockingly soft, shockingly warmer than the rest of him. My whole being is fixed on the sensation of his mouth on mine, all the world around us a strange and whorling dark. Threads of magic burst before my eyes, a shower of silver. I can taste his power and it isn't cold, like he is, but fiery as the sun.

I gasp and break the kiss, my whole body raging and wild.

He watches me through silver lashes but does not pull me back for more.

I am on fire, and I find I cannot look at him any longer. I drop my eyes, fighting to think about anything besides my flaming skin and the mad pace of my heart.

I push to my feet and the Jökull rises, too, bits of grass clinging to his trousers and the tails of his long coat. He seems all at once awkward and uncertain, like a half-grown boy caught at his game of pretending to be a man.

"You've had your price," I say, heat pouring through me. "Now leave me alone."

A hardness comes into his face, and he is the untouchable Winter Lord once more. "Very well, Satu North. But I will not be so kind in our next meeting."

I bristle. "When have you ever been kind?"

His eyes flash with something I can only read as sadness, and then he turns and is gone in a cloud of snow.

I'm shaking as I whistle for Honey, as I climb numbly onto his back. I ride through the night and on into morning. I ride until I can stop wondering what reason the Jökull would have to be sad. Until the ache of my father's farewell has dulled enough that I can almost bear it.

FIFTEEN

WHEN I AM A DAY PAST the ruins of the House Under the Mountain, I build a fire in the quiet dark, and I call for Fann.

The magic threads inside of me have grown a little stronger, and they reach out for him, carrying my voice to whatever darkness he's trapped in.

Wake up, Fann, I call to him. *Wake up.*

There's a shimmer in the grass and then he's there, gasping, his ghostly form seeming to glow in the firelight. He shudders and he shakes and it takes him awhile to lift his head, to seek my eyes with his own.

"Satu!" he breathes.

Joy floods me. I wish I had enough magic to make him solid,

so I could touch him, hug him. But it's enough, for now, that he's here.

He collects himself and comes closer to me, his translucent body—as always—making no impression in the earth. "How long has it been?" he asks. He's shaky, breathless, and it makes me ache.

"Another week, give or take." I swallow past the lump in my throat. "Are you . . . are you all right, Fann?" It's not really what I mean to say, because *of course* he isn't all right, but I don't know how else to ask if . . . if he's losing himself in the nightmare. If there will come a day when he will not wake at all.

His eyes are unfocused; he understands the intent of my question. "When I'm not with you, Satu, it's—it's dark and it's cold and . . . it tethers me. It's harder and harder to break free of it."

"And the cord between us is broken," I say softly.

"I'm afraid, Satu. I'm so, so afraid, that the next time the darkness takes me—" His voice breaks, and a sob catches in my throat.

"The Winter Lord did this to you—resigned you to the realm of nightmares." Just saying his name aloud makes me bristle and flush. I grind my jaw. "I'm not going to let him win."

Fann raises his eyes to meet mine, and his face is awash with hopelessness.

Magic stirs inside me, still tenuous, still new, but ready to answer my call. I'm going to hold on to Fann. I'm going to keep him here—I refuse to let him go back into the dark.

The fire crackles and the stars blaze.

"Close your eyes," I say.

He obeys. The firelight flickering over him makes it seem as if he is in constant motion, a creature born of flame, though he is sitting perfectly still.

I close my eyes, too, and reach for the threads inside of me. I am distantly aware that I don't need the Jökull now to see the magic. I tug at one of the threads until it comes loose, shimmering cerulean wound with flecks of gold—my father's magic, melded with mine.

I pull it out from my heart and into my palm, where it coils warm and restless. *Go to him,* I command my cerulean-gold thread. *Bind him to me. Keep him here.*

The weight of the thread curls out of my palm, slips through the air. I watch as it twists into Fann's heart, and I feel the sharp tug of the knot, pulling tight.

He gasps and my eyes fly open to find him clutching at his heart, gulping for air. But the next moment he's breathing easily again, and his gaze fixes on mine. His eyes reflect the firelight.

"You've found your magic," he says, awe in his voice.

"Part of it." I tell him briefly about the House Under the Mountain and gathering the first threads of the North Wind's power. I don't mention the Jökull at all—I don't want to think about him, about the price of his helping me or the sadness in his eyes. About the heat of his lips and his magic.

"I can only give you one thread for now," I say all in a rush when I've finished. "But it should keep you from the dark, or at least give you a path back to me in case the nightmare calls again. And when I collect more of my father's magic, I'll give you more threads, until there are enough inside of you to hold you here for good. Make you whole again."

I'm nervous, babbling, but he smiles in the dark and my heart warms. "You are the kindest and bravest soul I have ever met," he says quietly. "Thank you. I can't—" He swallows. "I can't even tell you how much."

"I'm sorry it can't be more."

He laughs a little. "You never need to be sorry. Set your burden down. Remember?"

I give him a wobbly smile.

We talk, late into the night, and I find myself telling him about my village, about my disastrous only day of school, about Madam Zima's offer to give me a job.

"Do you think," he muses, staring up at the sky, "that maybe it wouldn't have been so bad, in small pieces? Maybe you could have gotten used to it, little by little. Maybe it would have been a good thing, in the end."

I think about this, shame twisting my stomach into knots. "Maybe."

"Change doesn't always have to be bad. It's just—change. It's life. It's living." He sighs.

Fann exists, in his fragile, tenuous form, but he's not living. Not really. I can't help but think that I haven't been really living, either. Maybe Fann is right. Maybe Madam Zima was right. I want to do more than exist. I want to live, to be, to do. When all this is over, I want to be more than a girl alone on a mountain.

"Thank you," I say after a while. I'm lying on my back on one side of the fire, Fann on the other. I turn my face to him and he looks at me, the firelight dancing in his eyes.

"For what?" he asks.

I wish once again that I could touch him. "For seeing me," I say. "For understanding."

He smiles. "I'm only trying to do for you what you keep doing for me."

The fire lulls me to sleep, and I wake in the morning to a cold, driving rain. I'm relieved to find Fann still here, the thread between us taut and strong. He shines in the wet, but the rain doesn't touch him.

"Not fair," I grumble as I pack up my soaked supplies onto an equally soaked pony.

"One of the few advantages of being mostly incorporeal," he agrees, grinning.

We pick our way doggedly east, following a road churning with mud. I'm not sure who is more miserable: me or Honey. I'm more than grateful to have Fann there, walking along beside me. If I shut my eyes I can see my thread of magic in him, cerulean and gold, knotted tight in his heart. I still don't know what he is, *how* he is, if it's truly possible to save him. But I'm not, not, not letting him go.

The rain goes on for days. It's too wet for fires, too wet to sleep, too wet to do pretty much anything. Sometimes, during the day, Fann sings, his voice a thread of light in the drizzling damp—old ballads and folk songs I've never heard before. He talks, in halting phrases, about sisters and brothers and a house by a great wood, though sometimes he grows confused, brow wrinkling as he tells me that no, his house was by the sea, and he only had one sister. His memories tug at my heart and they clearly trouble him deeply. He resorts more and more to just the old songs, and as the hours spool on, to silence.

At night, I tell Fann my father's stories. He listens, but says very little in return, face tightening as if he's in pain.

"What's wrong, Fann?" I ask him, the third night of the awful rain. We're huddled under the branches of a dripping tree, which offers a little shelter, but still not enough for a fire. If I were truly the North Wind, I would blow all this wet away and revel in the delightful sensation of being dry again. I'm beginning to forget what that's even like.

"It's not enough," he says quietly, all hunched in on himself, his arms wrapped around his knees.

My heart twists. "What's not enough?"

He can't quite look at me, staring instead into the muddy earth. "The thread, Satu. The nightmare is calling me back, and the thread isn't enough to hold me here."

I worry at my lip. The magic inside of me pulses and whispers. I've felt it grow, the last few days. I can spare more, now, and

I'm stricken that he didn't tell me earlier. "Close your eyes," I say.

"I can't ask you to—"

"Close your eyes," I repeat firmly.

He sighs but obliges, and I close mine, too. I pull out two threads, this time. They come singing into my hand, cerulean and gold, twined together. They obey me easily, twisting into Fann's heart, knots pulling tight enough to make him hiss with momentary pain.

"All right, Fann?" I ask, when it's done, breathing a little heavily myself.

He nods, his eyes brighter than they were a moment ago. "Better," he says. "Thank you."

"I'm going to keep tying threads into you until you're solid enough to feel as wretched in all this rain as I am," I inform him.

He laughs at that, and warmth spreads to my toes.

It's *STILL* RAINING THE NEXT afternoon when our muddy road leads to a village, through tall wooden gates and onto cobbled streets. There's an inn just past the gates, a modest building with a stable butted up against it. Honey pricks his ears at the smell of grain and hay, while my own stomach wrenches with hunger—I finished the last of the food from my pack yesterday.

With Fann at one shoulder and Honey at the other, I squelch my way up to the inn's door. A half-grown girl with yellow hair peeking out from under her kerchief appears to take Honey from me. I grab my pack and relinquish the pony, then step inside.

I'm instantly assailed with heat and color, noise and lights and voices all vying for my attention. The breath squeezes from my lungs as panic claws up my throat. I wheel around to go right back out into the wet, almost welcoming the thought of starvation, but Fann is there, the rain falling through him, his brows raised.

"It's all right, Satu," he says gently. "You can do this."

I chew on my lip and give him a shaky nod.

"You there, girl! If you're not here for a room or a bite, I'll ask you to kindly stop dripping mud on my floor!"

I turn back. A skinny yellow-haired man who bears a striking resemblance to the girl who took Honey glares at me from behind the polished wooden bar.

I suck in a breath and approach him, wincing at the dreadful sound of my filthy boots on the wood floor. Slowly, the details of this cramped room are sorting themselves out: long tables and benches crammed in tight by the fire, half filled with men drinking vodka or beer, the strong scent of alcohol nearly overpowered by the bowls of cabbage stew at their elbows. They're laughing and loud, a few of them singing snatches of a raunchy song that makes my ears heat. Lanterns spin dizzily from ceiling beams. A stairway carpeted with a red runner leads to the upper floors. The door by the bar swings open and the yellow-haired girl hurries out of it, tray heavy with more vodka and stew for the patrons.

"Can I *help* you, miss?" says the innkeeper behind the bar, his irritation as palpable as the potent cabbage stew.

I force my attention to him, fighting to form coherent words amidst all the clamor in the room, in my mind, feeling absolutely horrible at the mess I've made with my boots.

"A hot meal, please," I squeak out.

"What was that? You'll have to speak up."

I take another breath, to quell my frustrated tears at having to repeat myself after it took so much effort to say anything at all. "A hot meal," I say, as loudly as I can without shouting. "And— and a bed in your stable for my pony and myself."

The innkeeper frowns. "If you can't pay for a room, you can't stay."

I shake as I pull damp and crumpled bills from the leather wallet in my pack and lay them out on the bar—the money I made selling honey to Madam Zima.

His whole demeanor changes. "There are rooms available, Miss—?"

"North."

"There are rooms available, Miss North. You can stay several nights if you wish."

The light and the noise, the heat and the reek of alcohol thud in my head while the magic inside of me pulses and twists, unsettled by my anxiety. I think of Fann, so sure that I can do this, and take a deep breath. "Just one night, please," I manage. "And I prefer the stable."

He shakes his head but takes every bill I've offered him. "Very well. You can have the loft. My daughter will bring you your meal—just a moment." He turns toward the kitchen and shouts, "Dasha! Another stew!"

I force myself to wait by the bar, gulping air and trying not to look as panicked as I feel. *Breathe, Satu. Breathe.*

What feels like an eternity later, Dasha appears with stew, bread, and ale on a tray. I stammer my thanks and take it, slipping back outside and shielding my dinner from the rain as best I can.

The interior of the stable is dim and quiet except for the comforting rustle of its equine inhabitants. I say hello to Honey, who is contentedly munching on grain in his borrowed stall, and then settle down in the aisle to eat my own meal. I practically inhale it, only coming up for air when every crumb is gone.

Fann stares dismally at my empty tray. "A marked *dis*advantage of being mostly incorporeal," he says with a sigh.

I quirk a smile at him and climb up into the loft, sneezing enormously from all the dusty hay. The rain drums overhead. Its steady rhythm is comforting now that I'm not out walking in it.

Fann comes up after me. He sits cross-legged, hard to make out clearly in the dim light from the single lantern that hangs below us in the stable aisle. I sense my threads, pulsing in him. I sense his sorrow, too.

"What's wrong?" I ask him, curling up in the hay with my pack for a pillow. I'm not sure I should give him more threads— the ones I have left feel thin and unsure—but I know I will if he needs them.

"When I deserted from the army," he says slowly, "I went to

the city. I was going to lose myself among all the people there, evade the soldiers who would be sent after me. I was going to change my name and apprentice myself to a painter."

My heart aches for him. "What happened?"

He stares stricken into the half dark. "I don't remember."

"What are you afraid of?" I ask him quietly.

"The darkness," he says. "The nightmares. Never finding out what I am. Who I am. Never tasting or feeling or *being*."

My throat catches and I blink back the sting of tears. "I won't let that happen, Fann."

I reach inside myself. I draw out another thread. I tie it tight to him.

"WHERE ARE WE GOING?" ASKS Fann as we leave the inn the next morning under a gloriously sunny sky.

We've been traveling east since I called him out of the dark—I consult a crumpled map every evening to mark my progress.

"Gradeslav," I tell him. "The river city."

We tramp along the road, all sticky, sucking mud now.

"I thought you would turn north," says Fann with a little shrug.

I look at him curiously. "North?"

"Isn't that where the bulk of your father's power must be, where the Wolf Queen wielded it for so long?"

He's right, of course. My stomach twists at the reminder of

my own cowardice. "I can't quite face it," I admit to him. "Not yet. I think she's not gone, Fann. I think some part of the Wolf Queen lingers at the heart of my father's power and—I'm afraid to face her, or whatever remnants of her are left."

Fann slips along beside me, his bare feet grazing over top of the mud. His eyes look far away, a breath of wind blowing grass and loose dirt through his incorporeal form. "What about the Unraveling?" he says quietly.

The breeze plays with the hair about my face and I breathe in the scent of sunshine and wet earth, shoving away all the uncertain parts of me. "Inna is in Gradeslav," I tell him. "So is her sister, Echo. She faced the Wolf Queen and defeated her. She'll be able to help, and she spent a lot of time with my father—I am sure there are remnants of his magic clinging to her."

"That makes sense."

I chew on my lip. Does he think I'm just making excuses for not going north? Am I? "Would you think very badly of me if I told you I'm hoping Echo will know how to fix everything? That our journey is almost over?"

He smiles and shakes his head. "I could never think badly of you, Satu. But I also know you're braver than you think you are. And this isn't Echo's story anymore, you know. It's yours."

I ponder this as Honey trudges down the soggy road. I'm not sure I quite believe him. I'm not quite sure I'm worthy of a story, no matter what my name is.

On the third morning since leaving the inn, the rain comes

again, gloomy and dripping. Our faithful muddy road grows wider the closer to Gradeslav we come, and far more crowded. Merchants and trappers pass me and my invisible companion in both directions. Headed toward the city, their heavily laden wagons creep along slow as snails, wheels hardly moving in the churning mud. Headed away from the city, the wagons are quicker, rattling and empty of goods. Groups of students pass us, too, going to or from the university, along with the odd farmer. Twice, a pair of soldiers ride by on flashy chestnut horses and they make me think of Fann deserting the army. He tenses a little when they pass.

Ahead of us, Gradeslav seems to rise from the ground through the pouring rain. Great stone spires pierce the sky overtop high walls, and the stench of the river reaches me even from a few miles away.

The road traffic increases, so there's scarcely space to ride without bumping into someone. People on foot, on horseback, or in wagons rush in both directions, seemingly heedless of the rain. My heart jangles in my rib cage as we approach the open gates. They're tall and wooden, painted in bright blues and yellows and reds that seem to shine even in the wet.

"Stay close, Fann," I say as we pass through.

"I'm here, Satu. Don't worry."

Then Gradeslav swallows me whole, the cacophony of noise and smells and incessant movement overwhelming my senses. I fight through the panic, tangling my fingers in Honey's mane, concentrating on every breath. Something tugs at my chest, a sharp, horrible pain that's cut suddenly off. Fann is gone, pulled back into his nightmare despite my binding threads.

I shout for him but it's no use, the tide of humanity sweeping me down the street like a leaf in a river current. I'm caught in a chaos of pedestrians and carriages, food vendors and stray dogs.

I can't think past the pounding in my head and I huddle low over Honey's neck, trying to breathe, to think, biting my tongue to keep from screaming. Rain runs down my neck. Someone's shouting at me to move, and I realize I've dislodged myself from the river of people and am blocking the entrance to a shop. I mumble an apology—or at least I mean to, but I'm not sure anything comes out—and numbly nudge Honey out of the way. I blindly turn off the main street and into a back alley that's dark and reeks of refuse but is blessedly, blessedly empty.

I slide off the pony and lean against his shoulder, wrapping my fingers in his coarse mane, breathing in the smell of him, mud and hay and earth and sweat. But I can't stop shaking and crying, can't ignore the panic screaming out in my mind. I don't need the Unraveling to fall apart. Just myself.

I collapse onto the cobblestones and am sobbing in the filthy alley when there comes a cold touch on my shoulder. It startles me enough to lift my head.

I stare straight up at the Winter Lord.

He is drenched through with rain but there is ice on his shoulders, the tails of his coat, the ends of his long hair. His expression is unreadable, but there is a strange sort of softness in his eyes.

I gulp air and try not to choke on the tears clogging my throat and my nose. My skin is still buzzing with panic, my lungs frantic, my heart beating too fast, too hard.

"Satu," he says. "What's wrong?"

He crouches beside me but I scrabble away from him, fighting and fighting and fighting to breathe.

His forehead creases but he doesn't move toward me again, just sits on his heels, his coat dragging on the muddy stones. Rain splashes into the alley. Honey paws at a puddle, anxious to move on.

Gradually, gradually, my heartbeat calms and my breathing grows easier. I am ashamed of myself, ashamed that the Jökull has seen me like this. But he doesn't mock me, doesn't laugh at me. He just crouches there, rain dripping from his eyelashes.

"Why are you here?" I say at last. "Did you send Fann away again?"

He winces. "Is that ghostly bastard still plaguing you?"

"I called him back. I tied threads to him to make sure he'd stay."

His face darkens. "That was foolish, North's daughter."

"*You* don't get to tell me what's foolish." I clench my jaw.

He pushes to his feet and holds out one hand to me.

I scramble up on my own, glaring at him.

"Why are you here?" I demand again.

For a moment, he doesn't answer, just watches me, that strange sadness tracing his features again. "Nightmares plague me when I sleep. But you face yours when you're awake, don't you?"

I gnaw on the inside of my cheek. "My nightmares are my own business."

"Of course they are. But it helps, doesn't it, to have someone wake you up?"

There's a tug at my heart and for a moment I shut my eyes, calling Fann back from the dark. "Yes," I say, staring straight at the Jökull again. "Yes, it does."

Fann tumbles into the alley, breathing hard, and it's a moment's work to tug another thread out of me, and tie it to him.

The Winter Lord stands straight and cold, ice creeping out from under his booted feet. Whatever softness was in him a moment ago is gone. "You are a fool, North's daughter. You are *worse* than a fool."

"*Leave*," I spit out at him. "I don't want you here."

For a moment he blinks at me, his hard eyes unreadable. Then he turns on his heel and is gone, snow swirling in his wake.

I go to Fann, who pulls himself to his feet, shaky as a newborn reindeer calf. It could be a trick of the dim light, of the gleaming rain, but I swear he's slightly more solid than he was before. My heart pulses with happiness.

"I was so afraid you wouldn't call me back," he gasps. "I was so afraid that *this* place is my dream, that that other place, the nightmare place, is real."

I shake my head. "*This* is real. This filthy, dripping alleyway in this deafening city."

He laughs without humor. "I'm a ghost who keeps appearing to the North Wind's daughter—what kind of reality is that? It's just a story. A story I tell myself to hold back the dark."

"We are all stories, Fann. Every one of us. That doesn't mean we're not real."

He takes a deep breath. "Then let's keep on with your story, Satu North."

The threads between us hum with contentment.

SIXTEEN

I T TAKES NEARLY ALL DAY TO cross Gradeslav. At first, I attempt to find Inna's house, working up the courage to ask multiple strangers directions to the address I saw so often on her letters while Fann stands encouragingly by. But I end up wandering in circles and decide to head toward the university instead. Inna's father works at the library there, and Echo's physician's office is only a street away.

The office turns out to be easier to find than the library, which is lost somewhere in the maze of the university streets and a press of people I don't have the energy to navigate. By the time I get there, the rain has slacked off and the sun is setting, sending fragmented orange light through the clouds. The office is a smart brick building with a bright blue door and gleaming brass knocker; the river rushes swift and gray just beyond. I only hope it's not too late in the evening for Echo to still be here.

"What will I do if I can't find her?" I fret as I slide from Honey's saddle and tie him to the iron fence.

"Look for lodging for the night," Fann answers sensibly. "And try again tomorrow."

I climb the steps, jittery with nerves, and Fann comes just behind. I rap the knocker and try to keep my breathing steady.

"Come in!" calls a voice from inside. "But I fear I won't have time to see you this evening—I'm late as it is!"

I creak open the door and step into a handsome room, the wood floor softened with a blue and green rug, a blue velvet sofa, and three mismatched armchairs clustered together on the right wall. A dark-haired woman sits behind a desk at the back of the room, practically buried in papers and scribbling things across the tops of them. Several opened ink bottles rest at her elbow, and there's a stethoscope looped around her neck.

"With you in a moment," she says, not looking up as she continues writing at a truly remarkable speed.

I glance sideways at Fann, who hovers at the door, looking unaccountably nervous.

I pace up to the desk. "Echo?" I say quietly.

She sets down her pen and raises her head, her scars shiny in the lamplight. She blinks at me for half a moment, and then a smile splits her face. "Satu?"

I nod, suddenly shy, and she laughs and stands, coming around the desk to crush me in a warm hug.

Or at least she tries. She can hardly reach me around her enormous belly.

I gape at her and she laughs more. "One would think you've never seen a pregnant woman before. What *do* they teach you on that mountain of yours?"

"Inna didn't *tell* me!" I blurt.

Echo shakes her head. "Oh, that girl. But she can be absolved of that, at least. She didn't know!"

I chew on my lip. "She's back then? She's safe?"

"As safe as a girl with one thousand punishments could be." Echo grins.

"Has she told you about the Unraveling?"

Echo puts one hand on my shoulder, glancing past me to where Fann waits by the door. For a moment, I almost think she sees him, but then her eyes find mine again. "She has, and I'm sure you have even more to explain. Come home with me—Hal will have my head if I miss dinner again. You can tell us all everything there."

Echo caps her ink bottles and blows out the lamp, then steps with me outside, locking the office door behind us a second after Fann slips out.

Honey whuffles at us from the fence.

"Handsome fellow," Echo greets him while I loose his bridle and Fann stands wary and silent beside me. Echo can't possibly see him—can she?

The clouds have broken apart further, and above the city spires, the westering sun washes the streets and the buildings with amber-orange light. We walk together, Echo and Honey and I, with Fann trailing a few steps back.

"I hardly recognized you all grown up," says Echo as we go, "even *with* all of Inna's description, although really you could be anybody under all that mud."

I have to smile at that.

She winces and puts her hand on her belly and I feel suddenly small and young and shy.

Echo catches me looking at her and laughs a little. "I don't know that I can take another month of this babe kicking my insides, but I suppose I'll have to. Oh, just here."

She leads the way down another street where houses march in neat rows and lamplighters are just beginning their night's work.

Echo stops at a little house with a blue door and a white gate. Opening the latter, she waves Honey through into the small courtyard beyond. She helps me relieve him of his packs and tack, and piles it all by the kitchen door. "I'll send Hal or Papa out to find some oats for him later," she says. "He can nibble at my garden for now. *I* certainly haven't had much success with it. I'm hoping I'll prove more competent with the baby." She laughs again, but I sense her nervous energy, and I'm dumbfounded that a woman who turned back time to save her love and defeat the Wolf Queen could be frightened of an infant.

And then Echo is opening the kitchen door and gesturing for

me to come after her and I do, sucking in a steadying breath.

The kitchen is tiny and dim, hardly room for the iron stove and a square of wooden counter. Beyond is the living space, lanterns bright on a round wooden table, the tantalizing scent of tea and beef and noodles wafting toward me. There's an upright piano crammed next to an empty fireplace, with a worn but comfortable-looking couch facing it, and a narrow hallway that must lead to the rest of the house.

Three people are sitting round the table: Hal, looking scarcely different than he did seven years ago, if a little more well-fed; the man who must be Echo and Inna's father, Peter, with white in his beard and the kindest eyes I've ever seen; and Inna, looking uncharacteristically kempt, her clothes clean and her braids neat, tied off with careful ribbons.

"I'm late, I know," says Echo, "but I have a good excuse. I've brought company."

"SATU!" Inna shrieks, leaping from her chair and hugging me with such force she nearly knocks me into the stove.

I laugh as I hug her back, relieved beyond words to see her again, safe and sound. Joy bubbles up, swallowing my anxiety for now.

"Take Satu to wash up," Echo instructs. "There should be something fresh for her to wear in the wardrobe."

I find myself ushered down the narrow hallway and into a tiny washroom, Inna leaving me to get to work with soap and rags. I've cleaned off several layers of grime when she comes back with a linen shift and a beautiful orange and gold sarafan. I wish I had time to take a proper bath and wash my filthy hair, too, but a clean face and hands and non-mud-encrusted clothes feel almost as miraculous.

Then it's back out into the tiny dining room, with Hal finding me a chair and Peter setting an extra place for me, squeezing me in between Inna and Echo. Fann lingers by the empty fireplace, his eyes flitting anxiously between Echo and Hal, but if Echo saw him at her office she doesn't seem to now, and there is no reason to worry even if she could.

We eat, more food than I've seen in weeks: noodles and mushrooms, tender beef and sour cabbage, with strong sweet tea from the samovar I suspect will keep me up all night. Conversation flows around me, too much to focus on, but I sense that all of them are giving me the space I need, no one asking more of me than I have to give.

"I am in an *awful* lot of trouble," Inna tells me ruefully when my plate is almost empty. "I'm only allowed to be here, school, or home for the rest of the *year*, which feels remarkably unfair."

"It's not," says Echo.

Inna ignores her. "*But*, I'm almost ready to submit my music transcriptions to the university, and both Papa and Hal says they'll be really well received, and I can tell everyone is proud of me, really."

"More furious than proud," Echo clarifies.

Peter frowns, and I sense he has not quite allowed his relief at

Inna's return to swallow his fear. He thought he'd lost Echo forever, when she was Inna's age, and then for Inna to disappear too—

"Don't look at me like that, Satu!" Inna scolds. "You're as bad as the rest of them. Except for Hal of course. *He* understands."

Hal's lips twitch, but he doesn't comment.

"I just can't believe it was all because of a boy," says Echo. "And not even an enchanted boy at that. Those are the *best* kind." She winks at Hal.

Inna launches into an insistent tirade about how she would have gone off on her adventure even if it *wasn't* for Illarion, and how her not being allowed to see him outside of school is more than unjust. She then whispers into my ear that it hasn't kept the two of them from lots of kissing in the coat closet, which makes me blush furiously.

The conversation turns to Peter and his work at the university library. He tells a long and rather uneventful story about a mis-shelved book, which leads to Hal launching into a rant about one of his students whose latest essay was rife with blatant historical inaccuracies. ("I was *there*. I *remember*. You can't get away with that sort of thing in my class.") Then Echo enthuses about stitching up a gut wound in her office today, which makes everyone recoil in horror.

And then somehow we're all sitting by the empty fireplace with more tea in hand, and Echo turns to me. "Forgive us, Satu. Here you are with important things to say, and we're all jabbering about nothing. Papa and Inna come for dinner every week, and we've always things to catch up on, but the rest will certainly keep. What's happened since you and Inna parted ways? Did you find the House Under the Hill?"

"Mountain," says Hal.

Echo grins—clearly an old joke between them—but doesn't glance his way.

"It's cold in here," Inna remarks.

I realize she's right, and glance toward the window that looks out onto the street. Frost traces the glass in lacy patterns, and my stomach wrenches. Fann is sitting, now, by the iron stove, his knees pulled up to his chin. He looks utterly miserable, and worry squeezes my insides.

Hal goes to lay a fire on the hearth, and I force myself to keep my eyes away from the window. When the flames are leaping merrily and he's settled beside Echo, I start my story, telling them everything that's happened since I left my mountain, with the exception of Fann—it feels wrong to discuss him when he's actually here—and the price the Winter Lord asked for at the ruins of the House.

Silence blankets the room when I've finished, Hal especially seeming drawn and quiet. Ice crackles thicker on the window-panes, obscuring the light of the street lamps.

"I have never heard of the Winter Lord," says Echo, thoughtfully.

"I have," says Hal. His forehead creases, reliving an old horror.

Echo's eyes flick over to him, and she takes his hand in hers.

"He was the Wolf Queen's right hand," Hal goes on. "Her guard. Her messenger. Her executioner. I never met him. Never even glimpsed him, really, but his magic was everywhere: in the voice of the winds guarding her realm. In the ice and the snow that shielded her. He brought her winter anywhere she bid him and stole or slew anyone she commanded him to. He was a demon, a creature as wicked as she was."

I realize I'm shaking, and I press my hands tight together to try and stop.

"The Wolf Queen is gone, though," says Inna, who's sitting cross-legged on the floor, unbraiding and rebraiding her long hair. "Her magic was taken away, all of her enchantments undone. If the Winter Lord was truly her servant—why does he still exist, why is he hunting you, Satu?"

I think of his words in the alley, the shockingly warm feel of his lips on mine. "He's not hunting me, exactly."

"Perhaps there are some things that cannot be undone," Peter says quietly.

I gnaw on my lip, thinking of all the things that will never be undone: Hal's entire family, dead centuries ago; the ten years the Wolf Queen stole from Echo. My mother's family, lost also to the Wolf Queen's whims and the sea of time. I can no longer see this as anyone's fault but my father's, mine. His words in the Temple of the Winds still haunt me—it was because of *me* he chose to bargain with the Queen and not the Weaver. My existence that impacted his choice. And whether that choice was made of fear or love or both, it led to many, many things that can never be undone.

"Satu," says Echo, one hand on her large belly, the other still caught fast in Hal's. "Don't look so glum. None of this is your fault."

Tears spark in my eyes and I blink them furiously away. "If I didn't exist, if my father had never—"

"But you *do* exist," says Hal, firmly. "And your father made his own choices, just as we all made ours." His face tightens again, and I realize he is still plagued with guilt for his own part in all this. It makes me impossibly sad.

"No more talk of guilt or blame," says Echo gently. "All that was forgiven, years ago."

Hal sighs and lays his head on her shoulder. Almost instinctually I reach into that place inside of me where my magic twists and grows. I can sense the threads between Hal and Echo, strong as braided cords, and my heart swells. There is none of my father's magic in them, only their own. "It's a boy," I blurt.

Hal, Echo, Inna, and Peter all look at me.

"The baby," I explain. "A boy. I can see his threads."

Echo smiles and Peter laughs, while Inna whoops and Hal pulls Echo into a fierce hug. When he draws away his eyes are wet.

"Do you have anything of my father's?" I ask Echo then. "Anything that might carry a piece of him or his magic?"

Echo thinks a minute, then nods and starts to heave herself off the couch. Hal kisses her forehead. "I'll get it, love. You've been on your feet all day."

"Ivan's book," she instructs him.

Hal is back a moment later with a copy of my father's book—he left it for Echo to find when she came down from the Wolf Queen's mountain. It's worn, battered about the edges, and the instant Hal places it in my hands, I feel my father's magic twisting through it, loose threads, waiting to be bound. I close my eyes and pull them inside of me, winding them about my heart where they pulse with power, strong and wild and *mine*.

I open my eyes again to find everyone looking at me, Hal with an odd expression on his face.

"Satu, you look . . ." He trails off, shaking his head.

My heart races, erratic and frightened.

"You're scaring her," Echo admonishes.

"It's just you look familiar," Hal says. "Especially now, with whatever magic you drew inside of you. You remind me of a painting I saw once, so long ago I'd forgotten it until now."

"What painting?" I say.

Hal's eyes are fixed on some distant point in a faraway time only he remembers. "It hung in my father's house," he says. "One of my siblings painted it, I think."

Echo considers her husband with a certain aching sadness. His memories hurt him, I realize. And so they hurt her as well.

Wind howls outside the house, and I catch the unmistakable scent of winter.

The clock on the mantel—an elaborate, beautiful timepiece in the shape of a bear—chimes midnight, and we all jump at the sudden noise.

"We'd best be home, Inna," says Peter, standing from his chair. "You have school in the morning, and I'm not about to lessen your punishment because Satu is here."

Inna pouts and doesn't move from her place on the floor. "I feel as if I'm to be wildly ill tomorrow, Papa. Can't I stay?"

Peter smiles but shakes his head. "Not tonight, dear heart."

"Illarion would miss you at school," Echo points out.

Inna turns bright red and pushes to her feet. "Fine," she grumbles. "But Satu, you'd better not leave without saying goodbye."

Everything in me aches at this reminder that I can't stay here, with all of them, that my quest is far from over, my journey far from complete. "I would never," I say.

Inna sighs dramatically, then hugs Hal, Echo, and me. "I'm going to try and convince Papa to let me go with you when you leave," she whispers in my ear.

I laugh—that would take actual magic. "Good night, Inna."

Then she and Peter call their farewells and slip out the front door, a gust of snow blowing in after them.

Dread grips me.

"He's here, isn't he," says Echo, glancing from the snow on the floor to her husband, who has gone horribly, horribly pale. "The Winter Lord."

I nod miserably, fear beating through me. "Do you think it's possible," I say, with a worried look at Hal, "that the Wolf Queen isn't wholly gone? That part of her magic—that part of *her*—remains?"

Hal's eyes go wild and Echo holds tight to his hand, tethering him here, to the relative safety of this moment.

"Perhaps," says Echo. "But there is more than one evil in the world. The Winter Lord may very well be his own separate piece of it." She kisses Hal's cheek. "Go and find extra linens for Satu, won't you, love? We'll put her up on the couch."

He goes, tense and sad, and I want to throw up because I didn't mean to upset him.

Echo touches my arm. "He'll be all right. Don't worry. But come out into the garden, Satu. I think there's something you need to show me."

SEVENTEEN

IT'S QUIET IN THE GARDEN, STARS peering white over the roof-tops, with no sign of the Jökull's snow. Honey is dozing on three legs, having thoroughly devoured the vegetables.

"Nothing can touch us out here," says Echo, coming slowly through the kitchen door. "Your uncles look in on us, every now and again. They wove a protection magic about the house and the garden, just in case."

"Just in case?" I repeat, nerves jumbling together in my belly like a swarm of moths.

"The Wolf Queen was strong. Impossibly powerful. I think, perhaps, there was always a chance that the bond the Winds laid on her would fail. That she would claw her way back to magic again. Seek to rebuild her domain."

The moths flutter and dive. "Do you think that's what's happening? The Unraveling, the Winter Lord—do you think it's all her?"

Echo shakes her head. "Maybe. And maybe not. There's only one way to know." She gives a little cry and grabs her belly, sagging suddenly in the door frame.

I'm at her side in an instant, ready to catch her if she falls.

She takes deep breaths, steadies herself. "Don't worry, Satu," she gasps. "False birth pains. This boy has another month before he makes his way into the world."

I worry my lip, not quite believing her and wondering if I ought to shout for Hal.

But the next moment the tension leaves her face and her breathing grows easy again. "See?" she says, overly bright. "I'm just fine."

I'm still not convinced, but the pain truly seems to have passed. She sinks to a seat on the stoop. I sit beside her.

"When I first met you," she says, "you were a babe, not even a year old. I looked at you and I thought you were wonderful, but I never imagined I would have a child of my own. I couldn't think of it, not with the journey still ahead of me. And now here I am with new life growing inside of me, and here you are, a young woman in your own right.

"The journey is always ahead, I think, the path always changing. It takes you to places you don't expect, don't think you're ready for. But it has a way of shaping you, preparing you, so you *are* ready, when you get there.

"I used to think that if I could erase my scars, I would have my happy ending, like all those princesses and woodcutters' daughters in the fairy tales. But I consider my scars badges of honor now. I wouldn't change them. Because if I did, I would lose everything: being a doctor, marrying Hal, our child. Even you, Satu—I would never have gotten to see you all grown up. I would still be trapped in the Wolf Queen's court, forever her prisoner. All that to say"—Echo shakes her head, her fingers reaching up almost unconsciously to trace the lines of her scars—"all that to say, you know which way your path lies. And I have complete faith that you will be ready for whatever awaits you at the end of it."

"Even if it's the Wolf Queen?" I have to shove the words past my tight throat.

"Even then. Now." She gives me a sideways smile. "Do you still have that mirror sliver? The last piece of the library?"

I do, having transferred it from the pocket of my ruined skirt to that of the borrowed sarafan. I pull it out now, unwrapping the cloth so the glass winks out at us.

Echo's eyes light up. "I'm hoping the House has one last gift for me. Come on, Satu. Let's go and find it."

She's touching the mirror fragment before I can even answer, and it swallows her whole.

Hal pokes his head out the kitchen door just then, worry tugging at his face when he sees I am alone.

"Library," I say helplessly, gesturing to the piece of glass.

He sighs and rubs his temples. "She *would*. Best not leave her alone in there, or we'll not have her back again."

He touches the mirror and it takes him, too. I go last of all, shuddering at the cold wrench of broken magic.

"This place is a *wreck*," Hal is saying as I open my eyes in the ruined library. "No offense, love, but good riddance."

Echo stands looking morosely at the shattered mirrors, hands in the pockets of her skirt.

"None of the mirrors work," I tell her apologetically. "I tried them all. The one to the Temple of the Winds is gone now, too."

Hal laces his fingers through Echo's as they circle the room, Echo brushing her free hand over the ruined mirrors. She kisses her husband's cheek. "I know you spent nearly a century trapped in the worlds of these books and I'm sorry for it. But all the adventures we had—it's how I fell in love with you, you know. Twice."

"I wouldn't have it any other way," comes Hal's soft reply.

I am awkward again, a stray thought in a story that's not my own. But Echo glances back and gestures to me. "Walk with us, Satu. Help us look."

I do, though I'm not sure what it is we're looking for. Partway round the room, Echo gives a shout and crouches down in the rubble—slowly, because of her belly. She pulls something out from under the dust and broken glass: a blue leather pouch. Hal pales as Echo opens the pouch with trembling fingers: Inside lies tiny golden scissors in the shape of a bear, a gold thimble, a shining needle, and an empty spool. These are the tools Echo used to help the wolf bind the House together. Tools of old magic.

"I thought they were lost," Hal says.

"The House knew we needed them," Echo replies. She looks at me. "That Satu needed them." She fastens the pouch shut again and hands it to me. "For you, North Wind. To stitch the universe back together."

"There isn't any thread."

She just smiles. "You'll find that, too, in due time."

Her words sober me, but I tie the pouch onto my mother's belt, and it feels right.

Around us, the library starts to shake, the last remnants of book-mirrors falling off the walls and smashing on the floor.

Hal stands up, tugging Echo to her feet. Both of them look at me, stricken, but unafraid.

"Find the rest of your father's magic," says Echo above a sudden rush of wind, the shaking room, the shattering mirrors. "Bind the Unraveling world. And save us, too, if you can. I'd like to go on living." She places one hand on her belly, the other still caught tight in Hal's. "But I understand if our story is finished. As long as we can end it together."

Hal says something low in her ear and wraps both arms around her. She leans into him, a determined set to her jaw.

Panic sears through me. "We have to go!" I shout, beckoning to the mirror on the door that leads out of the library. "Before this whole room collapses!"

"It's not collapsing, Satu," says Echo.

The back wall comes apart, thread by thread, fading into whirling dark.

"PLEASE COME WITH ME!" I scream.

But the darkness touches them, reaches out with dragging fingers. They cling to each other as the room shakes, as the wind roars, as they Unravel, until there's nothing left.

A feral cry rips out of me, but it's too late.

Hal and Echo are gone.

The floor falls away, the walls plummet into nothingness. I throw myself at the mirror, hurling through the glass and the broken, freezing magic.

I fall on my shoulder into Echo's tiny courtyard, Honey still dozing beside the ravaged garden.

Inna comes flying out of the house, her braids undone and her face frantic.

"What are you doing here?" I demand, engulfed in tears of horror and helplessness. "You shouldn't be here!"

"I snuck back when Papa went to bed—I was afraid you would be gone by morning. But what's wrong, Satu? What's happened? There was a horrible noise."

Fann unfolds himself from the doorway behind her, panic in his eyes.

I'm shaking and shaking and I can't stop.

And then I realize it isn't me that's shaking.

It's the courtyard, the house, the *city*.

"Satu?" Inna's eyes are wide with fear as she clings to the lattice by the door, where white roses bloom. She's shaking, too.

"No," I say desperately. "INNA, NO!"

Her face crumples as she Unravels, thread by thread. "Satu?" And then she's gone.

"NO!" I scream. "YOU CAN'T HAVE INNA! SEND HER BACK!"

But she's *gone*, she's gone, she's gone, just like Echo and Hal and the herders. Just like my parents.

And the city will soon follow.

"Satu, you have to go." Fann's words are rough and raw. "Before the Unraveling takes Gradeslav, and you with it."

"But she's *gone*," I wrench out, choking on my tears. "She's gone."

"*Satu*." His voice is frantic. "*You have to get up.*"

I drag myself off the ground, the world a blur before me, numbly wrapping the mirror shard in my kerchief and shoving it back into my pocket. I sling my pack over one shoulder and grab Honey's tack, but the city, the *world*, is shaking so much I can't saddle him.

"SATU!" Fann shouts.

Behind him, Echo's house is Unraveling, threads dangling loose in the night, whatever protective magic my uncles wove about the courtyard wholly broken.

I tug Honey through the gate and out into the street, heart skidding and skipping, too heavy to hold. Snow blows about the cobbles and the houses are unwinding themselves, one after another, given over to the raging dark. Fann flickers like a candle flame, his eyes wide with fear. I tie another thread to him, quick as blinking, and then leap onto Honey's back.

The pony springs into a gallop, the threads in Fann yanking him along like a toy on a string. He gasps in pain. My heart wrenches and I send more threads into him, tying them up so tightly that he's pulled onto Honey behind me. Almost, almost I can feel the weight of him at my back, his body something more than phantasmal now. Magic pulses between us, sparking and strong.

Honey runs and runs, away from the Unraveling city, following the line of the rushing river out onto the star-frosted plain. My heart beats double-time to the pounding of his hooves.

The Winter Lord blocks our path in a cloud of snow and Honey skids to a stop before him, Fann and I tumbling to the ground.

"What have you *done*, North's daughter?" The Jökull's voice is low and seething.

I pull myself upright, wind in my veins and magic in my heart. I'm not afraid of him. "I don't answer to you, Jökull. Let us pass."

His eyes flick to Fann, who stands by Honey, more solid than he's ever been before.

The Winter Lord's face twists. "You don't know what you've done."

Around and beneath us the world shakes. The Unraveling has

swallowed a whole city and is not yet satisfied.

"Give me the North Wind's magic," says the Jökull. "Tear it out of him and give it to me. Let me fix this."

I feel the Unraveling threads, creeping across the ground, sucking up the river, blotting out the stars. There isn't time.

"Get out of my *way*," I growl. "Come on, Fann."

I turn to call for Honey.

But the pony is Unraveling, looking at me with mournful eyes as the magic takes him, bit by bit.

I scream into the sky, the anguish ripped from my very soul.

And then a hot, searing wind whips through the frozen grass, raging all around us. There is a man in the gale, tall and copper red, with a white jewel bound between his eyes. His mouth is set in a grim line, and in one hand he holds a massive spear. Copper blood drips from wounds in his face and his neck. He is my uncle, the South Wind.

His eyes meet mine. "Go, Satu. While you still can. I will try to keep the Unraveling from spreading any further. *Go!*"

A glimmer of movement just above me makes me lift my head. I gasp.

"Fann!" I shout.

"Wait!" cries the Winter Lord.

But I pull on the threads that bind Fann to me and fling us both upward, onto the back of the shimmering horse who has come to me on a current of air.

EIGHTEEN

THE WIND HORSE BEARS US UP, up, into the night, so high I feel as if I could reach out and touch the stars. The strange gleaming creature is solid and yet not, wind between my fingers, soul sparking fire.

"What are you?" I whisper, as it bears us on and on. My grief is so heavy I don't understand how this being made of air can carry me at all.

At my back, Fann is silent and still.

I am the Sky Horse, comes its answer, not in words but in a sort of echoing music inside my mind. *Your father created me.*

Sorrow squeezes all my breath away. My father and my mother and every soul in my mountain village. Taisia and the herders. Echo and Hal. All of Gradeslav. *Inna.* Even Honey, my faithful companion. Gone. "Where are you taking us?" I thread my fingers through the Sky Horse's beautiful mane, which is both there and not there, glinting like sunlight on water.

Into the sky, it says.

"But where?"

The West Wind's House. Your father bid me watch over you, to come if you were in danger and bring you to a place of safety.

My throat clogs and the sky blurs. If I had known, I'd have called the horse sooner. I could have saved Inna. Everything inside of me is screaming.

"Why didn't you come before?"

There was not enough of the North Wind's magic in you until tonight, says the Sky Horse. *You could not have seen me. I could not have carried you.*

The words shame me. Wind curls past my shoulders and fans my hot cheeks. "Thank you for saving us."

Fann still says nothing, and I crane my neck around. He's here with me, eyes shut tight against the vast world below. I feel his fear, harsh and jangling inside of him.

"I won't let you fall," I whisper. "I won't let you fall." And I tie yet another thread between us.

Beware, little North, says the Sky Horse. *What will you do when you run out of threads?*

Unease curls through me, but I push it away. "Fann," I say, to the not-quite-ghostly boy at my back. "How do you feel?"

"Safe," he says. "Safe, with you."

His hand grasps mine and I gasp. He's solid enough to touch. But he's cold. He's so, so cold, like a dead thing. Magic whispers and whirs in my chest. I hold it tight. Dread squeezes my heart. No living thing should ever be that cold. What *is* he?

The Sky Horse bears us through the stars as below dawn breaks red on a world of glittering ice. All the while I don't let go of Fann's hand, even when I can no longer feel my own. He can't be dead. I won't *let* him be dead. I will use all the magic I have, to save him. I will use more.

The horse flies into the rising sun. I fear it will burn us, but it does not. Tendrils of light caress my cheek, slide past my shoulders, whisper in my hair. The magic inside of me stretches and stirs, responding to the light's touch. I remember my father's stories, how the Four Winds are the children of the Sun and the Moon, and I feel the truth of it, now. I am humbled, awed—my heritage is light, as well as wind.

Warmth floods my body, feeling coming back into the hand caught fast in Fann's. He cries out and snatches his fingers away, as if I've burned him.

"Satu," he gasps. "You're glowing!"

I look at my hand to see light, pulsing under my skin.

The Sun is pleased to see you, says the Sky Horse. *It is long since there was a child in the heavens.*

I peer into the light, straining to see the true form of my grandfather—I have the sudden, desperate wish to know his face.

"Have there been others before me?" I say. "Wind daughters?

Grandchildren of the Sun?"

You are the first, says the Sky Horse.

And then we're beyond the Sun, burnished yet with his great light.

"Did I hurt you, Fann?" I ask the boy at my back.

"No," he whispers.

But he does not reach for my hand again and it guts me.

We fly into what I can only describe as a rain country. Rain falls around us, sweet and silver, washing away the dust of the earth that still clings to me, but not the ache of my sorrow. This place drips with beauty and impossibility. Green things grow in the air, trees and islands and huge gray and blue creatures that swim between them.

My father gave up all of this, I think. *For my mother. For me.*

The Sky Horse flies up, up, through the rain country, to where a great house sits on a high white cloud. It is made of flashing bronze and I can hardly keep my eyes open against its brilliance.

"Don't let me go, Satu," whispers Fann, suddenly frantic. "I can feel the nightmare calling. Please. *Please* don't let me go."

"I won't," I tell him fiercely. "*Never.*" I tie three more threads to him, fast and strong. I won't surrender him to the dark.

We come to the very edge of the West Wind's House and step from the Sky Horse's back onto a wide courtyard paved with great slabs of bronze.

When you are ready, says the horse, *I will be here for you, wind daughter.*

And then the horse is gone, back down into the rain country. I turn to Fann. He is almost wholly solid, only his edges a little bit blurred. He looks frightened and small.

The threads inside of me murmur and twist, almost all of them, now, tied to Fann. I hope they are enough. They *have* to be enough.

We pace side by side to the great bronze door of the West Wind's House. It swings inward with the tone of a deep-throated bell, beckoning us into an echoing hall so vast I can't see the end of it in any direction. Stone arches stretch up into darkness, and yet the whole chamber pulses with shimmering light.

Waiting for us beneath one of the arches is not my uncle but a tall woman. She has long silver hair and bright violet eyes, her nose and jaw all sharp, angular lines, her ears large and lupine, furred with gray. I know her, too, from a story: Mokosh, the Wolf Queen's daughter. She wears a white ring on her finger.

"Well met, Satu," says Mokosh, striding forward to greet us. "I am sorry my husband is not here, but the Unraveling splinters far and wide, and he could not be spared."

I blink at her. "Your . . . husband?"

She flashes a smile that is sharp but not unkind. "Yes, my husband is the West Wind, but that is a story for another day. Come, we will eat as we talk, but we must do it swiftly."

I nod, too stunned for speech.

With Fann just behind me, I follow Mokosh through the enormous hall, then into a narrow stone passageway mortared with jewels, and out onto a wide terrace emblazoned with bronze. It looks out over the rain country, and the sun is vast and bright beyond.

A table is laid for three, heaps of fruit and bread and other foods I can't identify on waiting platters. I sit across from Mokosh, while Fann hovers at my elbow.

Mokosh pours a foamy pink beverage into etched bronze cups. She hands one to me. "Who is your companion, Satu?"

I nearly drop the cup. "You can see him?"

"Of course I can. He brims with magic, though none of it is his own." She looks at Fann. "Sit, won't you?"

He takes the seat next to me, every line of him exuding discomfort. "I'm Fann," he says.

Mokosh nods thoughtfully, studying him. "I knew of someone with that name, long ago."

His forehead creases as if with pain, but he doesn't say anything further.

I shift in my chair, taking an experimental sip from my cup. The drink is sweet, and fizzes pleasantly on my tongue.

"Now then, Satu." Mokosh turns to me. "You know where your road lies."

I nod, insides writhing. "North, to where the Wolf Queen once ruled. The seat of my father's power."

"Yes," says Mokosh. She serves me fruit and a savory pastry that smells of spices and summer days. I don't eat any; I don't know how to stomach food right now.

She doesn't eat either, just cuts the pastry into pieces with a tiny fork and knife. "You should know, then, that my mother—" Her hands shake a little, and she sets her utensils down.

"Your mother isn't wholly gone," I say quietly.

Mokosh rises from her seat and paces to the edge of the terrace, staring over the rail to the rain country, shimmering and green.

I follow her, and Fann follows me, keeping a pace back, tense and uncertain.

"The Winds should have killed her," says Mokosh as I come up beside her. "Instead they showed her mercy."

"Mercy is not to be scorned," I say.

She turns her face to mine, stricken. "Of course it isn't. But it is also not without cost."

And now, it seems, the whole world is paying the price.

"They made her a beast," I say. "They took all her magic away. How could she undo all of that?"

Mokosh shakes her head. "How, I don't know. She must have had some failsafe in place in case the worst happened and she was unable to access her magic. Something that protected her mind, if not her body. She has been reaching out to me in my dreams, the last few weeks. Asking me to come to her. To free her. So there is some bond laid on her yet. She has not regained her full power."

A sudden suspicion darts through me, making my gut clench: a failsafe, something to hold part of her magic, something to bring her back to herself. Something—or some*one*. I shake, heart racing and skin buzzing. I gulp desperate mouthfuls of air and try, try, to shove my panic down into the depths of myself. I can't get the Winter Lord's voice out of my mind, demanding, over and over, that I give him my father's magic.

He has never hidden who he is or what he wants. Only for whom he wants it.

Mokosh touches my arm, concern in her eyes. "Satu?"

"It's the Jökull," I say, trying not to rattle apart. "The Jökull is her failsafe."

"My mother's wretched hound? Perhaps."

Bile burns in my chest. "You know him?"

Mokosh studies me, her face going soft. "I lived in my mother's court for many years, Satu. I knew the Winter Lord as much as anyone. He was bound to her. They all were. But that's not what's important." She grips my arms and I look up into her startling eyes to find that they're wet with tears.

"My mother has no claim to the North Wind's magic anymore. No matter how much power she's clawed back for herself, she cannot bind the wind magic again unless it's freely given. You must find the rest of it, Satu. Draw it into yourself. Become the North Wind and save us all."

Tears pour down my face and I turn away from her, ashamed. "I don't know how. I'm not strong enough or brave enough. I'm not—I'm not *enough*."

"Satu."

Her fingers on my cheek are sharp with claws, but they do not cut me. "You have always been enough. There is great magic inside of you, burning and growing. It's always been there: your *own* magic, Satu."

I bite my lip, still unable to meet her eyes.

"Your father's magic will strengthen your inherent power, but even without it, you were always destined to become the North Wind."

"But how do I wield it?" I whisper. "How do I wield such power when I don't even understand it?"

Mokosh laughs a little. "You have *already* wielded your magic, Satu. It's so ingrained in you you don't realize when you're using it. You made Fann solid; you called the Sky Horse. West told me you have kept bees without a suit since you were a child. Did you never wonder why they didn't sting you? Why they came when you called?"

I'm startled into looking at her. "My bees understand me. They always have."

She smiles. "That is magic, you know."

A strange, warm feeling stirs in my belly. *You clearly have some kind of bee magic*, Fann said at our first meeting. It seems he was right after all.

I swallow. "But when I *have* collected the North Wind's power—how do I stop the Unraveling, when even my uncles can't fight it? How do I stitch the world back together, and how—" The grief is back, hard and raw in my throat. I take a shaky breath. "Is there a way to bring them all back? Everyone who was Unraveled?"

Mokosh's face goes grim. "I don't know, Satu. But if there is, I have faith that you will find it. The Great Weaver is not cruel. Now then." She turns to Fann, who has been standing behind me this whole while, not saying a word.

She steps up to him and takes both his hands in hers but he jerks himself free, fear in his eyes. "Don't touch me!"

"Fann," I say quietly, going to his side. "She wouldn't hurt you."

"She's a monster," he says, shaking, "no matter she's learned to change her face." Tears glint on his cheeks.

I stare at him, horrified. "Fann, what do you mean? Why would you say that?"

"He's right," says Mokosh frankly. "I am a shapeshifter, like my mother was. I use magic to soothe my vanity, but I am not ashamed to appear as I was made." She gives a swift shake of her head and changes before me, no longer bearing the face of a woman. She is almost wholly wolf, now, though her large violet eyes and long silver hair remain.

"Take care, Fann," she says. "The magic that burns inside of you is not your own. I do not know how much longer you can endure in such a state."

Fann ducks his head, his shoulders tense.

"I'm going to help him," I say tightly, "make him wholly solid, make him himself again."

A tenderness comes into Mokosh's eyes, and her human face

smooths back over her lupine one. "It is well for the world, Satu North, that you have such a great heart. I wish you success in this as well."

Beneath my feet, the bronze terrace begins to shake.

"But we are out of time, I fear. Take this." Mokosh offers me something small and dark and smooth, horribly sharp on one end and strung on a silver thread.

"One of my mother's claws," she explains. "A piece of her magic, to use against her if her power has once more grown strong." She takes a shaky breath, as behind her the West Wind's House Unravels, thread by thread. "There can be no mercy for her, anymore," she says. "Do you understand that, Satu?"

I nod, throat too tight to speak.

"Then farewell, North Wind. It seems my time has come."

"Satu!" shouts Fann.

The Unraveling reaches out for us, carving darkness into the brass pavers, crawling up Mokosh's silver skirts.

"Goodbye," I choke out. "I'm sorry."

I grab Fann's freezing hand and jump with him into empty air.

NINETEEN

FOR THE SPACE OF TEN HEARTBEATS, I forget to be afraid. There is wind and light, a soothing weightlessness. I belong here, in the sky.

Then I realize Fann is screaming, his death-cold fingers digging into my arms as we hurtle down and down.

The fear comes, but with it, a fierce sort of assurance. *Sky Horse*, I call in my mind. *Save us.*

And the shimmering creature curls beneath us, slowing our fall. Fann stops screaming but he shakes and cries. I close my eyes and let the wind wash over me as I bid the horse to bear us to the ground.

We land lightly in the snow. Fann scrambles off and away from the Sky Horse, eyes wild with panic. I slip down more slowly, reluctant to be parted from this being made of air. It bows its head to me and I stride to where Fann sits with his knees pulled up to his chest. Snow clings to his trousers and his bare feet. I need to find him shoes, I realize, now that he can feel things again.

I crouch beside him, insides twisting as he shakes and shakes. I've miraculously still got my pack with me, grabbed in haste in Echo's garden, and I tug a blanket out, wrap it around him. He pulls it tight about his shoulders, tucking his feet inside the fabric. It's a blanket from the herder camp, woven in a masterful pattern of white reindeer on a dark blue background.

I can't bear his turmoil, his agony. But there is something I must ask him, and I must ask him now. It takes me some moments to work up the courage. I swallow past my pounding heart, my wrenching stomach. "Did you meet Mokosh at the Wolf Queen's court?"

"Yes," he says heavily. "Long ago. She was . . . not kind."

I glance at the Sky Horse, who stands tense in the snow, all motion and rippling wind, impatient to return to the air. Wind blows snow over my knees, but I don't feel the chill of it. "Did she curse you, Fann? Did the Wolf Queen curse you?" Just asking the question guts me utterly.

He shifts in the blanket. He doesn't look at me. "Yes." His voice cracks on that single word. "Only the North Wind's magic can free me from her."

My heart is a fluttering thing in my chest, uncertain and afraid. "How much of the North Wind's magic?" I ask him quietly.

He hangs his head and doesn't answer.

Tears drip down my cheeks. "I have to try and stop the world from Unraveling. I have to, Fann."

He nods; he still won't look at me.

The tears choke me. It's cruel, cruel. Because why must I choose between trying to save the world, and trying to save the one person in it whose soul is fixed in mine? "I'm going to save you," I tell him fiercely, desperately. "I won't let you fall back into your nightmare, Fann. I'm not letting you go."

He lifts his head, his own tears shining on his cheeks. "I don't deserve your kindness, Satu."

I take his freezing hand and briefly squeeze it. "Of course you do." The threads I bound into him tug at my heart, little twinges of pain like splinters under skin. I have no illusions now about what is holding him here. Or what it will take to wholly and permanently free him.

Loss pulses inside of me and it is all too much to bear. Tears freeze on my cheeks. Snow falls thicker, colder.

I stand and tug Fann up after me, trying not to wince at his touch.

"We have to go," I say. "We're out of time."

He nods miserably, eyeing the Sky Horse.

Both of us scramble up, me in front and Fann behind. The Sky Horse runs into the whirling snow, staying close to the ground, like I ask. For whatever reason, Fann cannot bear the sky.

In the evening, we slide off the Sky Horse to make camp out on the wide plain. The faithful horse dissolves into air—I know it will appear again when I need it to. We have to travel quite a ways east yet before we can turn north, and I hate that I am yet human, that I cannot transform myself all to wind and fly forever without stopping. I have wasted so much time, and there is so very little left.

But as it is, I nearly collapse with exhaustion, scrabbling for the crumbs of stale food I find scattered at the very bottom of my pack. Fann is quiet, crouching near me, and has been all day. Belatedly, I offer him a bit of dried meat, but he shakes his head.

"I am not quite human enough for food yet," he says. He sounds unhappy, and there are lines of pain in his forehead.

"What's wrong, Fann?" I ask, taking a bite of meat that's so hard I nearly break a tooth.

"I feel the nightmare calling again," he says softly. "I feel *her* calling."

I worry my lip, the threads connecting us pulling sharp and tight. "I won't let her take you, Fann. I won't let you go."

He flashes a sad smile in the growing darkness. I tug another thread out of my heart and send it into his.

Around me, the world seems to still. Fragments of ice appear, suspended on nothing, spinning and white, and through them comes the Jökull, his shoulders dusted with snow, his once immaculate coat ragged at the hem. Across from me, Fann doesn't move and doesn't blink, that sad smile frozen on his lips.

The Winter Lord stops a pace away from me, his ice crystals hanging between us. There is something like desperation in his pale eyes. "You have *got* to stop doing that."

"Doing what?" I demand.

He glances with disgust at Fann's perfectly motionless body. "Giving him your magic, thread by thread. What will happen, do you think, when it's all gone?"

Still Fann stares unblinking into the night, and fear eats at me from the inside. "What have you done?"

The Winter Lord waves a dismissive hand. "Frozen time, just for a moment. Bastard is solid enough now for my magic to affect him. But you need to listen to me, Satu. The Unraveling is getting worse. Give me your magic. Let me help you."

I glower at him. "Fann is under a curse. If he doesn't have the North Wind's magic, he will *die*."

"Is that what he told you? He's lying, Satu. He's using you. He's just driving you to—to *her*."

"And what are *you* doing?" I cry. "Why would you ever expect me to trust you after everything you've done?"

"I'm trying to save you," he says, low and tight. "Take my hand, Satu. Let me save you from the Unraveling world. Please."

I stare at him, his *please* tearing at my heart. I am struck again by the sorrow that weighs on him, by the way it makes me ache.

I don't move and he comes closer, until only a sliver of night divides us. I can sense the cold of him, but I remember the

warmth of his lips, the strength in his long hands. Suddenly, I
can't breathe. I want to tell him *yes*, I'll take his hand. I'll give
him my magic. Because what could I even do with it? I'm just a
small, scared girl who never would have left my mountain at all
if it hadn't Unraveled before my eyes.

And yet something in me rebels, that place deep inside that
pulses with magic and warmth, that spins my own threads and
my father's together and makes them hum with power. They call
to me.

"Please," the Jökull repeats. He puts his fingers on my temples. "Don't make me take it from you." I feel his magic, reaching
for mine.

I jerk away from him, furious, but he catches my wrists,
fingers holding tight. Tendrils of ice shoot up my arms, sear
through my veins. I can't move and I can't breathe and I can't
stop staring at him. There is anguish in his face but I don't care.
Tears cloud my vision. "This is you, I suppose," I wrench out.
"Not being kind."

He looks stricken, like my pain means something to him. But
he doesn't let go. He doesn't stop pulling at the threads of my
magic. "I'm sorry, Satu. I have no other choice. If I don't take
your magic now, *she* will get it. There will be nothing left of you
then, not even a husk."

"We always have a choice," I whisper. The tears turn to ice on
my cheeks. "You could make a different one."

The Winter Lord lets go of one of my wrists. He brushes his

fingers over my frozen tears and they drip salty and warm again, sliding down my neck.

"It would be easier," he says softly, "if *you* were not so kind. But this is my different choice. The only way to save you."

He tilts his forehead against mine. His cold pulses through me and I'm pulled toward him like a lodestone. A flash of his eyes and then his mouth is on mine and I'm kissing him like all the world is falling away, like nothing exists but him, but me, frozen in his moment of time with his drops of ice that do not fall. He is ragged and wild and the warmth of him shocks me anew. How can he be so, so warm? I breathe in the Winter Lord and he breathes in me. His ice and his fire tangle inside of me, and then I feel him once more reaching, grasping, *pulling* at my magic, because I will not give it to him freely.

It hurts, it hurts *so much*, and my pulse rages as I fight to keep my panic, my fury at bay. My free hand scrabbles desperately for my collar and wraps tight around Mokosh's gift.

The Jökull screams as I stab him in the neck with the Wolf Queen's claw, as I rip myself away from him and grab Fann's hand, pulling him free of the moment frozen in time. Around us, ice trembles. It starts to fall.

The Winter Lord writhes on the ground, choking and screaming, and I'm sick at what I've done.

But that does not keep me from running with Fann into the dark.

Fann gasps as the Sky Horse bears us into the air, higher and higher, out of the Winter Lord's reach. I feel his agony, thrumming through the threads between us.

"What can I do, Fann?" I whisper through fresh tears. "How can I help you?"

But he doesn't answer, groaning with pain.

I bid the Sky Horse to take us down again. I pull Fann onto solid earth, untouched here by the Jökull's frost. He shakes beside me, wheezing, and terror grips me. I can't lose him. Not now. He is the only friend I have left in all the world and I couldn't bear it if he—

"Fann." I wrap my arms around him. I hold him tight. "Breathe," I say. "You have to breathe."

But he just shakes and shakes.

I shut my eyes, reaching for the threads that bind us. The knots are causing him pain. *I'm* causing him pain, for all I've nearly emptied myself to keep him here, with me. Tears gush unheeded down my face. "What do I do, Fann? What do I do?"

"Not enough," he whispers through his pain.

"Not enough magic?" I choke out.

"This . . . little bit . . . is keeping me here . . . but it's not enough . . . I think it's killing me."

Panic races along my skin and now I'm shaking every bit as hard as Fann.

"Break the threads," he gasps. "Cut the cords between us. Let me . . . fall asleep again, and when you've gathered the rest of

your father's magic . . . call me. The magic . . . you leave in me . . .
will know your voice . . . and . . . I will come back. I will wake up.
I will be . . . whole again."

"But the nightmare," I sob. "The Wolf Queen's curse."

He makes an attempt at a smile, reaching up one hand to
caress my cheek. "I don't mind . . . so much," he lies. "It is . . .
only . . . a dream."

Tears choke me, and I think I might be sick.

"You'll be faster," he says. "Without me."

"Fann, no."

"Please, Satu." He rubs his thumb along the side of my face,
his coldness numbing every part of me. "Cut the threads."

"How?" I'm crying so much I can't breathe.

He touches the pouch at my hip and I remember what Echo
found in the ruined library. What her and Hal were Unraveled
for finding. With trembling fingers, I open the pouch and take
out the bear-shaped scissors.

"It will be . . . all right," he breathes, and tries another
wobbly smile.

I bite my lip so hard I taste blood as I shut my eyes, as I bring
the scissors to the threads that shimmer between us. I sever them
with one sharp movement.

Pain explodes in my chest and Fann winks out like a
candle flame.

TWENTY

I FEEL THE SEVERED THREADS INSIDE ME, ragged and raw, and though the initial mind-numbing *agony* of that first moment fades, the brokenness does not. I am half-Unraveled. Only part myself.

I want to call him back, to bind the threads together again, to be once more whole, tied securely to him. But I can't. Because I don't have enough magic to break his curse, and even if I did, I couldn't use it on him. Not yet.

Still the frayed threads murmur and itch, fiber splinters in my heart.

The Sky Horse bows its head to me, waiting. Numbly I climb onto it, wrapping my fingers in its shimmering mane. It bears me up into the sky but there is no joy now, in the air where I belong.

You are hurt, says the Sky Horse. *I am sorry.*

I bury my face into the horse's mane, letting wind lick up my tears.

But it is not only the loss of Fann that eats at me. I cannot shake away the Winter Lord's anguished face, the awful sensation of the Wolf Queen's claw digging into his neck. I know I have not killed him, but his blood and his pain at my hand haunt me. I can still taste his kiss, his magic—ice and fire twined together, a snowstorm on a mountain in June. I can still feel the pull of him.

The Sky Horse flies on. Above me, there are only stars. Below, a blizzard rages.

I do not think he would have hurt you, says the horse after a while, reading my thoughts. *He is nothing but a scared boy, adrift in the winter snows.*

"He tried to take my magic," I say into the wind.

But he didn't, did he?

Again I feel the claw cutting into his neck. I swallow hard. "I stopped him."

It is his mistress you must beware.

"You mean the Wolf Queen."

She seeks to claw her way back into this story.

Broken threads pulse inside of me, and I shut my eyes against the pain. Fann and the Winter Lord are both connected to the Wolf Queen. Fann is cursed, but the Winter Lord? What is he?

He belongs to her, body and soul, says the Sky Horse. *I saw it in him. He fights her, but I saw it still. She wields his power. Commands his fate.*

I ponder my unspoken promise to Fann that I will do whatever it takes to make him whole again, even if it means pouring all of the North Wind's magic into him.

"Could I free him?" I ask the Sky Horse. I don't mean Fann.

Would you want to?

I have no answer for that.

A little while passes before I peer out at the stars again through blurry eyes.

"If I sleep," I say softly, "would you carry me on through the night?"

Of course, dear heart.

My father used to call me that. I can almost hear his voice.

I let tears and wind and night lull me to sleep, and when I wake again it is midmorning, and we are still flying.

THE SKY HORSE CARRIES ME east, always east, but it is never fast enough, never far enough. My heart cries out to take the northern path, and I despair of ever reaching it.

The Jökull comes steadily behind me, the air ever icy, the earth covered in snow. The Sky Horse feeds me with fruits from the rain country, carried on its back in an invisible pouch. *A present from Mokosh,* the horse tells me. So I live on those fruits and water from the clouds. I sleep, wake, eat. I never have to leave the sky.

I lose track of the days and the nights, but it must be a week, two, before a familiar scent in the air tugs at me, sharp enough to make me dare return to the ground.

Wind wraps around me, fierce and cold, and I turn my eyes north to where my mountain used to be. There is nothing there, now. It is a blank spot in the universe, a wheeling horror of severed threads that seem to twist and scream.

"Power suits you, North. Perhaps I was wrong."

I turn to see the Winter Lord standing in the swirling snow, the ugly wound on his neck barely scabbed.

My stomach wrenches. Even now, I can't bear that I'm the one who caused his pain. That's what lingers, even more so than the pain he caused me trying to steal my magic. And yet my hand still goes to the Wolf Queen's claw, ready to wield it again if he comes near me. He doesn't.

Wind rushes around my shoulders. The Jökull crackles with ice. Behind me, the Unraveled mountain pulses in agony, no less brutal for being so fractured.

The Winter Lord's eyes haunt me. "Don't go to her court, Satu. Don't go to her."

I clench my hands, nails digging into my palms. Magic pulses inside of me. Wind whispers round my heels. "I'm not afraid of her."

He doesn't laugh at my lie. "Some things are not what they seem. Not her. Not me."

There is fear in me. But there is anger, too. "I think you are exactly what you seem."

Wind stirs through his hair; snowflakes catch in mine.

"And what is that?"

I think of the Sky Horse's words. "You are a coward, my lord. A frightened boy who throws a fit when he cannot have what he wants."

The Jökull laughs without humor. "What is it you think that I want?"

I drown in heartbeats, in my pounding panic. "The North Wind's power. The North Wind's immortality. At the cost of everything else, even the world."

"You're wrong, Satu." He takes a step nearer and I tighten my hand around the claw. "That is not what I want. Perhaps it was, at first, but not anymore."

"Then what?"

His pale eyes pierce through me. "I want the North Wind."

"My father is *gone*. He Unraveled before my eyes, or have you forgotten?"

"I do not mean your father," says the Jökull quietly.

The rest of my words choke off. I stare at him, overwhelmed by the memory of his mouth on mine, by the taste of his fiery magic.

He takes a breath, eyes darting away from mine as if he's *nervous*. "Don't go to the Wolf Queen's court, Satu. She will *destroy* you. Let me bring you somewhere safe, let me show you—"

"I am not going *anywhere* with you," I snarl. The Sky Horse appears at my shoulder, hearing my wordless call, and presses its billowing body cool against my side.

The Jökull's eyes glitter. "Do you think you are strong, wind daughter? Do you think you can wield the whole of your father's magic without it breaking you? You are half human, after all. You are not fully a creature of the old world."

"And I suppose you are?" I scoff. I climb onto the Sky Horse's back, one hand still wrapped around the Wolf Queen's claw. But I don't bid the horse skyward. I wait, like a fool, for the Winter Lord's answer.

It is his mistress you must beware, says the echo of the horse's voice. *He belongs to her, body and soul.*

The Winter Lord raises his hands, snow swirling from his fingertips. His eyes don't leave mine as a horse forms in his storm, an echo of the Sky Horse, though this one is made of snow, its mane and tail glistening ice. It stomps one foot, wind blowing through its icy mane in a tinkling, eerie music.

"No," says the Winter Lord.

I have nearly forgotten what we were talking about, mesmerized by his magic. "No?"

He strokes the Snow Horse, and it nuzzles his shoulder. "I am not a creature of the old world."

Wind rushes wild between us and the Winter Lord's long hair whips about his face, tangling with the falling snow. Neither of us move, and if not for the fluid motion of the Sky Horse and the Snow Horse, I would think he had frozen time again.

"I was human, once. Long before you were born. But the magic that has sustained my life, that has given me the power of a Winter Lord—it is almost gone."

I glare at him across our whirling storm, anger the only weapon I have against my confused tangle of emotions. "I have no care for your life."

"Yes, you do," he says frankly. "You care about everything. Crushed flowers and spilt honey. Your mother's grief and your father's guilt. The plight of a character in a story."

His words choke me. "How do you know that?"

He doesn't answer, just studies me through wind and snow.

I tell myself it is only pity and hatred I feel for him. I tell myself it is nothing more. "What bargain did you make with her, Winter Lord?"

His snow turns to ice and rains down around him in glittering, knife-edged fragments, but he does not answer.

"You are beholden to her magic. Dying from the lack of it. And so you seek to keep me from going to her mountain because you can't let your only hope at life slip through your fingers. Isn't that right?"

The wind is stronger now, and I get the sense that it is *my* wind, giving voice to my feelings. It rattles through the Snow Horse's icy mane, and the noise is jarring.

"I never thought you would be cruel, Satu North." His voice is barely audible, but his words are sharp as cut crystal.

My heart twists, tears sparking hot. I find I do not want to be cruel, not even to the Winter Lord. But what else can I be? I cannot help him, no matter how sharp my pity burns. "I have no time for kindness."

"You are kind to all things. The bees and the winds and the mountain. That awful apothecary woman, your pony, the ghostly boy who means to take everything from you. And yet I do not merit your kindness?"

"No," I say fiercely, to myself as well as to him. "No, you don't."

"Then believe me when I say, if you go to her, *she will destroy you.*"

"Her power is broken. And when I collect the final pieces of my father's magic—"

"What?" he scoffs. "You will be able to defeat her? You are a *fool*, Satu. She will take that magic, bind it to herself as it once was bound. The Unraveling will cease, but she will not repair the holes. And she will rule over the broken world and make all life bow before her. Nothing will matter, not then. *Please*, Satu. Don't go to her."

I grind my jaw. "You can't stop me."

I shout a word and the Sky Horse springs upward in a whirl of air, wind singing in my ears, power swelling inside of me. "Faster," I whisper to my mount. "Faster."

Then the world blurs below me as the horse leaps over the Unraveled mountain, as we turn north, north, to where my blood calls me.

I don't have to look over my shoulder to know the Jökull comes hard behind, but snow is not as fast as wind, unless it is borne on the wings of it. He can't catch me. Not now.

I try to push his warnings from my mind, try to ignore the pulse of fear that he's telling the truth, not just trying to manipulate me into giving up my magic.

On and up we go, and a sudden joy sears through me. Every fiber of my being seems to hum that this is where I belong, that my feet were never made to touch the ground. *I'm coming, Papa,* I think. *I'm coming, Inna. I'm coming, world. I'm coming to save you all.*

For the first time since all of this began, I believe it.

THE FARTHER NORTH I FLY, the stronger I begin to feel. Threads slip into me, winding about the spool of my heart, fragments of the old magic that once belonged to my father, and now belong to me. In these northern wilds, the very air seems to teem with it.

Inside of me the magic sings and sears, and I am afraid that this burgeoning power will fill me up and up until it pushes me out, until nothing of my old self remains. And yet I crave it, too, because the North Wind's magic feels like the missing pieces of my soul. But even all these gathered, growing threads can't soothe the constant ache of the cords I cut between me and Fann.

Below me sprawls the tundra, frozen and white, and the Winter Lord blazes across it, a plume of silver.

I am not afraid of him, not anymore. What does the North Wind have to fear from the winter? It is the winter that ought to fear the wind, which commands the way the snow falls, and how ice forms upon the trees.

Still, his warnings haunt me, and no matter how far I ride, I can't shake away that feeling of being drawn to him, like our threads are tangled together.

Every night, I urge the Sky Horse up and up, until we fly among the stars, cool glints of fire brushing my cheeks, singing in my ears a glittering song. They welcome me as a sister of sorts, for there is light in my blood.

When dawn breaks every morning, I rest my head on the horse's neck and slide into a half-sleep, always aware of the wind around me, of the horse moving on through the sky.

I do not set my feet on the earth again; I don't give the Jökull the opportunity to trap me with his frozen words, to lure me with the strange inner warmth of him I do not understand.

The thought of Fann is a constant torment, the cut threads rubbing me raw. He has been long in his nightmare now. Will he be the same when I at last call him out of it? Can I save him?

There comes a morning when a frozen lake spreads out below me, so vast and wide it might as well be a sea. It tugs at me, and I bid the Sky Horse to take me down, down. For the first time in days I slip from its back, my feet grazing the surface of the ice.

It is not as smooth as I first thought. Some of the ice lays in furrows like a farmer's field, dusted with snow, their insides shining a bright, impossible turquoise.

I catch my breath, kneeling on the frozen lake and brushing

my fingers across the beautiful blue-green ice. It teems with magic, and I remember a line from Echo's story. *Jewels from the North Wind's crown*, my father told her. He didn't bring me quite this way when we traveled together to the Wolf Queen's mountain. I wonder if he knew, even then, that these jewels would reach out to me, that I could sense their magic, that I would yearn to draw it inside of me.

It is these jewels that called me down from the sky. They sing to me now, whispering that they no longer want to be bound in the ice.

With a thought, wind curls around my shoulders and twists out from my fingertips. It is stronger now than ever before. How much of my father's magic is buried here? I am terrified and overjoyed, and I cannot untangle either emotion from the other. I am not strong enough, to hold all this magic. How can I dare claim it? Yet how can I not? I ache for it in marrow, in bone, my heart crying out to be filled.

I whisper to the winds and they run across the ice, blowing away the snow, uncovering lines upon lines of glittering blue. I can scarcely breathe for the awe of it.

"Come to me," I say, quiet on the frigid air. "Come."

I am afraid. So terribly, terribly afraid. But I am ready, too.

The winds—*my* winds—whirl over the ice and fracture it to pieces, setting loose the threads within. They come and come, coiling around my heart, stretching me to make room. The magic is more powerful than any I've felt yet and it terrifies me. But I do not stop it coming.

What if it breaks me apart?

But what if it makes me stronger, better, wiser? What if it makes me into the thing I was meant to be, a girl able to hold on to her heart, to not sense and feel every fiber of emotion in the universe?

The magic swells inside of me. I do not break. Tears drip down my cheeks—I am still a fragile thing, still a breath away from being shattered.

One block of turquoise ice remains. My winds coil around it, breaking it, too. These pieces don't dissolve into magical threads. They twist and mold and make, forming a circlet of ice. The winds bear it up, set it gently on my brow.

I am so full of wind magic now my feet no longer touch the frozen lake; I hover an inch or two above the ground, and it takes a monumental effort to sink down again.

I touch the crown with hesitant fingers. It is not cold, like the ice it was made from, but warm, pulsing with power.

I shake and shake. My ears buzz and my heart races and I can't stop the tears that scald my cheeks. I want to tear the crown off. I want to claw all this magic out of me and bury it again in ice.

The Winter Lord's voice twists through my mind: *Do you think you can wield the whole of your father's magic without it breaking you?*

It is already breaking me, and there is yet more to gather. There are pieces missing; I feel their absence like lost limbs. I am not the North Wind. Not yet. Just a girl crying on a frozen lake, filled with power I can't wield, and don't even understand.

But I can't stay here. If I do, the world will fracture, and I will fracture with it. I don't know if I can save it. But I am so, so close. I have to try.

I tell myself a story.

Once upon a time, there was a girl who was brave enough to lift her head. She continued on her journey because she realized that there are things more important than herself.

I breathe in and breathe out. I open my eyes—I don't remember closing them. The world seems a little clearer, and I realize I do not want to go the rest of the way alone. With all the magic now inside of me, I don't have to.

Once more I kneel on the ice, wind wheeling around me. I grasp the severed threads and I *pull*.

"Fann," I whisper. "Fann, wake up."

I scream at the wrench of jagged, broken magic, white-hot pain searing through me.

And then the pain is gone and he is here, gasping, gasping, digging his nails into the ice, his eyes dark and wild. A strange scent lingers around him, like flowers and fire.

"Fann?" I say carefully.

There's a mutter of thunder behind us, and I glance back to see a dark cloud on the horizon. The Winter Lord is coming—we haven't much time.

"Fann." I scoot over to him, my pulse frightened and quick.

He throws his head up, scrabbling backward. "You have woken me too early," he gasps. "You have not got all the magic yet."

"I have enough," I say. "Enough to help you."

Pain twists his face. His eyes snag on my crown.

"I promised I would help you," I tell him, "and that's what I'm going to do." I look back—the cloud boils nearer. "No more nightmares." I tug at the broken threads in him; I tie them to the broken threads in me. Then I send more magic into him, more and more until it isn't a struggle, any longer, to keep my feet on the ground. I hold out my hand. "Now come on. Get up."

There is joy in his eyes as he takes my hand, as I pull him to his feet. The frigid cold of his touch burns me, but I don't let him go.

I tug him with me up onto the Sky Horse, who billows and dances over the ice. Behind us, a blizzard rages, the white and silver form of the Winter Lord riding hard within it.

TWENTY-ONE

WE FLY OVER THE BREADTH OF the vast frozen lake, over the glittering ice caves I traveled through with my father as a child.

The Jökull comes hard behind. He is not airborne, like Fann and me, but his Snow Horse is fast across the ice, and faster still over the mountains.

We hurtle on, wind chased by snow, and with every breath I feel another thread of my father's power seep into me. I marvel he could hold it all. I am terrified I cannot.

Behind me, Fann hisses and writhes, each moment seeming to cause him pain.

No, Fann, I think fiercely. *I'm not losing you, too.*

The threads slip into me, winding tight about my heart, and

as we fly, I pull them out again and tie them to Fann. I tie so many, so quickly, that my head begins to pound, my heart beat slow and sluggish, my body weigh heavy, heavy.

It is too much, wind daughter, says the Sky Horse in my mind. *It is too many. If you pull out any more threads, I will no longer be able to carry you. Any more than that, and you will both die. That much magic cannot be split between two souls.*

I bow my head over the horse's shimmering neck, tears falling thick. The North Wind's magic continues to wind into me, but I tie no more threads to Fann. He is solid behind me, as cold and as heavy as a block of ice.

"I'm sorry, Fann," I whisper miserably.

"It is enough," he answers. "For now, it is enough. But you must hurry. I don't have much time left."

None of us have much time left, I think. I urge the Sky Horse faster.

My blood calls me north, north! My father's magic sings through the air, becomes my own. I am terrified of what awaits me, but I am ready to face it all the same.

Ahead looms the Wolf Queen's mountain, a mass of dark green that resolves into a dense cover of pines as we draw closer. I can sense the magic that burns in the heart of it, wild and ancient and strong.

The Sky Horse bears us to the top of the mountain, where the trees swallow us up, and red flowers grow bright as blood despite the snow. Their perfume drenches the forest, overpoweringly sweet and tinged with the sour hint of decay. I press my hand over my nose.

Fann slides from the Sky Horse's back, collapsing in the snow. His body wavers from solid to translucent and back again, in dizzying repetition, and every shift *pulls* at my heart, jagged fractals of pain.

"I'm losing myself, Satu," he says through clenched teeth. "It isn't enough."

I crouch beside him, fear buzzing under my skin, the whole world wheeling beyond me. The wind in the trees, the sickening fragrance of the red flowers, the insistent pulse and pull of magic, the pain of Fann's shifting form—I cannot hold it all. Yet my mind drinks it in, in, every detail, until I clap my hands over my ears and bite my lip to keep from screaming.

I breathe, ragged, slow. I fight to hold myself here. I have come too far to fail now.

Slowly, my heart settles into my body. Slowly, my thoughts become clearer.

I open my eyes. Fann writhes in the snow, thin enough to see through. I pull threads from my heart and put them in him, not tied between us but given to him wholly. I do it again and again until he grows solid and stays that way, and the splintering pain in my chest dulls to an ache.

Fann looks up at me with a quiet smile and slowly stands.

There is magic yet inside of me, but only a very little. There is more in Fann than in me. I realize I cannot see the Sky Horse anymore, and grief clogs my throat.

Fann steps up to me, folds my hand in his. The cold of him slips thick and awful into my veins, and I find I am afraid. But there is no turning back, now.

Together, we stride deeper into the wood. The air is hushed and reverent, as if the trees form the arches of a great cathedral. The bones of this mountain are primordial, I think. I get the sense that this is the first place, the place where life and humanity and the old magic itself began.

I tug my hand out of Fann's, no longer able to bear the cold of him. I follow the pull of the magic my heart yearns for. Stones jut up out of the snow. More of those red flowers ramble everywhere, drenching the wood with their sickly perfume. It is the same scent, I realize, that clung faintly to Fann when I pulled him out of his nightmares. Dread folds over me like a second skin.

We come to a wall of trees that stretch up, up, their tops swallowed by the sky. They're birch and ash, bare trunks twisted together, and within them is cut a crude door. I clench the Wolf Queen's claw tight in one hand. I step through, onto molded leaves and a dusting of snow. Fann comes behind me.

The pulse of magic is stronger here, sharp and insistent, tugging at the threads of me. I know I have found it: the Wolf Queen's court, or the remnants of it. But where is she? *What* is she, now? What will it take to claim the last fragments of my father's magic?

"I told you you needed to stop doing that."

I jerk my head to the right, where the Jökull sits upon his Snow Horse, its icy mane rattling in the wind. I don't know how he's gotten here ahead of me.

"Giving up your magic," he clarifies. "Giving up *so much* of it. It'll kill you, Satu. You can feel that, can't you?"

I square my jaw and start forward, slogging through the snow. Fann, wordless, keeps pace with me.

"I'm glad you've kept the crown," the Winter Lord adds. "It suits you."

I ignore him and press on, snow clinging to my skirt. The reek of those awful flowers grows stronger, mingled now with the scent of a putrid fire. I realize it's coming from Fann.

My fear sharpens, chased by a dawning sense of horror I can't shake.

"You can still leave this place," says the Winter Lord quietly. "Take back your magic, Satu. Run while you are still mostly free from her."

I can't look at him, I can't, but his words spool through my head: *I want the North Wind. I do not mean your father.*

He dismounts and walks beside me in the snow. I still don't look at him.

"Satu."

There's a strain in his voice, a desperation that snags at my heart.

"I can't protect you from her. I can't save you. Please."

His eyes catch on mine and I harden myself at the fear I see reflected there.

"I don't need you to save me." The remaining threads of magic in me are uneasy, twisting and writhing. I am nearly sick with terror. But how can I stop?

"Don't listen to him," says Fann on the other side of me. "He's nothing but a bitter hound who failed to slip his leash."

The threads tied still between me and Fann tug, pull, tear. When they're gone, what will be left of me?

What are you, Fann? says each pulse of my heart. *What are you?*

Above the Wolf Queen's court, night comes swift and strange, though there should be many hours of daylight left. Stars shine green and cerulean and scarlet, dancing and swirling, their very essence undiluted magic, like the ones outside the Temple of the Winds. I am seized with a sudden fear that the power the Queen once wielded is still in effect, that years or centuries have passed in the world below since I set foot on this mountain.

I swallow a cry and lunge ahead, stumbling and nearly falling on the mound of roots and twisted branches that rises from the ground at the far end of the hall. The mound blooms with dozens more of those red flowers, their putrid scent so strong it makes me gag. I scrabble backward, nearly bumping into the Winter Lord.

Fann steps around me, dropping to his knees beside the mound. Fear and horror pound through me as he plucks one of the red flowers, as he pricks himself with a long, wicked thorn.

I hiss with sudden pain and find blood beading up on my own finger in the place he pierced his.

"Don't!" says the Winter Lord.

But Fann ignores him, jerking up and grabbing my hand with his frigid one. He presses my bleeding finger against the twisted roots.

The Winter Lord grasps my arm and yanks me back but it's too late: The mound is opening, roots and branches drawing back to reveal a slumbering woman on a bed of thorns and shredded red petals. She's naked, her chest rising and falling in a steady rhythm, her silver hair pooled around her like liquid shadow.

Fann's body writhes like smoke, like flame, and his eyes are burning. "Release her!" he snaps at the Winter Lord.

The Jökull obeys, dropping my arm and taking a step back from me.

I stare at Fann. "What are you?" I whisper. I am afraid of him—horribly, horribly afraid. I felt safer in the Winter Lord's grasp. There is so much of my magic in Fann, and so little of it in me. I'm a fool, and the whole world will pay for it.

Where is the rest of the North Wind's magic? I can sense it, somewhere near, but I'm not sure it is in this woman who slumbers on in the snow.

Once more, Fann kneels, bowing his head to the sleeping woman. The reek of him is overpowering, smoke and flowers and decay. "Wake," he says.

The woman opens her eyes.

TWENTY-TWO

S HE JERKS UPRIGHT, BARING HER TEETH, and as she does so her body shifts, silver fur covering her pale skin, knife-edged claws growing from her fingertips, wolfish ears showing through her silver hair. The flowers that grew on her bower bind together to make a dress for her; it flows from her furred shoulders like a bloody river.

She snatches Fann by the throat, her claws biting deep. He chokes and gasps but she does not wound him, does not make him bleed. He cannot bleed, I realize with horror—there is nothing in him but magic.

I feel her rip it out of him, the wrenching agony yanking at my own heart. I watch that magic fill her, watch color come into her cheeks and a crown of ice fold over her brow. She takes and takes and takes, every single thread I put in Fann, until there is nothing else left. He hangs limp from her hand and she flings him away from her, a desiccated body broken on the forest floor. He is shrunken and gray, only the barest scraps of skin clinging to his bones, like he's been dead a long, long while. The horror of it fills me up. I can't stop staring at the shell of the ghostly boy I thought was my friend. Tears choke me, and I am numb, numb, to anything else.

"Well," says the woman—the Wolf Queen. Her head swivels to where the Winter Lord stands, looking for all the world like a terrified boy. Drops of ice cling to his cheeks and I realize with a start he's been crying.

"The prodigal son returns." She steps past Fann's body, trodding carelessly on his outstretched hand. The crunch of bone makes me gag.

The Wolf Queen stops a pace away from the Jökull, who trembles before her. She smiles, showing jagged teeth, and rakes her claws down the side of his face, shattering his frozen tears and leaving little lines of blood in their place. He stands perfectly still and lets her hurt him, his eyes wild, a muscle jumping in his jaw.

"You thought because I was, for a little while, powerless, that you could be free of me? You were wrong—here you are again. At my mercy."

He bows his head, his pale hair whipping about him in the icy wind.

She strikes him hard across the face and he yelps and stumbles backward, blood flowing freely where her claws bit deep.

"Leave him alone," I whisper.

She turns to me with her cruel smile and burning eyes. "Ah yes, the little girl who presumed to claim a magic far too heavy for her to hold. You were so obliging to my servant, so sympathetic to his ghostly plight you neglected to realize yours. What a tender, foolish heart beats in your fragile chest."

I clench my fists, fighting to keep down the bile that burns in my throat. "Who was he?"

The Wolf Queen frowns. "Who was who?" She follows my gaze to the body on the ground. "*Him?* He was no one, some foolish boy who made a deal with me so long ago I have no recollection of what it was. He's been dead a long while, just a corpse in the ground, but he still belonged to me. I needed someone like that, someone whose name and history I didn't remember. I borrowed both, to prey upon your kindness—I am delighted that it worked so well. But who he was isn't important. He doesn't matter. His words were mine and his actions mine. He served his purpose. He drew you here, holding your magic, so freely given, ready to return it to me. It's quite fortunate you gave it to him instead of my fool of a winter demon. *He* wanted it for his own ends—to free himself from me. Can you imagine?" She laughs with the crackle and burn of a devouring flame. "But the Winter Lord has succeeded only in driving you here, and he will pay the price for his rebellion."

"Will you kill me, then?" he says quietly. Blood still drips down his cheek, pooling in the hollow of his neck.

She looks at him with cold scorn. "Death is far too easy for you, Fannaris. I will bind you to me tighter than before. You will never be free from me."

His brow creases at the sound of his name, his *name*, and around me the world seems to still with every beat of my heart and *I can't breathe.*

"Come to me, little lord."

He obeys, as if yanked on a string. He's breathing hard, the wild fear in him making my heart wrench.

"I still don't understand," I say, desperate to stop her doing whatever it is she means to do—to him, to me. "I thought my uncles destroyed you. Took away all your magic, undid all your spells and made you into—"

"A beast?" she finishes. "So they did. But I had a failsafe they did not know about. One of my enchantments was not undone, one piece of my magic was not taken."

My eyes fix on the Winter Lord. "The piece that was in you," I say quietly.

Wind whips through his long hair and ice slides through my veins. He bows his head, unable to look at me.

"The piece that was in him," the Wolf Queen agrees. "It took him a while to combat the warmth that settled over my domain, to find me in the cursed form your uncles forced upon me and undo their magic with the magic I gave him. But even then, the greater part of my power was gone, lost and loose, scattered along with your father's. I needed it back. I needed *more*, and I had to preserve what little was left to me."

She paces as she talks, blood-red flowers springing up beneath her bare feet, their stench making me want to gag and gag and gag.

"But then my little lord ran away. And so I tore a more willing servant from the ground, put a piece of myself inside of him, and sent him to find the North Wind. Then I fell asleep, to dream in peace, until the North Wind was brought to me. I did not expect his child to be atoning for his sins, and yet here you are. Almost completely powerless."

My eyes flick to the Winter Lord, and every line of him is hard and still, like he is carved from a solid block of ice. He does not lift his head. Does not look at me.

"What hold do you have over him?" I ask the Wolf Queen.

She grins into the wheeling sky. "He owes everything he is to me—his life, his breath, his very being. He made a bargain with me, as all do, in the end. I am afraid, however, that I cannot offer you one. When I take the last threads of power inside of you, there won't be anything left of you to bargain with."

"You can't have my magic." I lift my trembling chin, the power inside of me wary, afraid. Panic nibbles at the edge of my vision and I fight to keep it at bay. "I gave those threads to *Fann*, not to you, and I'll have them back, now. I need them, to fix the world."

"Fix the *world?*" says the Wolf Queen. "There is nothing left of your world to fix."

She points above us and I look up to see the green and scarlet and cerulean stars eaten by Unraveling darkness.

"When I have seized the rest of your power, I will let this world *burn*. I will find another—it is not hard, if you have enough magic, if you know where to look."

There are shards of glass in my throat. The world spins around me and I can't breathe. I stumble where I stand. I can't do this. Why did I ever think I could do this? Hysteria scratches at my mind and I let it in.

The Wolf Queen laughs and my head pounds and panic buzzes up and down my skin and there is nothing, *nothing* else.

"Satu."

A hand on my shoulder. Cold hair on my cheek.

The Winter Lord looks into my eyes and gingerly pulls me to my feet again. "I'm sorry," he says. Miserably. Helplessly.

"Has my little snow wolf lost his heart?" crows the Queen. "Bring her here to me, boy. It is time to end this. Don't worry— you're coming with me to the new world. My right hand. My faithful hound."

The Winter Lord's jaw pulls tight. His eyes bore into mine. He doesn't move.

"Fannaris!" the Queen snaps. *"Come to me. Bring her. Now."*

His hand locks around my arm. He hauls me toward her. Tears drip from his eyes and freeze on his cheeks. He never stops looking at me, his free hand grazing across the wound in his neck, his gaze begging me to understand.

I give him a brief, terrified nod.

My heart pounds as we draw near the Queen, as she closes the remaining distance between us.

Now, I don't dare look at the Winter Lord. A spot of snow touches my cheek, and in the space of a heartbeat, I rip the claw Mokosh gave me from the thread around my throat and shove it into the Jökull's hand. He lunges at the Wolf Queen, driving the claw into her neck as they crash together into the snow.

TWENTY-THREE

THE WOLF QUEEN SHRIEKS AS BLOOD bubbles up, as the red flowers all around her hiss and shrivel, as the trees seem to draw back, unable to protect their cold mistress. She screams and screams, more than such a small wound seems to merit.

And then she is still, her body leaking crimson in the winter wood, and all the magic she tore from Fann comes rushing like a tide into me. I stagger backward under the force of it, gasping in pain as it twists into my heart, filling me up, overflowing. Wind whips wild through the forest. *My* wind. I gulp air, undone.

The Winter Lord drops the claw he used to kill her, turning to me with an awful blankness in his eyes.

I look at him, stricken, two bodies on the ground and only him and me left against the Unraveling world. My winds *rage*.

There is blood on the Winter Lord's hand and it is too red against the whiteness of him. He holds that hand out to me.

"Come, Satu." The Snow Horse materializes beside him, blowing and stamping in my harsh wind.

There is no fear left in me anymore, only sorrow and an overwhelming sense of helplessness incongruent with the power that seethes inside of me.

I take his hand. I climb onto the Snow Horse and he comes behind me, his chest hard against my shoulders. I feel again the impossible heat of him.

He speaks a word to the horse and it springs away, bursting through the wall of trees and out onto the mountain. We hurtle into the world below, ice and wind tangling in my hair.

Sky and earth blur together, wind and snow slicing past my ears. Beneath me, the Snow Horse pulses with cold, with magic. But from the Jökull, there is only heat.

Fannaris, the Wolf Queen called him, and he'd looked as if his heart had been torn out and trod upon. *Fannaris. Fann.*

The Wolf Queen had stolen his name and his history. She'd given it to a body she tore out of the ground, to prey upon my tender heart. The painter who ran away from the army wasn't my ghostly friend. It never had been. Who he was, who he used to be, before the Wolf Queen desecrated the shell of him, I will never know. Grief weighs impossibly heavy. Because whatever else he was, no matter how much of herself she'd put in him, he was my friend. No one should end like that, their body used against their will. I can't help him now. I never could.

My translucent boy is forever gone.

There is only the Winter Lord, warm at my back.

We race across a snowy plain, ice splintering out before us with every hoofbeat. My mind is a whirl of confusion and horror and grief, driven by a deep panic that wherever we're going, we might already be too late.

The Wolf Queen is dead.

The Winter Lord killed her.

I helped him do it.

There is blood on my hand where he touched me. There is blood on my soul.

I try to understand what happened, try to work out if the man whose heart is thudding against my shoulder is an enemy or an ally or both. He saved my life. He kept the Wolf Queen from taking my magic, from killing me. *He killed her for me.*

Who is he, now his mistress is gone? Who was he before?

"Why did it kill her?" I whisper into the snow, the wind.

"Her own magic, turned against her," comes his voice, warm at my ear. "That isn't meant to happen, so it only took a scratch."

I think of a kiss in a moment of frozen time, of the claw in my hand and blood trickling from his neck. "If her magic is inside of you, why didn't it kill *you?*"

To this, he makes no reply, and burgeoning dread gnaws at me.

"We must go faster," he says instead. "Time is almost gone."

I glance behind us; the sky is Unraveling, the ground Unraveling, a dark yawning void nipping at the Snow Horse's heels. I send wind into its heart, its lungs, its bones, to lend it magic, to lend it *speed*. We hurtle fast as falling stars; we hurtle fast as life and death and time itself. And yet I do not think it is fast enough.

We come to a choppy, dark sea, black waves crashing over ice floes and chipping away at glaciers that rise like giants from the deep. The Snow Horse doesn't pause. It dashes over the water, icy hooves skimming the waves. I realize it is my wind that carries us, allowing us not to sink into those dark depths. I am humbled that the wind answers me, that it *knows* me, even though I am not quite wholly what my father was.

There is still one piece of magic left, one piece I've yet to claim. I realize, now, where it is.

It beats against my shoulder blade, fiery and wild, and the dread drags me down, down as I begin to understand what I have no wish to understand. What I cannot bear to.

The Snow Horse runs and runs, winding through the glaciers, leaping across the ice floes. We have come to a place that is neither land nor sky, that seems to be nowhere at all. The glaciers pulse with terrible cold, a brittle, unstoppable magic. Where is the Winter Lord taking me?

Behind us, the Unraveling fractures the world; I don't know how there are any threads left at all, to sustain us.

Then the Winter Lord guides the Snow Horse up onto a glacier so vast it seems to swallow the sky. He slides from the horse's back, his heels grinding into the ice. He holds his hand out to me. "Come, North."

Wind and snow tangle together in my hair as I hesitate, as I fight against the awful, whirling *pull* of this place.

It's the earnestness in his eyes, the desperation, that softens me. I take his hand, let his fingers tangle in mine as he helps me down. The cuts from the Wolf Queen's claws still score his face, long red lines I know must cause him pain.

The Snow Horse bows its head to the Winter Lord, and the Winter Lord bows back. "Thank you for your service, my dear friend."

The horse dissolves into snowflakes that blow away on the wind, and the Winter Lord's jaw tenses. I am struck again by his sadness. I wonder how I didn't realize before that it is steeped in every part of him.

He strides up the glacier and I come with him, calling my winds to hold tight to both of us, to not let us slip and fall. Around us, waves break over the glacier, the sea raging because we are, for now, out of its grasp.

It is only when we have climbed partway up the jagged mountain of ice that I see it: the bones of a ship, broken and frozen into the glacier. It's gray with age, hung with ice. Half of the hull is visible, a fractured mast hanging at a wrong angle. The remainder of the ship is lost somewhere in the deep.

The Winter Lord's hand tightens on mine.

I look askance at him. My heart jerks at the sheen of moisture in his eyes.

I am not brave enough to call him by his name. To ask him how it was taken from him or if he will take it back. *Fannaris.*

We have come to a flat stretch of the glacier, its jagged peak looming above us, the bulk of it rooted under the sea.

"Why have you brought me here?" I ask softly.

The Winter Lord lets go of my hand, and I hate that I want to snatch it up again, longing for his warmth in this blue frozen place.

"To show you the missing piece," he says. "To make you what you were always meant to be." His voice is rough. Broken. "Dig, North. You must dig."

I swallow hard. "With what?"

He says a cold word and stretches out his hand. Ice dances on his palm, drawing together to form a knife-edged spade.

I take it from him and kneel on the glacier. I look back.

He stands tall and grim, my wind whipping his pale hair in his face. He looks tired, worn out, impossibly young and impossibly sad. The knowing strengthens inside of me, makes me sick.

Above us, the Unraveling world roils and screams, reaching down, down, to sweep us up in its eternal nothingness.

"I am sorry I cannot help you," says the Winter Lord. "I am scarcely able to *be* in this place at all. But I will at least hold back the Unraveling for as long as I can. I think—I think it will be long enough."

He raises his hands to the sky, snow swirling from his fingertips. For a moment, it arches over his head, but whatever it is he is attempting to do fails; the snow falls back to earth again. Fear shows stark on his face, and he tries again. Snow and ice twist from his hands, but again it falls, his magic not obeying him, perhaps, here at the end of the Unraveling world.

Out of nowhere, a great wind rushes over the glacier, a current of magic that does not belong to me. Understanding flickers in the Winter Lord's eyes, a realization that escapes me. Once more he sends snow and ice from his fingers, and it weaves together to form a dome over the glacier, a shield to keep the Unraveling at bay.

Dread seizes me. I grip the ice spade. I begin to dig.

My winds assist me, blowing fragments of ice and snow out of the hole I chip with agonizing slowness. It is staggeringly hard work. Sweat slides down my back. My hand cramps.

Magic pulses strong under the ice, calling out to me. I do not want to find it but I must, I must.

I glance back only once to where the Winter Lord stands, maintaining the protective magic with his eyes shut, his hands outstretched, his lips moving soundlessly. There is pain in his face—his magic is not without cost, and I can't bear it to be in vain.

So I turn back to my work. I dig, dig, dig. When the spade shatters, I don't ask the Winter Lord to make another one. I claw at the ice with my hands, seized by an awful desperation, a horrible certainty.

I blink back tears and dig harder, faster, until my hands are bloody and raw, until I feel all of me has been stripped bare. There is only the ice and the wind and the Winter Lord's strange and steadying power. There is only this moment, and there will only ever be this moment. I cannot bear it.

Then I see the dark shape under the ice. Horror tangles up in my bones.

No.

I keep digging, scratching at the ice, clawing it up as fast as I can. My winds rush over the glacier, helping me.

I don't want to uncover that shape.

Yet I must, I must.

I dig in a haze of tears, the blood from my hands staining the snow. All at once I pierce through an icy dome and it shatters, fragments of ice sharp and sparkling as diamonds.

I'm sobbing as I brush them away, as my winds bear them up and fling them into the sea, as the shape buried in the ice is revealed to me.

I do not want to look. I do not want to *see*, to *know.*

My winds dry my tears. The Unraveling world pulses above me, in sorrow, in wrongness, in rage.

I take a breath, and let my eyes see the thing I do not want to see, the thing I already know.

The Winter Lord lies frozen in the glacier, utterly still, as if in death.

And there is a shard of the North Wind's glittering turquoise ice piercing his heart.

TWENTY-FOUR

I DON'T UNDERSTAND HOW THE WINTER LORD can be here, frozen and still in the ice, and yet there, warm and alive and holding back the Unraveling world. And yet he is.

I stare at the motionless body, pale hair and paler skin, the angular face I first glimpsed in childhood. His clothes are ragged and loose-fitting. His eyelashes are rimmed with ice. I glance at the man who brought me here, teeming with magic, his hands still stained with blood. Beyond these few differences, they are one and the same. Perfect copies of each other. I am gutted, wholly lost. Because how can this be?

"The last piece," says the Winter Lord, his voice husky. He's deathly, deathly pale. "Take it."

He means the ice shard in the body's heart—in *his* heart.

I tug his frozen self out of the glacier. I cradle his heavy head in my lap and trace the line of his cold brow, my fingers lingering at the hollow of his throat. There's the barest whisper of a pulse, a few threads of life yet in him.

"He's alive," I say softly.

"Only just," says the Winter Lord. "For a few moments more. The Wolf Queen's spell and your father's magic, sustaining him." He swallows. "Sustaining me."

My eyes fix on that piece of glittering ice.

"Take it, Satu," he says. "Please. Take the last piece freely. It's why I brought you here: the only chance for you, for the world."

My own pulse beats ragged and I can't stop staring at the ice shard, at his body, trapped in this glacier for centuries, frozen in some living death. I shake. "If I take it, it will kill you."

"I'm already dead, Satu." His voice is gentler than before, almost tender. "Or as good as."

I can't quite look at him, absorbed in the frozen horror of his motionless self, a block of ice weighing heavy on my knees, a fragile heart barely beating within.

The Winter Lord crouches down beside me, tucks a stray strand of my hair behind my ear. I turn my eyes to his.

His are wet, bright.

Above us stretches the translucent dome of the Winter Lord's magic, keeping the Unraveling at bay. The dome shimmers and shifts; it won't last forever.

"I don't understand," I whisper. It hurts. Everything *hurts*. I blink at him. I try to see through his enchantment but there is only him, pale, solid. "You're Fannaris," I say. "That's your name, isn't it?"

He sits back on his heels, boots grinding into the ice, and looks at the frozen form on my lap with a helpless sorrow. He hugs his knees to his chest like an overgrown boy. "His deepest wish was to be a painter," says the Winter Lord quietly, still staring at his own motionless body.

I bite my cheek hard enough to taste blood, but it doesn't keep the tears from coming.

The Winter Lord goes on. "His father, the duke, had other plans for him. So he was sent to the army. The Tsar had need of soldiers to fight in his great wars, and it was a noble profession. Far nobler than that of a painter."

I shake, choking on grief and a hurtling helplessness.

"But Fannaris Wintar couldn't bear a soldier's life for more than a few weeks—his every movement dictated to him, from sunup to sundown, no time to catch his breath, let alone indulge himself with the painting supplies he smuggled into the training camp. So he ran away to the city, his determination as fierce as his hope. None of the painters would take him as an apprentice, deserter as he was, and he narrowly escaped arrest, which would have meant prison, and a death sentence.

"He fled the city and snuck aboard a ship, hoping to win renown at sea and earn himself a pardon. But he was sailing for only three weeks when a storm blew the ship off course, farther north than any ship has ever gone. Into the Wolf Queen's domain."

Tears course down my cheeks and I want to scream and scream. But I am quiet. Because if he can bear to tell this story, I can bear to hear it.

"The ship ran aground on the ice. The sailors froze as the waves swallowed them up. But Fannaris clung to the mast, held aloft out of the icy water. He wept and he begged and he screamed for a miracle, crying out for someone to save him." The Winter Lord's eyes bore into mine and they are filled, now, with a dark and drowning anger. "But the salvation he wanted did not come, and he was left to the mercy of the Wolf Queen. She needed a guard. Someone to watch the borders of her land and keep a close eye on her enemies. Someone to wield a piece of the North Wind's magic.

"'Will you be that for me?' she asked him. 'Will you make that bargain?'

"And Fannaris clung to the broken mast as he felt his life slipping out of him. No one else was coming. No one else was going to save him, and he did not want to die. 'I will do anything,' he told her, 'if you save me.'

"Then she smiled, and he would never forget that smile. He regretted his words, realizing in that moment that it would be *better* to die than to live, and serve her. But it was too late.

"'The bargain is struck,' she said. 'You serve me, now.'"

I am weeping uncontrollably.

The Winter Lord touches my chin with one warm finger and

tilts my face up. I look at him through salt-blurred eyes.

His anger has faded to something richer, stranger. Sorrow and resignation and a hopeless tenderness that wrecks me utterly.

"She drove a shard of the North Wind's magic into my heart," he says softly. "She made me her Winter Lord, trapping my body here, in the ice, to dream forever of dark and frozen things, while she made for me another form—a form that could bear the cold and wield the magic. A form that could travel in the winds and the storms and the snow. *This* form."

He drops his hand from my face, the heat from his fingertips lingering. Everything I am is screaming, yet my body only shakes, tears choking me.

"I served her for centuries, Satu, making her snow and her ice and her storms where she would. Guarding her lands with her voice and her power. Bringing her servants and playthings, wreaking her havoc where she willed. I forgot who I had been. Because it didn't matter anymore. How could it? I wasn't myself. I was only *hers*."

His jaw is tight and hard, but his eyes suddenly grow clear. "Yet there was beauty in the storms, in the snow. There were a thousand shifting colors in the ice that, sometimes, I longed to paint. And the magic"—snow swirls in his palm and he blows it gently away—"the magic was intoxicating. I had power, more power than I ever could have imagined. I had no fear of men anymore—neither my father nor the Tsar. Both of them grew old and died, and I lived on. I would always live on."

My heart breaks, over and over again. "Weren't you lonely?"

The sea lashes angrily at the glacier; above the Winter Lord's magic dome, the Unraveling rages.

"I am always lonely." His shoulders slump, and his eyes fix on his frozen body. "When Echo defeated her—when your uncles took her power away, I thought I would be free. I thought I could leave her; I thought I would belong once more only to myself.

"But I was wrong. Because it was not her magic that bound me to her—it was the North Wind's." His glance flicks to mine, and it's filled with sadness, with shame.

"Only the North Wind's magic could free you," I say.

He nods.

"So you broke the enchantment that bound the Wolf Queen into the form of an animal—acting as her failsafe, as she intended. And when she sent you from the mountain to find the North Wind—"

"I went," he says heavily, "but not for her. For myself. I was never going to return to her side."

"You went looking for my father. You found me instead."

His eyes meet mine. "I always knew where you were, Satu. *Who* you were. Don't you remember?"

I do remember. Of course I do. "You made me the snow pictures when I was a child. You caught me when I fell from the mountain. But why did you make them? Why were you there?"

"I was often there, in the old days, until the Queen's magic was broken. She sent me to make sure your father did not mean to reclaim his magic. I was there the night you were born and many, many days after. I watched you and your father on your long journey north. I was on the path the night you took a step into the Wolf Queen's domain." His throat works. "I was under her command, then. I would have brought you to her, and she would have destroyed you, if your father hadn't—hadn't, for an instant, broken me out of her control."

"You let me go," I say quietly. "My father couldn't have over-powered you—he hadn't any magic."

He nods and takes a breath, his ice-encrusted hair clattering in the wind. "And I made the snow pictures because—because you looked lonely. And I thought you would like them."

I don't know how to reply to that. I stare down at the Winter Lord's body, heavy and cold, the threads of his life fast fraying. I shake and shake. I think I will rattle all to pieces.

"Even the nightmares she stole from me," says the Winter Lord.

"Your nightmares?"

"When I sleep, I dream of this," he says. "Being trapped in the dark and the cold, never dying, never breaking free, pinned inside this frozen rock for all of time. Hearing her voice, calling my name, reminding me of my bonds, laughing. Always laugh-ing. She took that from me, too. Gave it to that walking corpse to prey upon your kindness."

I shudder and gag, though part of me will always hurt for the ghostly boy whose true name I will never know.

"How I envied him," says the Winter Lord quietly, "that nothing boy who meant everything to you."

I bow my head over the body in my lap, the glittering ice shard calling to me. But I can't claim it. I can't kill him. Can't take from him the last beats of his heart. It isn't right.

"And when I saw"—he chokes, takes a breath, then steadies himself and tries again—"when I saw him in that little house in the city, there with you, there with the man who was my youngest brother, sustained impossibly in this time that is not our own, it broke me. Even though no one could see him, he was there when it should have been me."

"What did you say?" I whisper.

When he looks at me, his cheeks are wet.

"Hal is your *brother*?"

"The last son of our father the duke. He was hardly more than a baby when I was sent off to the army. I never really knew him. I was away on the Queen's business when she ensnared him, or I swear to you I would have stopped her, I would have found a way to save him. Now he's gone, Unraveled like all the rest, and this time—*this* time, I will atone for the evil bargain I made with that witch. Even though I had no other choice but to make it."

My throat hurts so much I can hardly breathe, my eyes caught and held by the last piece of my father's magic.

"I was angry with you for a long while," says the Winter Lord. "I wanted you to suffer, as I had suffered for so many years. But none of that matters now. I was wrong. I've always been wrong.

And I want nothing more than for you to become wholly who you were meant to be."

"Why were you angry?"

The Unraveling world seethes above us; the devouring sea rages below.

He does not answer, just says simply: "We are out of time."

The ice shard glitters, a frozen knife at the heart of the world. "I'm not going to kill you."

"I don't mind," he says. "Not as much as I thought I would."

"We'll find another way."

"Satu."

My name on his lips makes me tremble.

He crouches down beside me, touches my cheek with one warm hand. "There *is* no other way," he says gently. He wipes my tears away with his thumb, his heat and his magic burrowing under my skin.

"I'm sorry, Satu," he says. "I'm so very sorry. Forgive me."

There is a flash of movement, and then a blinding, searing pain as the Winter Lord rips the ice shard from his own cold heart and thrusts it into mine.

PART THREE:
North Heart

TWENTY-FIVE

WHAT AM I?

Threads of magic, wound too tight. Light and shadow.
Nauseating pain.

What am I?

Unmade, unwound, unwritten.

But

thread by thread

made again.

Magic—

pulsing from my heart and in my blood.

Knotted in every cell of me.

What *am* I?

Icy, numbing cold.

Power.

I am power.

No.

Salt on my tongue and wind in my lungs and I cannot breathe, cannot breathe.

I am:

A child in a room that bursts with stories, overwhelmed with light and heat and too many voices.

A girl sobbing on a mountaintop, a pounding head, a raging heart.

Never calm, never silent, never still.

But that is not all.

I am:

Bees and laughter and songs on summer breezes. Honey in jars and bright wool in carding baskets. My mother and father, their love and their grief.

I am all these things.

I am *more*.

Wind rushes through me and around me. Wind *is* me, and I am Wind, and we are at once everything and nothing, formless and yet throbbing with *being*.

I have always been too small to hold everything inside of me, to drink in all the maddening details of this loud and overwhelming world.

But I understand now that this is what I was always meant for.

This is what I am:

The North Wind.

A girl whose heart and mind are never quiet.

And the magic doesn't fracture me, because it is mine, mine. I choose it. I claim it. *Mine.*

The power settles inside like a cat curling up in a sunbeam. It stretches and it yawns and it falls asleep, warm and purring.

The pain in my chest, in my *being* subsides.

I open my eyes.

A garment of wind cascades from my shoulders, shifting colors of blue and purple and silver. The North Wind's crown rests heavy on my brow. I lift my hand to my sight line—there is a hint of silver in my light brown skin, magic flowing through my veins.

This, this is what I am.

And then I suck in a sharp breath, stunned.

For a moment, I'd forgotten.

I am changed.

But the world is not.

There is only the glacier and the frozen bones of a long-dead ship. The angry sea, the Unraveling sky.

The Winter Lord's body, cold at my feet, no ice shard in his heart now, the threads of his life spinning out, out.

And the Winter Lord himself, standing before me, staring, his eyes wide with awe, tears frozen on his cheeks.

But no, the Winter Lord is not his name.

Fannaris.

The man who killed the Wolf Queen to save me.

The man who gave his life for mine.

"Satu," he says. "You're *shining*."

And then he fragments, turning to crystals of ice, of snow, the pieces of him blowing away into the wind. I leap after him, his name on my lips, barely keeping myself from tumbling over the edge of the glacier.

The Winter Lord as I knew him is no more.

I turn back to the body I dug out of the snow but he isn't there, nothing left except the impression he made in the glacier. The last beats of his heart ran out, his form melting away, perhaps, at the exact moment his other self's did.

I collapse to my knees, sobbing in the snow, because I am the North Wind, and he's gone, and I am utterly alone against the Unraveling world.

I cannot help the Winter Lord—*Fannaris*—cannot save him, cannot call him back. Not here, not now. His death was written long before this moment.

I climb to my feet, glancing up at the Unraveling sky. Fannaris's magical dome is still there, protecting me, but it's beginning to crack, pieces of it falling around me like hail.

I can almost see him in the place he stood, his impression lingering like an afterimage behind my eyes.

This isn't right. It isn't *right*, and I refuse to let it be the end.

I am the North Wind.

I can change it.

I climb to the very peak of the glacier—or perhaps I fly. I'm not certain. I *move*, but it is different from how I moved before.

I stretch out my arms, feel the magic pulsing through my veins, the power that has rewritten every part of me. I peer into the wind currents, searching for the threads that belong to me now that I am the North Wind.

I find them.

They are vast beyond my comprehension, even in my new form. They twist through all the other threads, holding them together, impossible to separate from life and magic and *being*. Because that is what they are: the oldest of all the old magics, save, perhaps, for love itself.

I allow myself a final look back, to where Fannaris, in both of his forms, died in the snow.

Horror and pity twist through me. Fury hardens me. Fannaris was bound against his will—forced to serve the queen while his body was frozen in a glacier, trapped in his nightmares for centuries. He gave me the very last thread of his life. But I can't let him end that way: broken and hurting, drowning in sorrow. I *won't*. I am pity and duty and anger. I want to heal his pain. To repay him for his great sacrifice.

I am not immune to the fury of the Unraveling world, chipping away at Fannaris's protective dome. But I am the North Wind. The world will wait for me to save this one soul, to right this one wrong. I will turn my attention to the world when I am ready.

Tears freeze on my cheeks and I brush them away.

I step from the glacier and seize the Threads of Time in both my hands. I pull on them.

And they pull back.

TWENTY-SIX

THE THREADS OF TIME ARE A sea, a symphony, a sky full of stars. They are the hexagonal cells of an infinite honeycomb, the glittering sands of an eternal desert. They are beautiful and terrifying and more powerful than I ever could have imagined.

And they are mine.

Yet even so they overwhelm me with light and noise, engulf me in a thousand emotions I cannot name and cannot carry. They make my head roar and my heart rage, my part-human body shake. They whisper to me *let go, let go*. They want to pull me all to threads, to keep the loose pieces of me scattered forever in their endless waters.

But I don't let them. Because I will not accept what happened on the glacier. I have the power to change Fannaris's fate, and even if the Threads of Time rip me apart, I'm going to try.

I am the North Wind, I tell them. *You belong to me.*

Then command us, they say.

So I do. I tell the Threads of Time to take a form I can comprehend and can navigate. They become an ocean, unfolding out and out beyond the unreachable horizon. I ask my winds to build me a ship and they do, glittering strands of air weaving together to create a vessel as beautiful and impossible as the Sky Horse. I step into the wind ship and it holds me, for I am no longer merely flesh and bone. I am something less, and I am something more.

I bid the ship slide into the Time Thread Sea, bid invisible sails to swell and all the winds under my command to propel me forward.

And then I am adrift in Time.

I pass shining islands and vast, sinuous beasts that rise and fall beneath the waves, some with teeth and some with wings, some that are made of glass and some of smoke. There are walls of flame and moondust stairs. There are whirls of light in a sky that seems to be made of ribbons, all fluttering loose. There are doorways upon doorways, scattered in the sea, and I know where they lead: to every moment of time in every world that was ever spun out on the Great Weaver's loom. I could go anywhere at all, could lose myself in another time, another world, like the Wolf Queen meant to. I don't have to try and fix mine if I don't want to.

But I know my destination and my course. I will not stray

from it. I am made of wind and stars as well as flesh—the sirens of Time will not tempt me.

Fannaris, I command. *Take me to Fannaris.*

The Threads bear me fast and far to a different part of the sea, where the water is dark and swirled with silver. The air is colder here and seems to pulse with sorrow. A doorway looms, a great archway made of twisted blue ice. I am terrified. I am resolved. I command my wind ship to slip through.

The Threads move slower, here. Images are tangled in the weave of Time's tapestry—no, not images. Moments. Lives. Memories.

I am not to Fannaris's life, not yet. But I peer at the moments caught in the Threads, and the immensity of them overwhelms me.

I see babies born and mothers cry, soldiers take their last gasping breaths. I see a composer pen her greatest symphony and a boy with huge eyes ride his father's enormous warhorse. There are earth-shattering memories and quieter ones, with everything else in between. But each one is important, fragments of stories spinning out on the Great Weaver's loom. In all these moments I feel what the people in them feel: sorrow and joy, rage and guilt, hopelessness and relief. I feel and feel and feel, until I am all wrung out with emotion. Yet there is always, always more. I weep. I am not sure I will ever stop.

The moments come faster, some ancient, some new. Some I get the sense have not yet happened, at least from my limited perspective. I glimpse roaring machines on land and in the air, and strange iron ships billowing black smoke. There are impossible masses of people clustered together in metal cities so tall they scrape at the sky.

It is a relief, after all that, to see a boy sitting on a mountaintop singing to his goats, a strange girl with skin like tree bark in a dense, loamy forest, flowers growing out of her hair. A pale-haired boy standing on the balcony of a great house, painting the landscape that stretches out before him with deft strokes of his brush.

Fannaris! screams my mind. I command the winds: *There.*

My ship jerks sideways and slices through the moment, dissolving it.

I am disappointed to not find myself inside the memory, as I assumed I would be, but in a dark, narrow corridor, Time Threads twisting through the place where there ought to be a floor. A seemingly infinite number of doors line the corridor on either side.

I wipe the tears from my face and call my winds around me like a mantle. I'm trembling, terrified I'm not brave enough or powerful enough to be here. To do this.

But I think of Fannaris's sacrifice on the glacier and my resolve hardens. I'm going to save him. I'm going to undo the great wrong that was done to him.

I open the first door and step through.

I am in a hot room, a fire burning red on a stone hearth, a

woman in a high bed screaming. There are other women with her. There is blood in the bed and sweat on her brow and I realize with a wrench of my heart that this is the day Fannaris was born.

This is the business of bringing life into the world and it is not easy and it is not still. I weep for his mother's pain and I weep for my own mother's, because I did not know, I did not understand. It is horrible, but it is also miraculous, and when Fannaris comes wailing into the world and the midwives lay him in his mother's arms, for a moment I can't even breathe. His mother cries as she kisses him, pressing him tight against her breast. I feel her wonder and her joy, her exhaustion and her sorrow, her new perception of the world that has rewritten itself with her body, and with his.

I take a step toward the bed without meaning to, drawn to the threads of them, alive with the oldest of all magics.

His mother raises her face, squints in my direction.

"What is it, my lady?" asks one of the midwives.

For another heartbeat she studies me, curious but not alarmed. Then she bends her face to Fannaris and kisses his pale head. "Nothing," she says. "Just a breath of wind at the door."

I retreat into the corridor, my face still damp with tears, my whole body shaking with the enormity of the cost of *life*. Its sacrifice and love. Its magic.

I pace down the hall, tremulous, uncertain. It is here, now, that I feel the immensity of the North Wind's power. The ability to step inside someone's life. To alter it, when and if I choose. It sobers me. But it does not deter me from my path.

I cannot save Fannaris as a baby, as a child. It would change his life too dramatically, take all autonomy away from him. There is no reason for me to step into these early doors, to watch his childhood spin out before my eyes.

Yet I do step into them, because I find I have a hunger to know him, to *see* him, to understand where he came from and what burns most fiercely in his heart.

So I watch him take his first wobbling steps with his mother looking on in the garden. He trips and skins his knee, and I feel the hot pulsing pain of it. I see his first hesitant ride on his father's warhorse, snug and safe against his father's chest. I watch him follow his older brother around with adoration in his eyes and hold his younger siblings, tenderly, after they're born.

When he is six or so, shortly after the birth of one of his sisters, his mother, in a fog of exhaustion, yells at him for being too loud and waking the baby. He darts out of the great house with a sense of having suffered a horrible injustice, angry tears flowing down his cheeks.

I follow him, a Wind in the grass, my heart tugging for his hurt, though I am sure he will soon realize his mother was simply tired and overwhelmed, and meant nothing ill toward him.

But he keeps on running, his short legs carrying him farther than I thought, toward the wood.

Another story flashes through me, of a spoiled boy and a conniving enchantress. The Wolf Queen dwells in that wood, and she will harm Fannaris if he enters it. I know that she does not, that she *can*not, because he doesn't meet her here, now, but years and miles away. Yet fear still tugs sharp, sharp, and horror claims me as young Fannaris slips within the shadow of the wood, letting the trees swallow him up.

I forget myself and send a gust of wind through the forest ahead of him, blocking his way.

He stops but does not retreat, so I wrap him tight with winds and tug him back out onto the grass.

For a moment, he stares at me, and I realize I have inadvertently taken human shape.

I send myself away quick as a heartbeat, back into the corridor of his life. I sit for a while among the doors, pulse raging, angry with myself for interfering when I did not mean to.

Yet I do not regret pulling him from the wood.

I try to count the doors as I pass them, try and gauge how far I've come into Fannaris's life, but there are far too many doors, and it is impossible to tell. The only way is to open them, and look.

So I do.

I open door after door, careful, after the wood, to keep out of sight. I see Fannaris's mother give him his first set of paints for his tenth birthday and watch his first poor attempt at using them. I am flooded with his frustration and his wonder, his determination and stubbornness.

I watch as he learns and grows, impatient with lessons in his father's study, uninterested in the politics of governing a duchy, eternally relieved that that responsibility will fall to his oldest brother and not to him.

He is impatient with most things: riding and fencing lessons, history and mathematics and music. It is only when he picks up his paintbrush that he trains his body to be calm, his mind to be focused. With each door I step through, each successive moment in Fannaris's life, his skill grows and grows, until it seems he works magic with his paints, beautiful scenes unfolding from his hands like the Great Weaver making the world. His paintings seep inside of me, making me ache.

His favorite place to paint is on the balcony that overlooks the wide meadow, with the dark wood beyond. I take to sitting on the roof of his father's great house, watching him, mesmerized by the *swish* of his brush and the masterpieces taking shape on his canvas.

I am careful to be quiet and still, determined to not let him see me again. I haven't forgotten my father's story: The dog he tried to save for my mother died anyway, and his meddling caused her to lose her brother, too. I know I will only have one true chance to save Fannaris, that it is not here, not now.

But I also can't resist staying longer than I should, opening more doors than I need to. Sometimes, my foot slips on the roof tile, and he turns his head and catches sight of my gown made of winds. He must think nothing of it, though, for the next moment he always looks back to his canvas again. He must have forgotten his glimpse of me as a child.

Fannaris is seventeen when I find him one late afternoon, once more out on his balcony with his easel and paints. He looks scarcely younger than the body frozen in the glacier, than the cold Winter Lord I knew. His eyes are red from crying, and there is an angry mark from a hand on his face. I skipped the last few doors, so I didn't see what happened, but I can guess—his father has reprimanded him for shirking his lessons and has threatened to take away his paints. It's happened often enough, the last few years. I've felt his full range of anger and hurt, his frustration and disappointment, the feeling that what he is, for his father, will never be enough.

But this time, he doesn't pick up his brush. He climbs up onto the stone railing so his toes hang precariously out over empty air. He sucks in his breaths in little whistling gasps as he contemplates the drop. Beyond him, the sun is setting, sending long tendrils of light slanting across the meadow, gilding him in golden fire.

He grips the railing with both hands. He begins to scoot himself forward, then loses courage and stops. He shakes.

My heart wrenches, watching him, but I tell myself I don't need to interfere—I know very well he lives past this moment. He dies far from here, in an icy grave beneath an Unraveling sky. Grief catches in my throat.

He weeps into the glistening light of the setting sun. Without a word or a sound or even a breath, Fannaris flings himself from the railing.

A cry rips from my throat as he hurtles to the ground, and without a conscious thought I am there beside him, folding him in swathes of wind, catching him and bearing him upward again, as Fannaris himself, the Winter Lord, once did for me.

I deposit him safely onto the balcony, well away from the rail, and he sits with his hands pressed against the stone, staring at me in the fading light.

"What are you?" he whispers.

"Just a dream. Forget you ever saw me, Fannaris Wintar."

I turn to go but he snatches my wrist. Holds me back. His fingers are warm, pulsing with life.

I look at him, winds swirling round my shoulders, crown heavy on my brow.

"How could I ever forget you?" he whispers.

I should change myself all to wind and flee back into the corridor but I don't. I stay, gripped by his sorrow more than his hand. His emotions pulse inside of me, and it is hard to parse them from my own.

"Why did you jump?" I ask him. "Do you think your life worth so little?"

He bows his head. "My father means to send me to the army. I am to be a soldier for the Tsar and fight in his wars. The only paint I will see is blood." His voice is thick with tears, but he doesn't let them fall.

I crouch down beside him and wrap my arms around his shoulders. He's so solid, so *alive*, burning with grief and rage and helplessness. I have to fight to stay here with him, steady, in control. I have to fight to not let his emotions overwhelm my own. "Don't despair of your life, Fann. There may yet be good things waiting for you."

"Like *what?*" he says bitterly. "All I want is to be apprenticed to a painter, to become a true painter in my own right. I don't give a damn about the Tsar or his wars. I want to *create*. To capture the world on my canvases—the world as I see it."

I think of the Winter Lord and his ice storms, snow dancing in his palms. "You will."

"My father says it's no profession fit for *his* son. But what does he care? He has so many. Why doesn't he send one of my brothers off to war and leave me alone?"

I think of Hal, tricked by the Wolf Queen as Fannaris was tricked, bound to the form of a wolf and ripped away from his family forever. "Do you think your other brothers are more suited to war than you?"

His eyes flick my way and he shrugs a little petulantly. "They've never expressed a wish for anything else that I know of. Except my youngest brother, of course. He can't even talk yet."

My heart twinges, but I am not here to save Hal. He has already been saved, in a future far away, in a world that has not yet been Unraveled. "Have you asked them?"

"I certainly didn't ask *you!*" he snaps. He pushes himself to his feet and stalks to the balcony again, though he makes no move to climb over it a second time. "Who are you? How did you catch me? How do you know my name? It was you, wasn't it. In the woods when I was a boy?"

I step up beside him. "I'm just a friend."

He glares at me—I have not remotely answered his questions.

I have lingered far too long and interfered far too much already, but I can't quite bear to leave him in this state. I touch his arm and he doesn't shake me off. "Please take better care," I say softly. "The world needs you yet."

"Does it?" he scoffs. Then he chews on his lip and looks at his canvas, a half-finished landscape. "Might I paint you, Madame Wind?"

I gape at him. "What?"

He gestures at my living gown, billowing around me, at the cold crown on my head. "The old stories are filled with tales of the Winds, though I have never before heard of one who was a woman. Which Wind are you?"

"That doesn't matter," I say frantically. It will not do to suddenly alter the folklore of his time. "Just promise me you will not try to take your own life again."

He makes no promise, just says, "Can I paint you?"

I tell him no, but I don't leave this moment of his life. He picks up his brush. I don't stop him.

Fannaris paints feverishly, even when there is no light left to see by, the stars casting only the barest hint of silver over his canvas. When at last he stops, the moon is rising, peeking her full face above the rim of the world. Fannaris beckons me over, and I look at his work.

I hardly recognize the figure he has painted there: luminous and grand, clothed in wind and crowned with power. It stuns me and shakes me: I am practically a goddess to him.

A memory slices through me, Hal's words the night he and Echo were Unraveled: *You remind me of a painting I saw once, so long ago I'd forgotten it until now. It hung in my father's house. One of my siblings painted it, I think.*

The world presses in around me, panic pounding in my blood. This painting. *Hal saw this painting.*

I have already rewritten Time. Or Time has rewritten me. But if *Hal* saw this painting, that means that Fannaris did not first meet me as the Winter Lord. He first met me here, now. And though this moment has only just happened, for me, it was in Fannaris's past. He must have remembered. With every encounter, he must have remembered this one: me, in my full strength as the North Wind, catching him when he leapt from the balcony of his father's house.

TWENTY-SEVEN

FANNARIS STANDS STONILY IN THE COURTYARD of his father's house. There's a carriage waiting to take him to the army training camp, and his mother and siblings have come to see him off. The mark on his face has darkened to a deep purple bruise. His father isn't here—Fannaris will never see him again.

I tremble as I watch, nothing more than a Wind in the trees. I don't dare show myself again, not now I know how much I have already altered Fannaris's timeline.

In the courtyard, his mother embraces him, tears in her eyes, while his younger brothers and sisters hang from his arms and legs, all talking at once. His eldest brother, the heir, shakes Fannaris's hand in a manly fashion, and says he hopes Fannaris will do them all proud.

Fannaris says scarcely a word to any of them, not even the sisters who adore him beyond anything, not even his youngest brother, who has just learned to walk and is toddling about precariously—I keep forgetting he's Hal. Fannaris just gives them all a curt nod and climbs into the carriage, holding tight to his satchel, where he's stashed as many of his brushes and paints as he could reasonably hide. I watched him pack, peering in through his window and darting away any time he glanced in my direction.

The carriage lurches into motion. Fannaris's mother and younger siblings all start crying, and even the oldest turns away with wet eyes. I wonder if Fannaris ever knew how much he meant to them. It breaks my heart that his hurt and his pride keep him from bidding them a proper farewell.

He will never have another chance.

In Wind form, I fly awhile alongside the carriage, looking in the window. Fannaris sits on the floor, his head in his hands, sobbing like his world has ended. It *has* ended, really, and the knowledge wrecks me utterly.

I return to the corridor of his life and weep awhile between doorways. I don't quite know what to do—I don't quite know when to save him, when to rip him from the tapestry of his time and stitch him into an uncertain future in a world that might already be gone. My father's story about the dog haunts me—what if I save Fannaris, and he dies anyway? Or what if my saving him causes the world to Unravel sooner? And even if nothing horrible happens, the Fannaris I save now would not be the Fannaris I knew before. He would have never bargained with the Wolf Queen, never become the Winter Lord. He would only be a sad, petulant boy with shattered dreams, far from home. To him, I would only be the all-powerful North Wind who ripped him away from his world and his family. I don't know how to reconcile that.

So I pace on down the corridor that is his life, stepping through doors and watching from afar, torn, always torn.

I can hardly bear to visit many of his moments in the training camp. His misery eats at me, and my grief for him weighs heavier with every door I enter. His days are long, filled with grueling drills and shouting captains, his body honed into a weapon he has no wish to be. At night he steals out of his hard, narrow bunk to paint for a while under the stars, until his commanding officer catches him, makes him burn his canvas and his brushes, makes him pour his precious paints out into the dust. Makes him bear cruel lashes against his pale shoulders while his fellow soldiers laugh and swear at him, the son of a duke, crying over *paint*.

This is what breaks him, at the last. Terror grips me as I watch him sneak out of the camp, and before I can think about it properly, I send a gust of wind to smooth away his boot prints in the dust. I let the wind build and build, until a storm buffets the camp, giving him a few more precious hours before his absence is discovered. I tell myself that I haven't altered his timeline, that he could have run away without my help. I try not to think that maybe this is *how* he escaped—that I was always here, helping him, in his past and my future.

I follow from a distance as he journeys to the city, joining a merchant caravan and earning his keep helping to care for livestock. He reaches a great city, where he barters with the merchants for paints and clean clothes. He petitions every painter in the city, great and small, but none will have him. If he admits he's a deserter, he's turned away at once; if he lies and says his father sent him, he's turned away anyway, because he has no letter to recommend him.

The Tsar's soldiers are hunting for him. He sleeps in dirty alleys or doorways in poorer parts of town, awakened every morning by curses or brooms or stones. Everything inside me wants to grab his hand, pull him from his misery into my life, my world. And yet I think of my father's story, and I continue to hesitate. But it doesn't stop me from nudging the soldiers away from Fannaris with careful winds or buffeting storms. I don't let myself think about timelines. I just want to protect him.

There comes a night that I think Fannaris is asleep in a rubbish heap at the end of an alleyway. The moon is out, round and full, and it touches the stones and refuse with silver.

"You're always there, aren't you, Madame Wind?" he says unexpectedly. "Always watching me. I would say you're my guardian angel, but if that were true you haven't done the best of jobs."

"Of course I have," I say, startled into speech. "You're still alive, aren't you?"

He gives me a half smile that reminds me of the Winter Lord he will become. "I had thought my desertion was too easy—and I haven't been caught yet." He sobers. "Thank you."

"I can't stay," I tell him. "I'm sorry."

"Why? You see I haven't forgotten you, like you bid me. What harm can it do to sit and talk with me for a while?"

"Very great harm," I say. But I linger.

He picks himself off the rubbish heap and paces toward me. "Can I touch you, Madame Wind?" he asks softly, reaching out one hand.

"That's not my name." I evade his hand and his question, taking a step back.

He doesn't reach for me again. "What is your name?"

It is foolish to tell him, but I do anyway. "Satu North."

Fannaris smiles, moonlight making his face shine. "Not the sort of name I thought a Wind would have."

"I am only very recently a Wind," I explain.

He laughs. "And will you always watch over me, Satu North?"

Suddenly all I can see is his body, frozen and lifeless, snow blowing into the sea. My heart constricts and tears press behind my eyes and I *can't breathe*. I turn away.

But he catches my hand. Holds me back.

I look at him.

"Why are you crying?" he asks softly.

I taste salt, his moonlight-gilded face blurring before me. "I am trying to save you, Fannaris Wintar," I whisper. "If there—if there ever comes a moment when you are trapped, when you are . . . frightened, know that you are not alone. Know that I am coming."

He stares at me, sober, serious, my hand still caught fast in his. His pulse beats warm in my palm, and I wonder what, really, I'm waiting for. There is nothing to stop me from saving him here, now.

"Will you come with me?" I ask him.

"Yes."

I take a breath. I pull him down the alley, commanding the Threads of Time to let us into the corridor. But though I sense them all around me, they don't reveal themselves, don't part for us.

Let us in! I demand.

But they say: *It is not time. You cannot take him here. You cannot pull out his thread too early or the whole of Time will unravel.*

LET US IN! I cry.

It is not time. You cannot take him.

I drop to my knees on the filthy stones, an angry wind ripping through the alley.

Fannaris watches me, wary, but not afraid. "Wherever it is you wanted to take me—we can't go now, can we?"

I shake my head. "No. We can't. I'm, sorry, Fannaris."

He quirks a smile at me and offers me his hand. I let him pull me to my feet. "As you are only *recently* a Wind, I'll forgive you, just this once."

I try to smile in return but find I can't quite manage it. I need to go, need to return to his corridor and find the place the Threads of Time will allow me to pull him free. But I linger, watching him. He is so beautiful in the moonlight, and I can't bear knowing what comes next: his bargain with the Wolf Queen, his tomb of ice. In this moment, he is fragile and innocent, wholly human, no trace of winter magic, of death, of cold. I want to keep him from that. I want to hold him tight and not let him go. I want to kiss him.

This last thought startles me, and his eyes catch on mine.

We stare at each other in the dirty alley, wind blowing about our knees.

"Fannaris," I say. "Can I kiss you?"

He gives a little nod, his eyes suddenly wide, and my heart is a riot against my breastbone.

I touch his cheek with hesitant fingers, and he wraps his arms around me, tugging me tight against him. Then we're kissing like the world is ending, and some dim part of me remembers that it *is*: a blue glacier in a black sea, beneath the Unraveling sky. But here, now, his mouth is fierce and warm on mine, and our hearts beat in perfect rhythm. There is no magic in him and yet I feel it twining between us, threads pulling tight, never to be broken.

It's the Threads of Time that tear me away from him, tight about my shoulders, angry in my ears. I can't breathe, and my whole body shakes.

Fannaris stares at me, stricken, gulping for air. "Don't go.

Please don't go."

The Threads pull, insistent. "Fannaris—"

But then the Threads jerk me back into the corridor of his life. I sit with my knees pulled to my chest, dripping tears, numb with sadness. And I know, in the deepest part of myself, that the reason the Winter Lord kissed me at the remains of the House Under the Mountain was because I kissed him first.

AFTER THAT, I TAKE CARE Fannaris does not see me. I cannot interfere anymore, I cannot bear to, not until I have reached the moment the Threads will let me take him from his time into mine. But even so, I refuse to let him face his future alone.

I am there when he steals aboard a ship in a desperate gamble to avoid the Tsar's soldiers. I blow eddies of wind to distract the sailors from looking in his direction. His eyes glance skyward, searching for me. But I do not let him see me.

I am there as he turns green with seasickness, as he's discovered by one of the mates and put quickly to work with a great deal of shouting. As he peers through the portholes or over the ship's rails, day after day, night after night, looking for me. Not finding me.

I am there as a storm that is not mine whips cold out of the sea, as snow and ice rain down, as the ship is blown off course, so much farther north than it was ever meant to go. I taste his fear, hear his voice tangled with the sailors' screams. The sea swallows them up, pulls them down into black depths, but not him, not him. He is spared for a different fate.

I am there as he climbs to the top of the broken mast, splinters in his palms and terror in his soul. As he begs and prays, crying out for someone to save him. Crying out for *me*.

I hurl myself toward him, determined to pull him from his nightmare before it can begin, but the Threads of Time wind about my wrists, and jerk me back again.

Not now, they seethe through my mind. *Not here. This story is woven too tightly with too many others. If he does not meet the Wolf Queen, if he makes no bargain with her, Time will fracture, and there will be nothing left.*

I don't care! I cry. *Let me go to him!*

But the Threads pull tighter, tethering me unseen in this icy dark. They neither let me go to him nor bring me back to the corridor. I cannot get free, and I cannot help him, and I will be forced to watch the end of his mortal life.

Fannaris screams my name into the wind. I am torn apart, fractured to the depths of my being.

The Wolf Queen comes over the icy sea in a coracle drawn by a pair of black serpents with lupine faces. Their sides glitter with scales, and their long sinuous bodies dip in and out of dark water as they approach. The Queen is clothed in scarlet, a bloodstain against the frozen world, and her long silver hair spills down past her knees. The North Wind's crown flashes blue-green on her brow; knife-edged claws protrude from her silver-furred hands.

Fannaris stares at her as she looms near, tears freezing on his face, screams dying on his lips. He shakes and shakes and *I cannot bear it.*

I howl in anguish, but the Threads of Time slither down my throat and choke off my voice so that he can't hear me. He thinks he's *alone*, he thinks he's alone, that I haven't come, that I've betrayed him to this *witch.*

No wonder he hated me when he brought his storm to my mountain.

The Wolf Queen's lupine serpents bear her coracle to the broken ship and then, impossibly, up into the air where Fannaris clings to the splintered mast. She steps from her vessel and walks on nothing toward him, bending down as she reaches him, touching his face with her claws. He whimpers as blood beads up in thin red lines.

"Who are you?" he whispers, fingers digging into the wood of the mast.

"Fannaris Wintar," she says, "I am your salvation." She smiles.

I try to scream, try to rip myself from the Threads of Time, but they do not let me go. *Not yet, not yet,* they whisper.

Rage and horror splinter me apart, and I can't even clap my hands over my ears to shut out the Queen's voice, because the Threads bind me to the ice. I choke and I weep but I can do nothing to stop her, nothing to save him.

I watch as he agrees to her bargain. As she breaks off a piece of my father's crown and thrusts it into his heart.

He collapses, wheezing in pain, and she laughs at him, the sound echoing cruelly over the frozen sea.

I fracture, again and again, but the Threads hold me fast and I can't go to him, can't tear the ice from his chest and hold him, warm and alive, heart beating next to mine.

She encases his body in ice and buries him deep in the glacier. She calls his new form out of the snow.

Fannaris, the Winter Lord, pushes himself free of the frozen ground, shaking ice from hair that has grown paler, longer. He kneels before the Wolf Queen. He pledges his allegiance.

For a moment, the Threads of Time loosen their hold, and half a cry slips from my throat.

The Winter Lord raises his eyes, and they meet mine. He can't see the Threads binding me; he doesn't understand. Anger and confusion and terror burn in his gaze, but hatred swallows them whole.

His name forms on my lips. I stretch my hand out to him.

And then the Threads yank me back into the corridor, sliding apologetically around my shoulders. *It wasn't time, it wasn't time.*

A scream wrests out of me, a torrent of wind rushing down the endless hall. I want to tear the world apart with my fury; I want to rip time to shreds. But instead I sob and I sob, because Fannaris is bound to a fate worse than death, and because he thinks I could have saved him—and chose not to.

TWENTY-EIGHT

I DO NOT WANT TO OPEN ANY more doors. But the Threads of Time are silent, now. They will not tell me when and where is the moment when I'm allowed to save him. They will not tell me if there even *is* such a moment, or if my journey is fruitless and I am only deluding myself.

I pace the halls of Fannaris's life. The Wolf Queen made him immortal, and the corridor stretches on and on. I don't want to see him used as the Queen's weapon, forged into a cruel creature with nothing but ice in his heart. But I don't know how else to find the right time to save him.

And so I see Fannaris as the Winter Lord fortify the Wolf Queen's realm with an eternal, impenetrable winter. Sometimes, he stands beside her throne. Sometimes, he's sent into the world to carry out her orders. I see him break and bind the power my father gave to the Wolf Queen, see him scatter part of the crown over the frozen lake, magic to help the winter hold forever. The rest he binds as a gatekeeper at the House Under the Mountain, charged with guarding the wolf who was Hal.

I see him weeping, alone in the Wolf Queen's forest, when he realizes who Hal is and what the Queen did to him.

And I see him coming to look in on my father, making sure, as the Queen ordered, that the former North Wind had no intention of going back on his bargain.

I see him caught by my father, once, as he's lurking outside my parents' reindeer-skin tent. My father invites him in out of the cold to share a cup of tea and the Winter Lord, bewildered, refuses, melting away into the night.

And one evening, shortly before my own birth—I've seen my mother's belly, huge and bewilderingly tight—I step through a door to find the Winter Lord sitting on my rock ledge, his feet dangling over empty air. Snow swirls round him, ice falling like diamonds from his fingertips.

"I know you are there, Satu North," he says, without turning his head. "You are always there. Have you not had your fill, by now, of my torment?"

"I'm trying to save you," I say softly. "I'm sorry it's taking so long."

He jerks around, his eyes searching for mine in the dark.

But the Threads tell me: *Not yet, not yet* and I turn myself all to wind and flee back into the corridor.

I am too much of a coward to step through the next set of doors—I don't dare look into his life when I know he is watching mine. And I can't bear his sadness. His anger.

I peek through the doors, as quickly as I can, to gauge how far along his timeline I've come. I walk and walk and walk, until I find that his corridor has an end after all.

Ten doors stretch to a sudden stop, loose threads swirling into a tangled void.

Which one? I ask the Threads.

You will know it, they reply.

How?

You will know it.

Panic is a storm inside of me. I try to be calm, staring at the doors, counting them, considering them. I know what I will find through the last door—I was already there, the moment he stabbed me through the heart with the North Wind's ice, the moment of his death. It has to be before that.

Doesn't it?

My heart beats and beats, the answer just out of my grasp. I force myself to think it through, weighing life and death in my hands like a god. There was life yet in Fannaris's frozen body, for a few seconds, before the Winter Lord drove the ice shard into my heart, before I became wholly the North Wind and he turned to snow, the body that had been trapped in the glacier for centuries vanishing with him.

That is my moment, I realize. The only point in Time where I can save him.

My eyes are drawn to the door that's three from the end, and the Threads of Time whisper and sigh, relieved I've reached the proper answer.

I clothe myself in wind, and I pass through.

I do not take human form, do not set foot on the glacier. I am suspended in a place between earth and sky, just below the Unraveling that reaches for me, snarling. I don't let it touch me.

For a breath, the glacier is empty, the white bones of the dead ship the only hint that life ever touched this place.

And then a horse made of snow comes hurtling across the sea, the Winter Lord and my former self on its back. The Threads of Time murmur in my ears, telling me to be still, still.

So I watch. I wait.

"Why have you brought me here?" comes my voice, thin and quiet, from the glacier below.

"To show you the missing piece," the Winter Lord returns, tall and cold and grim. "Dig, North. You must dig."

He makes me the ice spade. He promises to hold back the Unraveling for as long as he can.

Above me and around me, the Unraveling spits and shrieks, snagging at me, trying to tear me to pieces. Below, the Winter Lord attempts his protective magic. Twice, the Unraveling sneers at him, dissolving his spells. I feel his fear, for himself and for the world, but most of all for my small self, digging in the ice, not knowing what awaits her there.

His fear makes me angry because he should not be helpless, not here, and I send a gust of wind magic toward him, joining it with his ice magic to form the dome that will shield me, and him, for as long as I am digging there—for longer.

He is startled and tilts his face upward. He can't see me, not in my current form, but he *knows*, and I remember that gust of wind, that knowing look, from before. Because it has always happened this way. Me here, watching over him, as he also watches over me.

His knowing sharpens into determination, and I understand that *this* is the moment his resolve hardens. The moment he knows for certain what he will do when the other Satu digs his body out of the ice. He knows what I have become, and he knows how I will become it.

It is agony, watching myself dig Fannaris out of the ice. Every moment that passes in which I don't save him feels like I am betraying him, again and again. But the Threads of Time hold me back, and I know the moment I'm waiting for is the right one.

Yet the waiting is unbearable.

At last, at last, the other Satu uncovers Fannaris, frozen, still. I feel every pulse of his heart, tremulous, unsure. There is fresh agony, now. He is there. Alive. And yet still the Threads whisper that it is not time, not time. I cannot save him before I become the North Wind. If I did, the universe would only unravel a different way.

Below me, the Winter Lord tells the other Satu his story. She listens. She weeps for him. But she refuses to claim the last piece of her inheritance.

The Winter Lord glances up for an instant, sensing me near, as he did so many times throughout his life. He trusts me, I realize. It humbles me. Terrifies me. After everything, *he trusts me.*

I am almost caught off guard when he jerks the ice shard out of his true body's heart, when he drives it into my former self. I cannot quite bear to watch my own transformation into the North Wind. I experienced it, and that is enough. I fix my eyes instead on Fannaris's body. I count his heartbeats. I'm terrified there aren't enough left.

I wait, wait, until Satu comes into herself, until she looks, for a moment, at Fannaris, cold and still on the ice. Until she turns toward the Winter Lord.

Now! scream the Threads of Time and my own heart together. *Now.*

I sweep down onto the glacier; I wrap Fannaris in winds.

Over my other self's shoulder, the Winter Lord's eyes catch for a moment on mine. "Satu," he says. "You're *shining.*"

And then I bear Fannaris's body up, up, into the air, away from the glacier and into the corridor of his own life. When my other self turns back to the place he was lying, she will see only snow, and think he disappeared when the Winter Lord did. But she—*I*—was wrong. Because he is here, with me. And there are yet a few beats of his heart remaining.

TWENTY-NINE

ET US THROUGH, I COMMAND THE Threads of Time, and they obey, tearing a rift in that moment, drawing us into the corridor of Fannaris's life. He is too cold in my arms, the space between his heartbeats growing farther and farther apart. I understand, as I didn't fully before, that the North Wind's ice was keeping him alive. That without it, his body can't endure.

There is something desperate in me, something wild and frantic, a different sort of creature than the one that drove me to try and save the boy who gave his life for mine. That was—pity, fury, duty, an impulse to right a horrible wrong, a desire to heal his hurt and erase his sadness.

But this—this is something else, something I do not quite know how to name, or do not quite want to. I know his whole life now. I've seen him at his best and his worst, felt his sorrow and tasted his joy. He is—he is *more* to me than he was before, and I know that if he does not wake, if he does not *live*, the broken thing inside of me will never be whole again.

He is almost out of time. But I refuse to lose him the same moment I've saved him. I am the North Wind, after all. And Time must obey me.

I shout a word to the Threads and they part for us, the corridor dissolving into the shore of the Time Thread Sea, where my wind ship is waiting. I lay him gently down into it. I tell my winds to bear us into the sea. And as the ship leaves the shore, I place my hand on Fannaris's heart, reaching for his pulse, reaching and not finding it.

But I scream at Time that it cannot have him. I send wind magic into his heart, into his lungs. I send winds whispering all around him, warming him bit by bit, until frost no longer traces the line of his cheeks, until his lips are red and not blue, until his chest rises and falls and his heart beats, beats, beats, steady beneath my hand.

The ship bears us on into the sea, and Fannaris stirs. Opens his eyes. A cry chokes out of me.

"Satu," he whispers, voice hoarse and dry with disuse.

Faster, I urge my ship. *Faster.* Time is a whirl of light and color around us.

He sits, carefully. He lifts one hand to touch my face. "You saved me," he says, with utter wonder. "You saved me from the dark."

But I feel the frozen ice of time scrabbling to claim him, and I know he is not safe here.

Faster! I cry to my ship and it obeys, all the universe clamoring outside of us, until we come to a veil of mist in the sea and sail through it.

I reach out my hand to Fannaris and he takes it. We climb together from the ship, and his brow furrows in confusion.

We step onto the rock ledge on my mountain, far away, a time and a place that no longer exist. But I have commanded it to and so it does, a frozen moment, eternal, forever. There is no time, here. And so here time cannot take him from me.

It's a summer afternoon, the mountain drenched in the scent of wildflowers and honey, of sun-warmed stone. Nothing moves, and so all is eerily silent, like the Winter Lord's frozen time outside of Gradeslav.

Fannaris's pulse beats between our joined hands, and we sit together on the rock ledge, not letting go.

"I always knew," he says at last, "that you would save me."

I turn to face him, studying the line of his jaw, the gray of his eyes, the white-gold sheen of his eyelashes. "Even when the Wolf Queen bound you to her service?" I ask quietly.

"I still hoped. Even then."

We look out across the tundra, motionless and strange, a moment of beauty preserved forever in amber.

I lay my head on his shoulder. "I wanted to save you sooner. I wanted to save you so many times. But the Threads wouldn't let me. There are some things even the North Wind cannot do."

"I know that now," comes the murmur of his voice, close above my ear. "I lost sight of my hope in my anger. I wanted you to suffer, as I had suffered, a just payment for your perceived betrayal. But I could not bear to see you hurt. And the thought of the Wolf Queen binding you, using you—I would have never let that happen."

The Threads of Time are whispering in my mind, tugging at me, telling me that I am the North Wind but I have not the power of the Great Weaver, that this moment is not forever, after all. I ignore them. I push them away.

"I am sorry," says Fannaris. "For the pain you bore on my account."

"It is all forgotten. All forgiven."

I lift my head and we stare at each other once more. Fannaris touches gentle fingers to my face, wiping away tears I didn't realize were falling. He tugs me to my feet and we pace to the edge of the rock, looking out into the world that used to be, but is no more. I try to ignore the coldness that shivers under his skin, waiting and wanting to consume him.

"Then you were aware," I say, "of the things you did as the Winter Lord, even though your body—"

"Was frozen in the glacier," he finishes quietly. "Yes. I saw everything. Experienced everything. *Did* everything. Only when that body was asleep did this body know the cold and the dark, feel the horror and the power of the ice in my heart."

A sob chokes out of me, but Fannaris squeezes my hand. "It was not your father's fault, Satu. It is not yours."

"I should have found another way to save you."

"There was no other way."

I gnaw on the inside of my cheek, fighting to keep the tears back. I let Fannaris thread his fingers through my hair.

"You have always been full," he says, "of life, of magic. You burst with it, you know. With the very oldest and strongest of magics. I felt it, from the first moment I saw you as a child."

There is ice creeping up his bare feet, pulsing in the pads of his fingers. A fractal of frozen blue curls across his cheek.

You can't have him! I scream at Time. But Time does not listen.

Tears pour down my face and Fannaris wipes them, gently, away. He holds me tight against him, strokes my hair with a hand that grows horribly, horribly cold.

"Thank you for saving me, Satu," he whispers. "For not leaving me to die in the cold, in the dark."

"I won't let you die," I wrench out. "I am the North Wind and *I won't let you die.*"

"This body wasn't meant to endure," he returns simply. "It cannot."

"But I want it to." I pull back enough to look into Fannaris's face, to see the whorls of ice, the frost on his eyelashes, the warm flush of his skin turning slowly blue. "Do you *hear* me, Fannaris? I want you to. I'm not letting you go."

He smiles as he smooths his thumb over my cheek. "If you had lived in my time, long ago," he says, "I would have invited you to a party at my father's great house. There would have been music, Satu, more food than anyone could ever eat, and dancing, such dancing! I would have danced with you until the dawn, and together we would watch the stars fade, the sun rise on a new morning. We will never have that moment, you and I. But we have this one. Dance with me, won't you? Until the dawn?"

I can't speak for crying but I nod my assent, and he guides my hands, one to his shoulder and one to his waist. He leads me through the dance, a seamless, fluid motion, and I can almost, almost hear music. It's Time, perhaps, that plays for us.

So we dance, as the Threads swirl angrily about my shoulders, reminding me of the Unraveling world, of the North Wind's duty, of the thousands upon thousands of souls that are waiting for me to save them, while I dance with a dying boy in a moment of frozen time.

"Please don't despair," says Fannaris, as ice freezes his veins, as his legs get heavier and heavier, making him stumble, making him fall at the last to his knees.

I crouch with him, holding his hands as the ice takes them, winding its way all through his body, taking back what I tried so hard to seize for myself.

"You saved me," he whispers, ice curling up his neck. "You saved me from the cold and the dark. From dying alone. You gave me this."

I wrap my arms around him, holding him tight, tight, as the Threads of Time rip us from this moment, send us whirling back to the place I did not want to see again: the glacier, frozen and blue, in the midst of an angry dark sea. Above us, the Unraveling rages, chunks of the Winter Lord's and my joint magic raining down like snow.

Fannaris's heart beats tremulous and quiet. Wind snarls in his hair.

"I'm free," he says, the words cracked and brittle as his throat freezes, too. "Of her, of my bargain. I'm *free*, Satu. You did that for me."

Grief pulls me all to pieces. I cling to him, and I realize the thing inside of me that is breaking is my heart. "Stay with me," I beg through endless tears. "Please, Fannaris. Don't leave me here alone."

He is almost completely frozen, now, and can no longer move his body, his head. But he smiles a little sadly and fixes his eyes on mine. "I am sorry, Satu."

"You can just become the Winter Lord again," I say desperately. "You don't have to die here. I won't *let* you!"

"The Winter Lord is here, Satu. In me."

"But his body—"

"Is here, Satu."

My hand goes to his chest, to where the North Wind's magic froze his heart. I feel the tiniest pulse of it still, beating inside of him.

And then the ice takes him wholly, and he is horribly, horribly still. Frost traces lacy patterns on his eyelids.

It wasn't enough. The journey and the wanting. It could never be enough. It was always going to end like this—Fannaris, dead in the ice. I am a Wind, but I cannot rob Time. I cannot undo what was already woven into the tapestry of the world.

I cannot bear it.

Wind rages around me, lending voice to my anguish. But I myself am still, gasping in the snow, my eyes fixed on the frozen form of him, crystalized in perfect beauty. I put a word to the broken thing inside of me. I give it a reason.

The ice of him shatters, and turns to snow, and blows away into the sea.

I jerk upright, screaming. "No! NO! BRING HIM BACK!"

But he's gone. He's *gone*, and the world is still Unraveling, and I have utterly, utterly failed.

I love him.

And he's gone.

THIRTY

I *LOVE HIM.*

It startles me. Staggers me. *I love him.*

Such a small word, *love.* And yet it is the oldest power in the universe. It is what the world is *made* of. It pulses and stretches inside of me, warm and strong and good.

Beneath me, the black sea claws angrily at the glacier, seeking to drag it into the icy depths. Above, the last of the Winter Lord's and my protective spell shatters, and the Unraveling world reaches down. In moments, the sea and the sky will meet in me, and I will be Unraveled, too. It will be a relief, perhaps, to reach the end. No more feelings, no more tears, no *more*—just peace.

But.

I love him.

Already I am used to the thought, as natural to me as the pulses of my heart.

He gave up his life for me. I tore time apart to save him. He's still gone, I'm still alone, but—

I can't let it be for nothing. His sacrifice. Mine. I can't let *all of this* be for nothing. I won't.

Somewhere out there, my parents and Inna, Echo and Hal, Taisia and the herders, and an entire world of people are trapped Between. Waiting for me to truly claim my birthright, to stitch up the tears in the universe, to bring them back.

I stand to my feet, winds whirling round me, fragments of ice hissing over the glacier. Threads of nothingness curl down from the Unraveling sky. They brush against my shoulders and I gasp in pain, scrabbling out of their reach. But I don't despair, not anymore. Because there is work to be done. And I am the only one who can do it.

Stories unfold inside of me. I am ready, at last, to take charge of mine.

I choose this, I think to the icy sea and the howling sky. *The North Wind's power. The North Wind's burden. I choose this.*

The Sky Horse shimmers into being beside me, its mane rippling in my winds. It bows its head to me. *My Lady North. Where are we going?*

I climb onto the horse's back, my fingers grazing across the belt my mother wove, the pouch that Echo once wore. I take out the golden needle, hold it tight in my hand.

To bind up the Unraveling world, I reply. *To end all this.*

You haven't any thread, says the horse.

I look to the place where Fannaris drew his last breath, and my broken heart beats, beats. There is love inside of me—not just for Fannaris, but for my parents and Inna, for every soul torn away from my fractured world. There is old magic wound about my heart.

Yes, I do, I tell the Sky Horse. *I have everything I need.*

And then we're flying, up into the depths of the Unraveling darkness.

For a moment, the Sky Horse bears me untouched through the broken threads. I breathe in magic and wind, feel the rippling coolness of the horse's mane on my cheek. I loose the golden needle from the pouch at my waist. I was made for this, and I am not afraid.

Then sudden, searing agony, as I am torn from the Sky Horse's back, as I spin out into writhing, fathomless dark. Broken threads claw at my hair and my skin, burning me in every place they touch. They pulse with sorrow and anger, with unspoken words and regretted oaths, with lost and fractured magic.

And then they rip me apart.

THIRTY-ONE

THERE IS DARKNESS AND A TERRIBLE, piercing cold. The dark is all-consuming, smothering light and touch and sound. There is no horizon, no boundary of space. I can't feel the pulse of my heart or the weight of my body. I don't know if I am moving or if I am standing still. I don't know if I have a body at all.

I don't know what I am, and it doesn't matter. I will dwell in this darkness always. This is my eternity.

And yet.

I remember stories and warmth and the scent of honey. I remember the rough feel of paper under my hand and ink spots on my fingers. I remember laughter, reindeer, music.

I remember a boy, frozen all in ice, pieces of him blowing away into a winter sea.

I *remember.*

And I do have a body because there are tears on my cheeks. A needle in my hand. Old magic wound about my heart.

Light, I realize. *I need light.*

I call for it and it comes, whispering and warm, pulsing through me—a gift from my grandparents, the Sun and the Moon.

And I see, all around me, an unending expanse of broken threads.

Despair crushes me.

The needle trembles in my hand. It is an impossible task, but I have come this far. I have to try.

I reach deep inside of myself, grasping for a thread of the old magic. I feel it beating in my heart and I pull it out, a length of shimmering, twisting silk. It hurts, hurts, but I slip the thread through the eye of my golden needle anyway.

I grab two broken threads, holding them tight in one hand even though they burn me. I pierce them with the needle. I stitch them together again. I grab another two. I tug more old magic from my heart. I sew them together, too.

And then there is only the work, the needle singing in my hand, the thread pulling from my heart, the pain of the frayed world, blistering my palm. I sew and I sew and I sew, weaving myself into the tapestry of the universe, lending pieces of my heart, my soul, my self. I am a river and a song. I am a tender spring leaf and a story spun out on a winter's night; I am the first blush of autumn, the last summer flower.

Threads of old magic pull out of me, more and more and more. I feel sorrow and joy and anger, laughter, rage, awe. I feel, feel, feel, but the feelings are never gone and the threads do not run out.

On I go into the Unraveled world, my needle singing and the universe sighing as thread by thread the dark recedes.

There is no time here, I think. No beginning and no ending. There is only the work to be done, the magic spinning out of me. How long does it take to stitch up the universe? I have only just begun, it seems, and yet I have been here, intent on my task, a millennium at least.

I try to hold on to the pieces of myself: stories and honey, paper and laughter. A boy made of winter.

I sew and sew.

I lose the pieces, one by one.

There is only the endless task, the hurt in my heart, my hands.

I grow wholly weary. Tears dampen my cheeks.

The needle slips from my fingers.

I collapse into darkness.

THIRTY-TWO

I SIT IN A HIGH COLD TOWER, and there is snow at the window. A tapestry billows over my knees. It is enormously complex and impossibly beautiful. Almost every thread of it is frayed.

There is a needle in my hand that flashes gold in the firelight, and it is threaded with a gossamer filament that spins out from my heart. I feel the tug and pull of it, and it hurts, but not more than I can bear. I glide the needle in and out of the tapestry, making hundreds and thousands of stitches. My heart-thread never seems to run out, which is good. Because the tapestry is infinite, ever more of it under my hands for me to repair. I have always been here. I always will be.

For a time, I am aware of nothing but the tapestry, the needle, the glint of gold and the constant ache spooling out of my heart.

I come to a patch of silver threads, and I glance up to see snow clinging to the window. Tears drip onto the tapestry, and I do not know why.

Gradually, as my hands become certain in their task, the clack of shuttles echoes near and I realize I am not alone in this tower room. I lift my head to the right and see a giant loom and a man sitting behind it. He is tall, but beyond that I cannot quite comprehend the sight of him. He works steadily at the loom, hands and feet moving with exquisite skill. It is from him that the tapestry flows, every thread in its right place, a tiny part of a vast, impossible beauty.

But somewhere between the loom and where I sit, the threads are ruined, torn. I peer down into the dark to see a great swarm of moths attacking the tapestry, devouring every part they can.

The Weaver seems unconcerned about the moths. He just continues his task, as I continue mine.

Over and over, stitch after stitch, he creates, and they ruin, and I repair.

"Why do you not crush them?" I say, head bent over the needle, my heart aching and raw as the thread pulls and pulls. "Why let them destroy what you have made?"

"If I cease my work, so too will the universe cease," comes the Weaver's reply. His voice is warm as honey.

There is a hollowness inside, a grief and a horror that rushes up to overwhelm me. "Must I sew forever, then?"

"I did not say that."

My needle rises and falls, tugging the frayed threads back together as the shuttles clack and the moths unravel newly woven rows.

Tears pour down my cheeks because I have found another patch of silver in the tapestry. There is something in me that remembers—cold snow on my hot face, ice tangled in long hair, warm lips touching my own. *I love him.*

"Do not weep, little one," says the Weaver gently. "This is not the end."

But the tears come and come. I shake as this tower room closes in on me, as the whisper of the moths' wings burrows into my mind, as the thread pulling out of me hurts, hurts, hurts.

I remember a sad story in a dark room, crying on a mountaintop with children's laughter ringing in my ears, broken honey jars in the snow. I weep. "Take it away," I gasp. "Take it all away. Please. I know you can."

"Take what away, daughter?"

I bunch infinite fabric in trembling hands and prick myself with the needle. A spot of blood stains the threads; they shiver over my knees. "All of my feelings," I choke out. "They are too many. I cannot hold them all. They're destroying me."

"Are they?" says the Weaver. "Who would you be, Satu North, without your great heart?"

And I bow my head because I do not know, do not know.

There comes a step at the door. I didn't know there was a door, but it opens, and a man steps in. A man with wings on his shoulders. I peer at him, because I feel I should know him, but I don't. His face is streaked with gold blood.

He crosses the room, kneels on the floor where the moths whisper and writhe. He takes a spinning wheel from off his back and he crouches there, catching the moths, spinning them into gray thread that grows and grows until the heap is so big I cannot see him behind it.

We work, all three of us, the Weaver, the man with wings, and me.

And always, always, snow rattles against the window and tears drip into my lap.

Two other men appear at the door, one with a spear and one with a sword, both with jewels bound to their foreheads. They join the man with wings, gathering up the moth thread and setting it in baskets. The baskets are full to overflowing, and still the man with wings spins, still the other two gather his thread. Still I stitch, and still the Weaver's loom remains in constant motion.

How high is this cold tower, I wonder? Where does it dwell?

My heart stutters, and I gasp as the thread winding out of me breaks suddenly off. I collapse over the infinite tapestry, choking for breath. The beats of my heart grow still. The room fades around me, and I am swallowed up. But I am not afraid. All I can think about is the snow at the window as I go into the dark.

THIRTY-THREE

I AM IN A LOW CORRIDOR OUTSIDE a plain wooden door. There is
frost tracing the curve of my cheek and I can still taste the salt
of my tears. It is very dark, but a line of light seeps from under
the door, and shadows stretch long down the hall.

I am not alone. I tilt my head up and look into the face of
the Weaver. I can comprehend him no better than I could in the
tower room, but there is sorrow in his eyes and wisdom in his face
and he is clothed in stars or mountains—I cannot quite tell.

"How can you leave your loom?" I ask him, and the darkness
swallows my words.

"My work is finished now," he answers in that honey-rich
voice. "The thread eaters are gone and the tapestry repaired and
the world will spin on as it ought to."

"What were the thread eaters?"

"Brokenness," he says. "What you would call loose magic."

I tremble. "Who were they? The men in that room who helped me?"

"The other Winds," says the Weaver. "They were always there, in the Unraveling, helping you, even when you could not see them. You have never been alone."

Tears drip down my cheeks. "Why am I here, now? Is . . . is my work finished, along with yours?"

"Yes, dear one. And you are here because I did not think you could find the path on your own."

"The path?"

He nods, shimmering, solemn. "The path Between."

My heart jerks and I gasp at the sudden wave of grief that engulfs me.

"You have lost many," he says gently. "The other Winds have gone before you, seeking those they lost. I offer you that same chance."

Memory and sorrow swell inside of me, scraping at my raw heart. "Can I save them? Can I bring them back?"

"The way is long, wind daughter; the souls are many, and the path will shut. We must go quickly."

I nod, teeth clamping down on my lips to keep from crying. I taste blood, and the tears come anyway.

I walk with the Weaver down the long hall, and I have the dim impression of a ceiling, high above, of many different corridors that branch off this one, of thousands upon thousands of doors. But the Weaver goes straight ahead, and so I do not turn aside. The light follows us, chasing at our heels, illuminating, ever so slightly, our path.

"What is this place?" I whisper.

"My house," answers the Weaver. "I am sorry for the darkness—if I lifted it completely, the light would destroy you, Wind though you are."

"I don't understand."

"You tread the very fabric of the universe, Satu North."

My heart stutters. "This is the tapestry I stitched up."

"Yes."

"But how—"

"Because you *are* a Wind, despite your humanity. I am able to bend the rules of space and time for you. You've bent them yourself."

"The Time Thread Sea."

He dips his head, glimmering in the darkness.

"But what *is* the Between?"

"A room, of sorts. A place where all the stray bits of magic, loose threads that no longer fit, are gathered."

I start to shake. "What happens to them?"

"They are bound," he says quietly. "The room is sealed. So the loose bits cannot harm the world."

"Can't you stop it?"

"I cannot exist in the Between; I cannot go there."

"Why?"

"I am magic bound, and the Between is magic unbound—both cannot dwell in the same place."

Our path descends, winding down and down. We pass doors, or something like doors, swaths of fabric that ripple in the breath of my winds.

"Here," says the Weaver, and stops abruptly.

There is nothing before us, nothing at all. Fear bites at me.

"Slip into the space between warp and weft," he says. "May you find the ones you seek."

He turns to go.

"Wait!"

He glances back, a steady smile on his lips. "You have something to ask me, North Wind?"

I stand trembling, more tears slipping down my cheeks. "If my father would have come to you, instead of the Wolf Queen, what price would you have asked him to pay? Would you have denied his request? Would you have forced him to stay the North Wind when that wasn't what he wanted, when it would have meant losing my mother, losing me?"

A sadness touches the Weaver's fathomless eyes. "What is it you really want to know, dear one?" His voice is infinitely gentle.

"If it weren't for me—" The words scrape my throat, brittle and sharp. "If it weren't for me, everything would be different, wouldn't it? If I didn't exist—"

"But you do exist, Satu North. You live your own story, make your own choices, as your father did."

"Would you have helped him?"

"Yes."

My heart wrenches. "Then all of this, *all of this*, could have been avoided?"

"Dear one." He puts a hand on my shoulder, and it is heavy with warmth, with peace. "What may have been does not matter now. Whether or not your father made the right choice, this is the story that both of you find yourselves in. Your father loved you before you were ever born. His choice was made of fear, yes, but it was also made of love. I would have helped him. But I do not condemn him."

The Weaver's face blurs before my eyes.

"Now," he says. "Go and find your father and all the others. Stitch them back into the world again."

I can hardly speak for crying. "How do I save them?"

"You will find a way," he says. "Farewell, Story North. Take heart. All will be well."

And then he is gone, and I am alone.

THIRTY-FOUR

I STEP BETWEEN WARP AND WEFT, WELCOMED by tendrils of darkness, frayed threads brushing my shoulders and whispering past my face. I ask for light and it floods through me, a soft glow emanating from my skin. I call the Sky Horse. I am not sure it exists anymore, not sure it will appear, but it does, all flowing, breathing wind. It bows its head before me.

"I am glad to see you, friend," I tell the horse. "We need to find them. All of them."

I am ready, it returns.

I climb onto the horse's back and nudge it into the darkness, reaching out for the threads of everyone dear to me: my parents and Inna, Echo and Hal and Taisia. I reach and I call them, and the dark shivers around me.

The horse bears me slowly through the Between, and I have the vague impression of a great, impossible room, the walls made of fabric, golden stitches running through the floor. It will not hold for long; I must find them and save them before it collapses around me. And when I *do* find them, I will need a way to carry them home.

Even as the thought sparks, I glance behind me to see a long line of Sky Horses, each a little different than my horse, with proud hooves and manes made of wind. I am not sure I made them, not even sure I called them, but they are here, and my dread eases a little. I gave so much of myself in that cold tower room, but my heart remains within me. I am not yet empty.

Bring me to them, I command the threads of this place.

The Between bends around me, and I slide from the Sky Horse to kneel at the side of a woman who lies slumbering in the dark. There are threads wrapped all around her, binding her to the fabric floor. The Weaver's voice slides through my mind: *They are bound. The room is sealed. So the loose bits cannot harm the world.*

Fear throbs in my chest, and my hand goes to the pouch still at my waist, fingers loosing the golden scissors. I snip the threads that bind her, uncovering her legs and torso, her face. To my surprise I find Madam Zima, the apothecary, and I feel a pulse of pity.

I touch her brow and she wakes, peering up at me with confusion. I lift her up with my winds and settle her gently on a Sky Horse. *Bring her home*, I tell it. *Let her think this all a dream.*

The horse bows its head to me, leaps into the air, and is gone.

I pace on into the Between, finding more villagers bound to the floor, all sleeping, all unaware they were ever Unraveled. I free each one with the scissors, wake them, set them upon a Sky Horse, and send them home.

I cut Taisia loose, and when I wake her, she peers at me for a moment with tears in her eyes, then brushes her fingers across my brow and bows to me.

"You are powerful indeed, my Lady North."

It feels wrong for her to bow, and I grab her hands and pull her to her feet again. "Is this what you Saw?" I ask her softly.

She smiles a little. "Not even my Sight stretched this far."

"But still you saved me. You sent me out of the camp at the cost of all the others."

Taisia shakes her head. "The Weaver is merciful, dear one. I did not doubt him. I did not doubt you."

Her unwavering faith makes tears well in my eyes.

"Come and visit, when you can," she says. "I would love to hear the whole of your story." Then she climbs upon a Sky Horse of her own accord and flies away into the dark.

I free and wake person after person whom I realize, after a while, must hail from Gradeslav. How many cities, I wonder, how many people, are trapped, here Between? Is it truly all of them?

I cut another woman free and find Echo, slumbering peacefully, her belly round and tight beneath her dress. Tears choke me as I wake her, and she looks at me with profound relief.

"Satu," she breathes. "You saved us."

"I'm trying," I say, horribly aware of the unease of the Between, the floor rippling beneath us, binding threads growing up to snag at our heels.

She hugs me tight and then pulls back, her eyes tracing the crown on my brow. "You've claimed your birthright."

A Sky Horse appears to take her home, but she frowns and shakes her head. "I'm not going back without Hal."

"Echo, it isn't safe."

She smiles, one hand pressed to her belly. "Nothing is ever safe where Hal is concerned."

So she walks beside me the next little while, watching with ever increasing grimness as I cut the threads binding soul after slumbering soul, freeing them from the Between, sending them home.

I can sense her rising panic as we fail to find Hal, Inna, Peter. The same panic boils inside of me.

"What if they're gone?" she says tightly. "What if the binding threads have taken them away?"

I grip her arm to keep her from stumbling over the rippling floor. "We're going to find them, Echo. *All* of them. We're not leaving until we do."

She nods, tears pouring down her cheeks. "I can't lose him. Not now."

I think of Fannaris, my Winter Lord, blowing away into the sea, and my heart snags. I see snow on the window in a cold tower room. I fight to keep from crying but the tears fall anyway. Where has he gone? Is he here, somewhere, Between?

But no, of course he isn't. Because Fannaris wasn't Unraveled. Fannaris is dead.

We find Inna, the threads falling to the sharp edges of my scissors. She springs up from the floor, hurling herself first at me and then Echo.

"Where are we?" she says. "What is this place? Are we somewhere magical? *Satu!* You're wearing a *crown!* Why do I always miss everything exciting? Where's Papa? Where's Hal?"

A Sky Horse appears at her shoulder.

"Time to go home, Inna," I tell her.

"Like hell I'm going home!"

"Inna!" says Echo, laughing in spite of everything.

The Sky Horse paces away from her, and I don't press my friend. I don't *want* her to go.

Echo tries to answer Inna's flood of questions as we pace on into the Between. There are holes in the floor now, patches where the threads have worn through, and we're careful to step over them, swaying on the uneven fabric.

Peter is the next person revealed when I cut away the binding threads. Inna wakes him and pulls him to his feet, and he wraps both his daughters in a fierce embrace.

Fear chokes me—where are my parents?

A Sky Horse comes for Peter, and he tugs a reluctant Inna onto it in front of him.

"I'm sorry," I tell her. "I'll come and see you as soon as I can."

"You'd better! I've so much to tell you, you know—I dreamed music, the whole time I've been here. I'm going to write it down and—"

The Sky Horse bears them away, through the fabric of the Between, and then my friend is gone.

There is never a moment, I don't think, when I'm not crying.

Echo holds tight to my arm and I want to be strong, for her sake. I feel her breaking beside me, crumbling with grief and despair.

And then at last, *at last*, it is Hal we find beneath the binding threads, sleeping with his arm for his pillow, his light hair flopping over his eyes.

Echo crouches awkwardly beside him, reaches trembling fingers to his shoulder. "Hal," she whispers. "Halvarad. Wake up."

He opens his eyes and looks up at her with wonder, tears trembling on his lashes. He touches her face and pulls her tight against him, crying into her neck as they cling to each other. Then he helps her to her feet, their fingers interlaced.

I call them a Sky Horse and it appears beside us, dipping its magnificent head. Both Hal and Echo hug me, and then Hal boosts Echo onto the horse before climbing up behind her.

"Don't be long, North Wind," says Echo. "Come back to us soon."

"I will," I promise, but the words stick in my throat.

Then they're gone and I'm alone again but for my own horse, still pressed up against my shoulder.

I told Echo not to despair, but I feel it eating at me, wrapping around my heart, tearing at the old magic still coiled inside.

A wind passes through the Between like a great, heavy sigh, and I see two bound figures sleeping a few paces apart. I know they are my parents even before I cut the threads obscuring their dear faces. I kneel between them, calling their names, and they stir and wake and look at me. We huddle together, hugging and crying, and for a few moments the joy is fiercer then the sorrow.

"It suits you," says my mother, looking at my crown. She squeezes my hand and kisses my cheek. "More than it ever suited your father."

My father laughs, though tears gleam in his eyes. "It was always meant for you, I think, my dear heart."

All of the Between shudders, tears, the fabric no longer strong enough to hold us.

Fear grips me as I summon another Sky Horse, as my parents climb onto its back. "Wait for me," I tell them. "I've another journey to take you on, but there is one last person I must find Between."

My father's eyes meet mine and I realize that somehow he *knows*. "Godspeed, Satu," he says quietly.

The horse bears them out of the Between, and I turn and plunge deeper into it, running flat out over the rippling floor, urging my winds to hold me, to make me swift and sure.

"Fannaris!" I call into the dark. "Fannaris Wintar! It's time to wake up!"

I refuse to believe that my journey through the Time Thread Sea was in vain. I refuse to surrender him to death when I pulled him back to life with my own two hands.

I love him, and I *refuse*.

Behind and above and around me, the Between begins to Unravel, holes gaping, binding threads shriveling like grass in scorching heat. I leap onto the Sky Horse and urge it faster, faster, as swift as wind and stars and time.

The Between unravels all to pieces.

We outrun it.

"FANNARIS!" I scream.

And then I see him, just ahead. Like the others he is sleeping, caught in binding thread, but at my voice the threads snap and he springs to his feet. He holds out his hand, and as the Sky Horse hurtles by, I grab him and pull him up behind me.

He is cold with magic.

"Satu," he breathes. "I am not real. I am not here. You cannot save me."

I don't listen.

The Sky Horse leaps from the Between. We are swallowed up in wind and light.

But when I open my eyes to see the bright blur of the world, whole and certain below me, there is no one pressed up against my back.

He isn't here.

I am alone.

And the Between is gone, Unraveled forever in a burst of stars.

THIRTY-FIVE

I WAKE TO THE SCENT OF HONEY and wildflowers and the touch of warm wind on my cheek. I was dreaming, perhaps. A strange, long dream, the kind that captures you completely, unsettling enough to make you cry in your sleep. There are tears still trembling on my lashes.

My fingers go to my forehead, brush against the cold stones of my crown. Memory pours through me. Not a dream, then.

I am the North Wind, and the world is saved, and Fannaris is dead.

I open my eyes to a tear-blurred view of my mountain rock ledge, and find I am not alone.

My parents sit with my uncles and Mokosh on a blue and yellow blanket, eating sandwiches and drinking tea. The absolute absurdity would make me laugh if sorrow wasn't knitted so tightly in my heart.

My father sets down his tea mug and comes to pull me to my feet, welcoming me into the circle of six souls I never thought I would see again. It seems they've all been waiting for me.

Winds stir over my knees as I settle between my parents. I am a tangle of feelings I can't quite reconcile. I am overjoyed to have them all here, alive and well, but the memory of snow upon my cheek, of a boy with a shard of ice in his heart, breaks me, again and again. Of a single moment, frozen in time, where we danced in this very place. I'm fractured inside, the acres upon acres of binding thread I pulled out of my heart to sew up the universe leaving me utterly hollow. But that isn't why I bow my head in front of all of them and weep until I'm utterly spent.

It's Mokosh who lifts me to my feet, who paces with me to the edge of the rock shelf, the green and gold spring tundra stretching out far below.

I tell her about Fannaris—the Winter Lord—and how the Wolf Queen used the shell of a dead boy to deceive me.

"I thought he had the stink of my mother's magic about him, but I wasn't certain," she says when I've finished, sitting beside me on the rock ledge with our legs dangling. "If I had realized she put a *piece* of her inside him, I would have tried to warn you."

"Not your fault," I say, pressing my fingers into the rock to ground myself here, here. I take a breath of wildflower-scented air and wish for snow. "Fannaris is dead. I *know* he's dead, and yet—"

"Yet your vision of him in the Between taught you to wish otherwise."

I nod, miserable.

"Take heart, Satu. There may be a piece of him yet left in the world. He may find you again, like West found me."

"You were Between?"

"Yes, and almost lost to it. I have had many second chances in my life, and I mean not to waste them." She smiles. "Take heart," she repeats. "Come and visit me in my husband's house. I love him dearly, but I crave a friend as well. It is a *very* large house."

A friend. My heart squeezes. "I'll come."

We both stand and turn to find West waiting.

"Thank you," he tells me sincerely. Wind ripples through his white wings as Mokosh goes to join him. She kisses his cheek, and I don't miss the thin gold scars that trace his skin. We all bear marks from the Unraveling, seen or unseen. They will never fade.

West and Mokosh bid farewell to my other uncles and my parents, and then West unfolds his wings and bears his wife away into the sky.

East and South take their leave next, thanking me as West did. Then they, too, are gone.

It's only then that my father pulls me into a fierce, tight embrace, and my mother clings to both of us. We all cry together, the weight of our joined emotion too heavy for words.

"Tell us your story," says my mother, when at last the three of us pull apart again. "I want to hear every word."

"And you will," I say. "But there's something I have to ask you first."

I ask them. My mother's eyes shine, and my father kisses her, and that is their answer.

I TELL THEM MY STORY as we sail through the Time Thread Sea, every word of it, from the moment they were Unraveled, to the moment we were reunited on our mountain. My mother is especially awed at my time with Taisia and the herders, descendants of her family. It's a sign to her that her choice is the right one.

When I have reached the end of my tale, I fall silent, looking out over the Time Thread Sea. It pulses and swirls with memory, past and future. My parents sit in the stern of the wind ship, pressed close together. I am in the center, facing them.

My father holds out one arm to me and I move to his side, folding myself under his shoulder.

"I am sorry, dear heart," he says softly into my hair. "For all the sorrow you bore on my account. You are a braver, truer soul than I."

I listen to the pulse of his heart, drink in his scent: wind and stories. "If you had it to do over again, would you make a different choice?"

"To seek the Weaver, you mean," he says, "instead of the Wolf Queen."

I nod against him, and my mother shivers and sighs.

"It was the right choice," my father says quietly. "But I was not brave enough to make it."

I think about this as we sail on through the Time Thread Sea, wind stirring in my soul. "You looked ahead, didn't you?" I sit up and look into his dark eyes. "You knew what would happen if you went to the Wolf Queen. What would happen if you went to the Weaver. And you chose the Wolf Queen anyway."

My father is brave enough, at least, to not avert his gaze. "Yes, dear one."

"You must not blame him wholly," says my mother, tears rimming her lashes. "He showed me, too. I chose it with him."

Frustration burns in my chest. "What was the Weaver's price? Why was it worth all of this?"

My mother chews on her lip. My father looks out over the sea.

"I would have had my mortality," says my father. "Your mother and I would have been together, in her own time."

"And me?" My voice wavers.

My father folds his warm hand over mine. "You would have been raised in the Weaver's house, until you were old enough, and strong enough, to take the North Wind's power—a power kept safe and bound, away from the world."

"You would have been well," says my mother. "Protected. Beloved. But we would not have known you."

Tears prick and pour. My parents wrap their arms around me, tug me close, but I pull away from them.

"You hadn't any right!" I shout. "To keep that from me, to

make that decision for me! Did you look at every moment, Papa? Are you certain that is the future that was woven?"

"It is what we saw," says my mother.

I slump in the ship, deflated. "You destroyed the world to keep me."

The waters of Time lap against the wind vessel, bearing us on.

"You can't have seen everything. The Weaver is merciful. He would not have kept me from you."

"Perhaps not," says my father heavily. "But I couldn't risk losing you, Satu."

"Neither of us could," my mother says.

A glimmering archway appears over the sea, twisting with magenta threads. I direct the ship through it.

I am a tangle of grief and hurt and love, always love, even if I can't quite agree with my parents' choice.

We come not into a corridor but to the base of a vast mountain. A stone path winds steeply upward, the mountain's peak invisible in a swath of cloud.

I climb from the boat, winds coiling around my shoulders. My father helps my mother out, and then the three of us stand, looking up at the mountain. Threads coil through it, magenta and blue.

"Can you forgive me, Satu?" asks my father.

I throw myself at him, hugging him tight and crying into his shirt.

When at last I pull back again, I feel a little easier.

I lead the way up the stone path. There are countless other paths that branch off both sides of the main one: doorways to my mother's life. Partway up the mountain I stop at one of those paths, threads shimmering, singing, calling.

I turn to my parents. "The way is through there," I tell them softly.

"Will you truly not come with us?" says my mother.

I shake my head. "The North Wind is needed in her own time."

My mother's eyes still shine, her whole body trembling with joy. But there is sorrow, too, when she looks at me.

My father kisses her once more. "Wherever you go, my love, I will follow. As long as you will still have me."

She laughs. "If I was going to give up on you, Ivan North, it would have been long before now."

He smiles.

They hug me again, first my mother, then my father. There is far more sorrow, I think, than I can properly hold. My mother weeps into my hair. My father clings to me.

"This isn't goodbye," I remind both of them, and myself, too. "I am the North Wind. I can visit very often."

"You had better," says my mother. "I love you, Satu." She kisses my brow and steps onto the path. She doesn't look back.

My father gives me one last hug. "I love you, dear heart."

"I love you, too, Papa," I whisper.

He follows my mother down the path. I blink, and they're gone.

I stumble back down the mountain, my heart impossibly heavy. The whole way back through the Time Thread Sea, I weep bitterly. I don't want to be alone.

THIRTY-SIX

THERE IS A PALACE FOR ME, up among the winter stars—the great house of the North Wind. My uncle West comes to show me the way.

It has been only an hour since I bid my parents farewell, since I stepped from the wind ship onto the rock ledge, eyes swollen with tears.

The Sky Horse bears me up, up, through the night to a wide, shimmering terrace, my uncle flying just ahead of us. I lift my bleary eyes to the vast house, black as obsidian with veins of flashing silver running through it. It is beautiful beyond imagining, but I stay on the Sky Horse, my hands tangled in its whispering mane.

"I don't need a palace," I say. My voice sounds very small,

swallowed by the night and the shimmering magic.

"It is your birthright," says West, his white wings rippling. "From here, you can oversee your domain, make sure the world is spinning as it ought to."

I shake my head, fresh tears biting at my eyes. "Whatever I am now, I was born mortal, Uncle. I will live in my parents' house on my mountain. I will guard my village, and if I am needed elsewhere—my winds will tell me."

West smiles, a little soft, a little sad. "I had a feeling you might say that. But now you know the way, if ever you change your mind, or if ever you need a sanctuary from the world."

My throat hurts, and the palace blurs before my eyes. "Thank you."

"And please don't forget Mokosh's invitation. Come as soon as you like. As often as you wish."

I attempt a smile but can't quite manage it. "I will."

West bids me farewell and flies away to his own great palace. I turn the Sky Horse down again, to my mountain, to my empty house.

I sleep in my narrow bed in a room that seems smaller than it used to. I dream of snow and wake to find my pillow damp with tears.

IT IS EVENING WHEN I arrive at the Wolf Queen's mountain, the Sky Horse setting me gently down. Stars are beginning to prick through the newly darkened sky, and there is a stillness here that tugs at my heart.

The boy lies where the Wolf Queen discarded him, forgotten and used up, a boy with a borrowed name because his own was lost to death and time. She used him to manipulate me, but he was just another of her many victims, and he doesn't deserve to rot here, bones on bare ground. And whatever she made him, he was my friend. I gather him up and fly him to the base of the mountain where I camped with my father when I was a child. Wildflowers grow here, bright and sweet. I dig him a grave, deep in warm earth, and I lay him gently in it. I utter a benediction over him and surrender his soul to the Weaver. I hope he is at peace, with no nightmares plaguing him. One day, I will enter the Time Thread Sea and go searching for his name and his story.

I return to the top of the mountain, pacing to the spot where the Wolf Queen's body is crumpled on the ground, dried blood on her neck where Fannaris stabbed her with her own claw. She does not belong here on this mountain. She doesn't belong in this world. I find I pity her, for all her darkness. She is the one, I think, who truly has ice in her heart.

I wrap the Wolf Queen's body in winds and call for the Threads of Time. They answer, shimmering before me, opening a doorway into the great sea.

I sail for a while in the twisting waters, not seeking a door to a life but to a world—the Wolf Queen's. I ask the Threads to lead me there and they do, at the last, through a warm lavender waterfall, to a green and grassy shore.

I dig a second grave, deep, deep, on a hill overlooking a sprawling wood. It is a humble resting place, for such a powerful enchantress. But death has no care for the small or the great. I say a benediction for her, too. And then all that is left of the Wolf Queen is a patch of ground on a forgotten world.

I sail home, trying not to think of snow blowing into an icy sea, of the one grave I cannot dig, the one body that does not exist for me to offer a benediction. I do not think it will ever stop breaking me.

THE DAYS ARE LONG. SPRING darkens into summer, and the cold touch of winter has never felt so far away.

I teach myself to fold away my crown and garment of winds, to appear wholly human to the villagers. I tell them that my parents had to go away, that I have inherited the house. I can't quite bear to say that they've died even though, in this time, they have. Their graves are side by side on my mountain, the dates of their deaths etched in ancient stone.

I take up my mother's weaving, selling cloth for coins, and try to stitch myself into village life. No matter I still panic if I am indoors very long, am still overwhelmed by light and noise and the clamor of too many people. This is the life I've chosen. The people I've chosen. But there is no peace here, nothing to assuage the ache of my bone-deep loneliness.

My one small joy I discover housed in the inn's stable: faithful, sturdy Honey, munching on oats and whickering happily when he sees me. I am glad that he is not lost forever to the Unraveled world.

I spend hours on the mountaintop, or soaring on the Sky Horse through the heavens, listening to the stars sing until my heart is calm enough to return to earth.

There are no bees, anymore. No hives dripping with honey to give my hands the steady work I crave. I could send my winds out seeking for more, but it feels like a betrayal. I try to tell myself that this is what Fannaris was, that he took my bees from me, that he isn't worth my dreams, every night, traced with frost and tears. I don't listen.

The emptiness of my parents' house weighs on me, and I take to sleeping on the mountain, watched by wind and stars. I am listless, restless. I begin to wonder if perhaps the North Wind's great palace would be better, if everything would be easier, removed from the earth and the reminders of all I have lost.

I go to visit my parents every Sunday, and they come to expect me, with supper ready as soon as I appear over the ridge. We eat and talk and laugh together. We trade stories. I meet my grand-parents and my cousins, and I sit and weave with my mother. I help her finish the tapestry that hung on her loom the night she and my father were Unraveled. She asks me, every week, to stay, brimming with contentment, me her only missing piece.

But I can't. I am the North Wind, and I belong in my own time, watching over my domain as I am bidden. So every week, when I have lingered deep into the night, I bid them farewell and return to my ship in the Time Thread Sea. Back on my mountain, I lay fresh flowers on their graves, and sleep under the stars.

I visit Inna and Echo nearly as often. Sometimes I stay with Inna for a few days at a time, and we are up late into the night, drinking tea and laughing until I forget, for a while, my sorrow.

I am there when Inna presents her folk song transcriptions to the head of the university and is accepted on a full scholarship. I meet the infamous Illarion, and begrudgingly decide he *might* be worthy of my friend. They clearly adore each other, a thread of the old magic growing strong between them.

I hold Echo and Hal's baby mere hours after he's born, and he is both weighty and fragile in my arms. His eyes are bright and his tiny fist holds fiercely to my thumb. I look at him, and I *ache*. He's called Peter, for his grandfather.

I tell Hal in halting words about Fannaris, his brother. Hal tries not to show me his grief, but I feel it anyway, and it chokes me.

After that I don't visit for a while. I can't quite bear to.

I PACK UP THE HOUSE: my father's books in boxes, my mother's yarns and needles tied up in neat bundles. I can't stay here any longer—there is too much hurt on this mountain. I will go to the North Wind's house and teach myself, perhaps, to forget my sorrow. My loneliness.

But still I linger, not quite able to let go. I try to sell my father's books and my mother's loom, and I change my mind. My parents are alive and well, happy in my mother's time. And yet here, in this life, they're dead, gone. And these things belonged to them. How can I give them up?

I am still here in autumn, when the bees come back, merry and humming. I am on my rock ledge, face tilted to the warmth of the setting sun. I see them, and everything inside of me cracks in two. I drop to my knees, sobbing, as the bees whirl around me, whispering in my ears and snagging in my hair, their wings soft as snow. They know me, and I know them—they are *my* bees, the ones I thought were dead, frozen in Fannaris's ice. Beyond all hope, all reason, all possibility—he's sent them back to me.

"Thank you," I whisper to the air.

A snowflake catches cold on my cheek.

THIRTY-SEVEN

AYS PASS. WEEKS PASS. I DO not go to the North Wind's house. Winter comes, and snow blankets the mountain in white. I don't know why I expect to see him around every corner, but I do. And yet the snow falls and falls, and he doesn't appear.

Of course he doesn't.

He's dead.

The villagers don't need me. They have their school and their shops, the merry warmth of the inn, their friends and their songs. For them there is no lurking horror, no weight of sorrow. They don't remember the Unraveling or the Between. And if they ever wonder what, exactly, happened from summer through to spring, why there is no memory there to fill the gap, they never voice it. At least not to me, the strange woman who lives alone on the mountaintop and flinches at the slightest noise.

I understand my father more than I ever have, why he wanted to give up the vast, unending loneliness of immortality to spend a single lifetime with my mother. I long to have that choice, too. But even if I had someone to give up my power for, how could I, knowing the cost?

I try and try to fill my days. I work at the loom and write in the office. I make sure my bees are safe and snug in their winter hives. But my hands are not patient and my heart is not still and I am ever, always, restless.

My thoughts turn once more to the North Wind's house. It is the only answer, the only place that, perhaps, I can find some peace.

There comes a night in December, when I am sitting as usual on the rock ledge, staring out into the winter stars. The villagers have gone to bed with candles in their windows, ready to welcome the solstice with little flames of light. I hug my knees to my chest and think of the North Wind's house. I will go, in the morning. I will set myself free of the earth, let the magic wash over me completely, and soothe my mortal hurts.

Clouds knit together, blocking out the stars. Snow falls softly on my shoulders, and tears trace fiery tracks down my cheeks. I bow my head to my knees. I shake, shake.

"Please don't cry," comes a quiet voice behind me. "I never want to make you cry."

I jerk my face up to see a man standing there in a flurry of snow, his pale hair blowing about his shoulders.

A strangled cry tears from my throat and I leap up and throw myself at him, knocking him backward. We land in a snowdrift and I'm sobbing and sobbing and he holds me so tight I can feel the wild pulse of his heart.

"I'm so sorry. Please don't cry. Not for me. Not anymore."

"You left me," I sob. "YOU LEFT ME! I thought I would be alone forever. I thought I could bear it but I *can't*, I *can't*."

Snow and wind whirl around us, like we are caught in the eye of our own storm.

"Satu," he says, soft as a prayer. He smooths my cheeks with his thumbs. He kisses my forehead. "I could not bear it either."

I MAKE HIM TEA IN my parents' house, and he sits there at the kitchen table, real as the scratches in the wood, long legs folded up like a grasshopper's. I can't stop staring at him, can't stop chewing on my lip, the pain the only thing assuring me that this is real, that he is *here*.

"How?" I ask, sitting down across from him. Steam curls up from the chipped tea mugs between us.

He can't seem to stop looking at me either. I wonder if he is studying my differences, as I am studying his.

"How?" I repeat.

"You pulled me from the glacier before I died."

"But you—"

"Died anyway," he says gently. "I know. My body—that

body—was not meant to endure the cold. I could only have ever lived a few minutes without the North Wind's magic."

His eyes snag on mine, and my heart stutters. We froze those minutes. Made them last as long as possible, but they weren't enough. He grabs my hand and presses it against his chest. I feel magic there, life, pulsing together.

"There's still a tiny sliver," he says, "a splinter of the North Wind's ice, caught in my heart. Binding me to you. Did you mean to leave it there?"

Grief and joy choke me. "I don't know."

"It rewrote this body—the Winter Lord's body—just before death claimed me. And then I was Unraveled. The vision you saw of me in the Between—it was real. You saved me, Satu. You have saved me so many times." His voice breaks, tears dampening his cheeks.

And then I am on his side of the table, pulling him into my arms, letting him cry on me, as I wept on him in the snow.

"WHERE WERE YOU THEN, ALL this time?"

My question slips through the tides of the Time Thread Sea and I am content, though my grief is never far.

He sits in the bow of the ship, peering into the strange, incomprehensible waters, watching great silver beasts rise and fall beneath the waves.

"Trying to find my way back," he says softly. "The tiny

shard of magic—it wasn't quite enough to make me solid, in the warmer months. There wasn't quite enough of me to—to *be* anywhere, properly. It was only when the weather grew colder that my form returned. And my magic, too, at least in part. But I knew I couldn't come back to you without sending them first. It took a lot of power."

My chest tightens. "You mean my bees."

He turns away from the sea, a wan smile on his lips. "I didn't actually kill them, you know. I only wanted you to think I had."

"Why?"

"Because I was angry, Satu."

"Why?" I repeat, but my stomach roils and I already know.

He studies the tenuous form of the wind ship. "Because I knew you were there that day on the glacier when I was clinging to the mast and begging for you to save me. But you didn't. You left me to the mercy of the Wolf Queen."

I swallow down rising bile. "Time wouldn't let me take you, not then. I tried, Fannaris. It killed me to leave you to her. I'm sorry. I'm so sorry." Fresh tears choke me.

"Don't cry, Satu," he says softly. "I never want to make you cry. It wasn't your fault. Time was right. It was the only choice I could have made—if you would have saved me in that moment, everything would have fallen to pieces, and there would have been no world to save at all."

As I bid the ship on through the Time Thread Sea, I turn away from him, because I can't stop crying. I'm not sure I ever will.

He joins me in the midst of the ship. He threads his fingers through mine, and the heat of him both comforts and torments me. "Satu. Why are you crying?"

I can't bear to tell him. So I don't.

We sail on, past a chaos of starlight and Time Thread creatures. The ship stays true to its course, but I bid it not to hurry.

"Satu. Where are you taking me?"

It is the same question, said in a different way, and I realize that he already knows. That's why he didn't say anything when I pulled on the Threads of Time, when I asked him to come with me.

Too soon we come upon his archway; too soon the ship sails into the corridor that is his life. I raise my tearstained face to his.

He grips both my shoulders, a ferocity in his eyes.

"No," he says.

My heart slaps against my rib cage, so hard it pains me. "I'm setting it right, Fannaris. The very last piece."

"Don't send me back. Please. I can't bear it."

"You would forget me," I tell him quietly. "You would never remember that the Wolf Queen bound you and tormented you for centuries. You can see your family again. You can be happy."

He shakes his head. "As much as you may think me a coward for not wanting to face the Tsar's soldiers, I don't want that life, Satu. It isn't mine, not anymore. I miss my family, I *do*, but—" He cups my face in his hands, his glance filled with desperate urgency. "I can't give you up. Please don't ask me to."

Hope has wings and they beat inside of me. I take a breath. "Are you sure, Fannaris?"

"Yes. *Yes.* I have never been more sure of anything." He tilts his forehead against mine. "Besides, Hal is in your time. I should like to get to know my youngest brother."

It is hard to think beyond the winter-sharp scent of him. I struggle against the desire to pull him closer than he already is, to forget everything else. But. "Let me do one thing for you, at least."

I slip from his arms and step through one of the doors, coming back a moment later with paper and ink I found in his father's office. "Write to your family," I say. "Let them know you are well. Let them know you love them and miss them."

He nods solemnly, then sits cross-legged in the corridor and picks up the pen. He cries as he writes.

When he's finished, I leave the letter on his mother's vanity, tucking it between her mirror and a bottle of perfume.

And then Fannaris and I climb back into the wind ship together and sail back through the sea to our own time.

EPILOGUE

WE SIT ONCE MORE ON THE rock ledge. The snow has given way to a softly rising moon. I can hardly believe he is here. I'm not alone. He's *here.*

"Thank you," he says, looking out over the darkened tundra.

"For what?"

"For catching me when I jumped from the balcony. For concealing me from the Tsar's soldiers and pulling me from the glacier and the Between. For all the times you saved me."

I glance sideways at him, flushed with heat and tongue-tied by sudden shyness.

"I remember everything," he says, turning to meet my gaze. "Every time you came to me. I was . . . I was angry, for a long while. But even when you left your mountain, when you started your journey to become the North Wind, who would betray me—I couldn't hate you. You saw my childhood, my life. And I saw yours. I was still angry. Part of me wanted you to suffer for what you did to me the day I bound myself to the Wolf Queen. Something you hadn't actually done yet."

My heart jerks. "I will always be sorry I couldn't save you sooner."

"And I am sorry for all the pain I caused you." His voice is suddenly gruff, as if he's fighting tears again. "You saved me just in time, Satu North."

We dangle our feet over empty air and let the night, for a while, fill the space between us.

"What will you do, now that you're here?" I ask him.

"I don't know. I haven't been Fannaris, really, in so many centuries I'm not sure I quite know how to do it." He snaps his fingers and we both watch snow swirl and dance in his palm. His forehead creases. "You're immortal now. You know that, don't you?"

I do know. I think of the cold house waiting for me among the stars and I shudder at how close I came to letting it be the ending to my story.

"I am—" Fannaris takes a breath, tries again. "Whatever magic still sparks inside of me, the life I have left is a mortal one. You will live forever, Satu. I will not."

Tears clog my throat and I envy my parents, for having what I can't choose.

Fannaris drops his head into his hands, and sighs like his heart is breaking. "There are so many things I must atone for. So many wrongs I must right. It will be easier, I think, if I do them alone."

"What are you talking about?" I grab his shoulders, wrench him around to face me. His skin is warm beneath his ragged coat, though the air around him is bitterly cold.

He squares his jaw. "I have to go. I don't want to, but—I must find the descendants of all the people the Wolf Queen stole away or ruined or enchanted, everyone I had a hand in ruining. I have to atone for my sins. I am not worthy of you, Satu North. I never have been."

I *glare* at him. "Don't you *dare* assess your worth to me, Fannaris Wintar!"

"I'll come back to you," he says miserably. "When I can."

I shake my head. "No."

"Satu—"

"No," I repeat. "For good or ill, the choices we've made have led us to the place we are now. If there is atonement to be made, then atone we must, but when it is over there is, as there always has been, forgiveness. I won't keep you from the path you feel called to, but you are a damn fool if you think I'm going to let you go alone."

He tilts his head, a smile tugging at his lips. "There is nowhere I could go where you could not find me, North Wind. Nor would I want there to be."

"We have both been enough alone already," I say, and my

voice cracks. "The North Wind cannot do without her Winter Lord." I lift hesitant fingers to touch his face: his brow, his eyelashes, a freckle on his lip. "I *love* you," I tell him. "I love you. Don't you dare leave me alone."

He cups my jaw with his hands, and there is immense strength in his careful gentleness. He smiles, smooths his thumbs over my cheeks. "And I love you, Satu North."

In the moment before he kisses me, I realize the solution to the problem of my own immortality. When we have a child, and she comes of age, I will pass my birthright to her, if she is willing. I will become mortal and grow old with Fannaris beside me. I will not let him go into darkness alone. Not ever, ever again. It is the right answer, I think. But I do not have to tell him yet. We have a whole sea of time between now, and then.

A storm whips up around us, veiling all the mountain in wind and snow. His mouth finds mine, and he tastes of fire and winter and peace.

It is a long, long while, before the storm dies down, and the world is once more quiet.

In the morning, in the light of the newly risen sun, two horses leap from the mountain. One is made of wind, and one of snow. We go together, into the sky, to write our own ending.

ACKNOWLEDGMENTS

DRAFTING A BOOK IN A GLOBAL pandemic whilst trapped at home with my mostly-not-napping toddler during the hottest Arizona summer ever on record was an experience, to say the least! I could not be more grateful for all the help and encouragement I had along the way.

Thank you to my agent, Sarah Davies, for tirelessly championing my books, and for seeing the promise in this idea.

Thank you to my editor, Lauren Knowles, for believing in *Wind Daughter* from the start, for bearing with me as I merrily followed character chemistry instead of my outline, and for making me change that one aspect of the story even though I didn't want to (you were, as always, right!).

Thank you to the whole team at Page Street for making such beautiful books—I can't believe this is our fifth one together!

Thank you to R. J. Anderson, who read *Wind Daughter* as I was first drafting it, and who brainstormed with me about *that one thing* (you're a genius!). Thanks to Charlie Holmberg for her invaluable feedback on the second draft—it got better from there, I promise! Thanks to Hanna Howard, who read draft three as I was revising it, and fielded many, many angsty Marco Polo messages. Deep breaths, more tea! Thanks to R. J. (again!) and Jen Fulmer for reading and giving feedback on that third draft, and to Hanna (again!) for helping me Fix Time.

Thank you to Jenny Downer for constant brainstorming, cups of tea, deep discussions about everything under the sun, and work sessions—when we can squeeze them in.

Thank you to my mother-in-law, Joanie, for taking Arthur a day a week so I could finish writing and revising this book! I couldn't have done it without you.

Thank you to my husband, Aaron, for always believing in me, and for loving me—quirks and volatile emotions and sensitivity and all. I would turn back time to save you, just so you know.

And for Arthur, my ever-growing Bear—thank you for (sometimes!) napping, for always giving me the best hugs, and for telling me sternly to "go work" whenever your Oma comes over to hang out with you. Don't be in any hurry to grow up, okay?

Lastly, to my readers, old and new: Thank you for coming along on Satu's journey, and for allowing me to share a piece of my heart with you. Here's to the old magic.

ABOUT THE AUTHOR

JOANNA RUTH MEYER IS THE AUTHOR of young adult fantasies such as *Into the Heartless Wood* and the critically-acclaimed *Echo North*. She writes stories about fierce teens finding their place in the world, fighting to change their fate, save the ones they love, or carve out a path to redemption.

Joanna lives with her dear husband and son, a rascally feline, and an enormous grand piano named Prince Imrahil in Mesa, Arizona. As often as she can, she escapes the desert heat and heads north to the mountains, where the woods are always waiting.

ALSO BY
JOANNA RUTH MEYER

   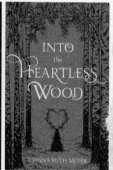